CLOUD PIERCER

Paula Welch

First Published in Australia through IngramSpark
www.ingramspark.com

This edition published 2022
Copyright © Paula Welch 2022

Editing and proofreading: Aurora House | www.aurorahouse.com.au
Cover design: Donika Mishineva | www.artofdonika.com
Typesetting and e-book design: Prepress Plus | www.prepressplus.in
Email: pjwelch.author@bigpond.com
Website: www.paulawelch.com.au

ISBN number: 978-0-6487655-5-4 (Paperback)
ISBN number: 978-0-6487655-4-7 (e-book)

A catalogue record for this book is available from the National Library of Australia

Dedication

I would like to dedicate this book to my family for all their support.

To all the plane buffs out there, the sky's the limit.

For you, Dad.

Prologue

On board Flight AN224

'She's up ahead!' Benjamin yelled.

'Fuck, she's big,' Marcus replied.

'Steady! Keep her steady!' Benjamin cried.

'I'm trying!'

Benjamin was rigid in his captain's chair as the plane flew closer to the foreboding peak of Elie de Beaumont. As it flew overhead, Flight 224 skimmed past its top with only twenty metres of depth to spare. The force of the aircraft caused the peak, covered in snow, to break away.

Benjamin quickly flicked the interphone on and yelled, '*Brace, brace, brace!*' He gripped the control column as if his life depended on it – which, maybe, it did. His heart was hammering in his chest. Fear gripped every part of his hardened body as he saw what was about to happen. His thoughts flashed momentarily to his children, but he didn't have the luxury to reminisce. He had to act. Fast.

Captain Benjamin Flynn pitched the nose down. The plane descended between the surrounding peaks of Mt Walter, Mt Green, and Mt Darwin. Benjamin heard a terrible noise. He knew that part of the left wing had just broken away. The plane turned sharply on its side, then hit the surface of the valley floor. Hard. Cushioned by the virgin snow-covered floor, which exploded all around the plane, it now continued its long descent down the Tasman Valley, skidding and sliding, bumping and jolting over the snow and ice as it began its journey down the valley floor.

★

One week before …
Christchurch Times
'News Bulletin – Massive Earthquake Rocks South Island of New Zealand'

Story by James Fleet

'The 7.6 magnitude earthquake woke the sleeping inhabitants of the South Island of New Zealand at 2:15 a.m. Scientists at GeoNet confirmed that the epicentre was over 50 km north of Christchurch, but the tremors were felt throughout the South Island and in the lower parts of the North Island. This recent series of earthquakes was just shy in magnitude of the Kaikoura earthquake that shook the South Island on 14 November 2016, just after midnight. Ruptures were felt over multiple fault lines. Geologists have been quick to compare both earthquakes with alarming concern. The Kaikoura earthquake was regarded as the "most complex earthquake ever studied".

'GeoNet – EQC Earthquake Commission in New Zealand, the national body which detects, analyses and responds to natural disasters such as earthquakes, volcanic activity, and tsunamis – have warned that the seismic activity is far from over.

'The GeoNet scientists are monitoring the 600-plus sensors around New Zealand that detect seismic activity and are alarmed to have learned that numerous fault lines have shifted more than their annual expectancy forecast. The New Zealand government has put all agencies on alert and advised the public to be prepared for more aftershocks in the coming weeks.

'Geologists have stated that their major concern is the Alpine Fault line, which runs down the West Coast of the South Island. With heavy snow on the mountains, avalanches are a great concern. The Ministry of Civil Defence, along with the Department of Conservation, have closed the Mount Cook National Park until further notice.

'The hypocentre (the point where the rupture starts) was at a depth of 14 km/8.6 m. The epicentre (the point on the Earth's surface above the hypocentre) was 6 km south of Pegasus Bay and 50 km north of Christchurch. It lasted approximately two and a half minutes.

'Yet again, the snow-covered mountains of the Mount Cook National Park have been rudely awakened from their winter hibernation by this latest earthquake. The Alpine Fault, which runs deep beneath the bedrock, along with a number of smaller fault lines, has begun to shift. To the naked eye, it is infinitesimal. However, this displacement – deep below the surface – will set off a series of aftershocks. The two affected plates are the Pacific Plate and the Indo-Australian Plate. Gas vents have been known to find their way to the surface from deep within cavernous pits below, silently expelling built-up vapour into the atmosphere around the National Park. GNS Science specialists are monitoring New Zealand's active volcanos in case the earthquake activity is a prelude to volcanic activity.

'Flights scheduled to arrive in Christchurch airport have been diverted due to the expected aftershocks. All flights have been cancelled until the FAA deems the airport safe to re-open.

'This latest earthquake could be only the start of a major shift along the fault lines, which could see the face of the National Park changed forever.

'Only time will tell.'

Chapter One

Blue Southern Skies, Bankstown Airport, 30 kms from Sydney
2.05 p.m., Thursday, approximately 11.5 hours before the crash

Once the pilot signed the fuel docket, he stowed his flight bag in the cockpit of the Pilatus PC-24 Learjet. The private charter was scheduled to leave on time from Bankstown Airport to Christchurch, NZ, at 4 p.m.

The pilot started his walk-around. He checked the fuel, tyre pressure, ailerons, rudder, and elevators during his inspection. But when he inspected the landing gear, he noticed something inside the hatchway. A small black box was attached to the inside wall. Irritated, he immediately called maintenance and demanded to know who'd left it there.

When the aircraft engineer arrived, he confirmed that it was not his or that of his maintenance crew. The engineer picked up the box and took it back to a maintenance hangar. When he opened the box, he was horrified to see a small device inside connected to a timer, already counting down a series of numbers. Beside the timer was some form of plastique. The hanger was immediately evacuated, the airport closed, and all incoming flights were diverted.

The police and bomb squad were called. They confirmed that the device was made of Semtex. It had been set to go off twenty minutes after the plane's scheduled departure.

The owner of Blue Southern Skies couldn't comprehend who would attempt such a ruthless act of sabotage. They had only been in business for two years and had a modern fleet of three Learjets. They were hoping to expand the following year. Surely it couldn't be an act of corporate interference?

The owner apologised to their clients, informing them of a maintenance fault that wouldn't be fixed until Monday. Both the owner and the pilot were still in shock by the time the federal police arrived to question them.

Upon their arrival, their first question to the owner was, 'Who were your passengers?'

Chapter Two

ANZAL (Australian & New Zealand Airlines) Operations, Mascot Airport
3.50 p.m., Thursday, approximately 9.5 hours before the crash

Margaret Tennyson knew that it was going to be a hectic shift. As the flight operations manager at Mascot Airport, she had already cancelled one flight due to a faulty sensor reading in the avionics bay on flight AN327 – which, when replaced, had shorted out several other sensors.

ANZAL had apologised to its customers profusely.

Although, the bulk of the airline delays were not entirely their fault. Another series of earthquakes in New Zealand's South Island, throughout last week, had caused Christchurch Airport to close for five days, and it had only just re-opened.

Flights had been grounded at Christchurch Airport while inspections were carried out. Now that the airport had re-opened, Margaret had to clear a backlog of very angry passengers. She authorised the use of their new A380-800 Airbus, which could carry up to 500 passengers. This would clear up the bottleneck of passengers from the cancelled flights earlier in the week. Turnaround would be swift. The aircraft would bring home passengers, waylaid in Christchurch, later that same day. ANZSAL's new Airbus was their shiny new star in a quickly expanding fleet. AN224 was scheduled to leave at 10 p.m. Sydney time, one hour before the Sydney airport closed. The flight time would be three hours and thirty minutes long and would arrive in Christchurch at 3.30 a.m. local time.

At fifty-two, Margaret was one of the most experienced flight operations managers in her profession. Today, she had much to do. She had organised the additional flight in record time, but now she needed a flight and cabin crew to man it. Margaret co-ordinated with the flight crew operations manager to ensure the legally required cabin crew would be available. Eighteen flight attendants would be needed on tonight's flight, one for each emergency door, plus one extra on each level of the double-decker Airbus.

Margaret knew that pilots hated having their schedules changed at the last moment – it was unproductive and time-consuming. However, she knew one captain who would be available.

Captain Benjamin Flynn was currently on leave, and probably bored out of his mind. Margaret knew that he would come in and fly the last-minute flight to Christchurch, as well as return her later that same day.

'Jeremy, it's Margaret. I need you to get in contact with Captain Flynn – I need him to fly to Christchurch tonight on AN224. I also need a co-pilot.'

'Will do. Marcus Whitby is on call – he can fly the second seat.'

'Perfect.'

Jeremy, a seasoned veteran at ANZAL, was accustomed to last-minute flight crew changes. Once he finished with Margaret, he started making calls.

AN224 had been arranged in record time. The flight crew, on their arrival at Mascot Airport, would head straight to the pilots' briefing room where Jeremy would make sure the pilots had everything they needed for their pre-flight checklist. From there, they would file their flight plan with Air Traffic Control.

Margaret rewarded herself with a self-satisfied grin and allowed herself a few minutes of 'me time'. She sat down and enjoyed a well-deserved coffee. She was relieved that her shift wasn't going to be as hectic as she'd first thought. Margaret's work colleagues didn't call her 'Tenacious Tennyson' for nothing.

★

4.00 p.m., Botany Bay

Benjamin Flynn was resting his arms over the balcony of his three-bedroom apartment in Brighton-Le-Sands. The sun had travelled behind him now, and it was growing colder as it continued its western circumnavigation of the planet.

He was looking out across Botany Bay. Benjamin could see Mascot Airport's two parallel 16/34 north-to-south runways. He marvelled at the sight of another Boeing as it lifted off and headed out over the sea, carrying passengers to amazing destinations or simply taking them home.

Benjamin had enjoyed his week off. He had spent it with his two adult children, Sam and Julia. He had been feeling restless for the last few months, maybe because his divorce had just been finalised a little over a month ago. His relationship with his ex-wife, Elizabeth, was better now than it had been for the last five years. But now that he had bought this new apartment, he felt lonely. At least with its three bedrooms, there was plenty of room for Sam and Julia to come and stay on the weekends.

Benjamin's children had taken the divorce well. In fact, they all had. Benjamin and Elizabeth had become friends again, although some nights he missed having his family around him. Listening to the hustle and bustle of their busy lives. But he knew, as Elizabeth did, that they were better off apart.

The Australian Air Force had been Benjamin's calling from the age of eight. Retired four years ago, and now at fifty-one – and with the onset of grey hair at his temples – he was starting to tire of the aviator's life. Not the flying part – never that – but the lonely long-haul separations. His divorce had been inevitable. He couldn't blame Elizabeth, as he had hardly ever been home. The Air Force had separated them with assignments and deployments during their marriage, and while working for ANZAL had improved their time together, his long-haul flights still saw him away for days at a time.

Benjamin's children were living their own lives now, but he still loved them dearly, and he was realising now – too late – how much of their childhoods he had missed. He had no intention of missing any more.

Benjamin walked back inside and closed the door. He decided to take a long walk along the beach before dinner. He grabbed his keys and mobile. As he made for the door, his mobile vibrated in his jacket pocket. It was Flight Ops. Benjamin was tempted to let it ring out, but then again …

★

5.25 p.m.

'You fucking idiot, their flight was cancelled. They found the bomb,' Wolf said.

'I'm sorry. I didn't think they'd find it. I waited until the maintenance team and the fuel truck left. I didn't know that the pilot would inspect the plane so thoroughly,' Jackal replied.

'A professional would have known. Our target was not supposed to return to Christchurch. You fucking *idiot*.'

'I'll take care of it.'

'*How?*'

'I'm on a flight back to New Zealand in a couple of hours. I'll be there in plenty of time before they arrive. I'll come up with another plan.' Jackal was starting to get anxious. He knew the consequences of failure.

'No. We had one chance. A downed aircraft in deep water would be hard-pressed to prove sabotage. Crash investigators would never find all the pieces. Anything you do now will draw attention,' Wolf said, angry at not having taken care of the problem himself in the first place.

'You paid me to do a job, Mr Wolf. Let me finish it!'

'You had your chance,' Wolf said before hanging up.

Jackal − a.k.a. Terry Burrows, as his mother had christened him − realised at that very moment that he, himself, was in very deep water. He could live with the downing of a small plane with a handful of people on board, but their targets would now be on a commercial flight carrying over 500 people.

He knew himself to be ruthless, but not a psychopath.

He needed to disappear for a while. A long while. Terry gathered his bag and headed to the airport. He needed to get out of this game. His employer was not a forgiving man. He had been chosen because they wanted a cleanskin to do the job. He was brought over from New Zealand to do it; fly in, fly out.

He cursed himself. Nothing was ever that simple.

As he exited the motel, he looked up and down the street for a taxi. One was sitting idle forty metres down the road. He raised his hand to summon it. After a long minute, the driver started the engine and moved forward to collect his passenger.

★

5.35 p.m.

'Mr Wolf,' said the driver. 'Is it a go?'

'Hold fast. We may still have use of him. Take him to the airport. If my plan isn't a go, we'll take care of him once he arrives back in Christchurch.'

'Understood,' said the driver. After hanging up, he started the engine and drove up to the motel to collect his passenger.

After disconnecting, Wolf made another phone call.

'I may have a solution to our problem.'

'Go on,' said Mr Fox.

'If the authorities believe it was an act of terrorism or corporate espionage, then let's finish the job.'

'*Go on*,' he replied, trying not to voice his irritation.

'I'll follow them to New Zealand. I'll text Tigress to let me know where the target's heading once he's off the plane. Once we know, I'll have someone intercept him at the airport. He won't be a problem for long.'

'And you're sure you can manage that?' Fox asked with growing sarcasm.

'Yes. Jackal is heading back to New Zealand. We'll use him as our fall guy.'

'That was our original plan,' he said, 'which I paid you handsomely for. Or have you forgotten?'

'No. I haven't. The job will get done, Mr Fox. This is but a small delay. Our target won't be in a position to report you or your organisation to the authorities. I can also make it look like Jackal was working for a competitor. He won't be alive to contradict the evidence.'

'Can it be organised in time?'

'Yes. I'll make a few calls.'

'Let me be very clear about this, Wolf. I want Henry Adams dead.'

'*No names*, please, Mr Fox!'

'This deal is worth billions to me. Once he's figured out the full extent of what I've done – which will be very soon – he'll head straight to the authorities. The sanctimonious prick already knows about Iceland.'

'That didn't take him long. What about Tigress?' Wolf asked.

'No loose ends.'

Chapter Three

The Sir Stamford, 93 Macquarie Street, Sydney, Suite 207
6.30 p.m.

'Why?' Henry asked.

'I don't know,' Gertrude answered. 'They wouldn't say. Just that our flight was cancelled due to a maintenance issue. Don't worry, ANZAL opened up a new flight to Christchurch tonight. I managed to get us two seats in first class, but we're leaving from Mascot Airport now.'

It went without saying – Gertrude was angry with Blue Southern Skies for cancelling their flight.

Gertrude checked her watch and saw that she had time for some bubbles and bubbly before going to the airport. Once back in her own room, she went into the bathroom to run her bath. She felt cocky and confident – her life and career were a glowing success. She had backed a winner in Henry Adams. She checked her messages before sinking into her bath. *Poor Henry*, she thought. *A brilliant man, but naïve and far too trusting.* She put her headphones on and listened to some music while sipping her champagne.

Gertrude chuckled to herself, Henry had no head for business. He was a scientist, a designer, and more importantly, a revolutionary thinker. Which meant he had no time for the rudimentary nuts and bolts of running a business. His company was floundering with him at the helm. It hadn't taken much persuasion for Henry to invite Gertrude to join his team.

Gertrude had orchestrated Henry through the design phase of his revolutionary new technology. Then she'd guided him into the hands of Jackson Myer, CEO of Cyber Systems. Now, Gertrude's assignment was almost complete. She would finally reap her rewards.

Gertrude had met Jackson a little over four years ago. She knew him to be resourceful, clever, and shrewd. His company was going places, and so was she.

Gertrude and Jackson were playing Henry like professional violinists – faultlessly.

As Gertrude enjoyed her bubble bath, she fantasized about how she was going to spend her future wealth. *Poor Henry*, she thought, again. *He never really knew how to play the game.*

Unfortunately for Gertrude, Jackson Myer only wanted Henry's technology. He didn't like loose ends, and Gertrude Simpson knew far too much.

She never heard the knock at her hotel room door.

Meanwhile, back in his own suite, Henry continued to work on his laptop. He didn't know what all the fuss was about. He would have been happy to fly business class, or even economy, just as long as he got back home. He never liked to travel outside of New Zealand, or even Christchurch for that matter. He preferred familiarity and routine.

He knew he shouldn't grumble. He would have been lost these past two years if Gertrude hadn't found him. She had turned his work and life around. He was grateful to her for getting his business off the ground. He was an engineer by trade and had realised early on that he had no head for business. Henry's new technology would revolutionise modern society, especially in the field of medicine. Luckily for Henry, Gertrude had introduced him to Jackson Myer at an AI conference. The rest was history.

Henry had been relieved when Jackson had backed his technology all the way. Henry had much to thank him for. Leaving the business side to them, he'd concentrated on the development of his chip, which was now about to become a reality.

Even though Henry left the running of the business to Gertrude, he still liked to have a hands-on approach. The business was his responsibility, and if it failed, it would inevitably be down to him.

He had been thankful of that prudence when he'd come across an illegal entry into their computer systems.

Henry had trouble believing that someone on his team would betray him, so he'd outsourced the investigation. Secrecy was paramount in his line of work. He knew something wasn't right. He trusted his small team of engineers explicitly, but it had been no mistake that the security of his system had been breached.

The private investigator had confirmed that the trace went back to an I.P. address in Iceland, of all places. Now, Henry needed to get home and find out what was going on. He was expecting an update on his return to Christchurch.

Henry had confided in Gertrude about what he knew. He knew that she was the one person he could entrust this information to. She'd appeared alarmed but had said she would help in his investigations once they were back home.

Henry's problem was that he never learned how to play the game.

He was zipping up his suitcase when he heard a knock. He walked over to the door of his suite and opened it to find two federal police officers waiting outside. They asked to come in.

'Could we please confirm that your company hired a Learjet from Blue Southern Skies to fly you home to Christchurch today?' the first officer asked.

'Yes. Uh, what's this about?' Henry asked.

'I don't wish to alarm you, but a small explosives device was found in the wheel assembly of the plane you chartered,' he said.

Henry was momentarily confused.

'Wait … a *bomb?*' he said finally.

'Correct.' The police officers allowed Henry a moment to compose himself.

'We do not believe the bomb was intended for Blue Southern Skies directly, but possibly for the passengers it was carrying,' said the first officer. 'Two separate parties had chartered the flight to Christchurch. Namely you and a Gertrude Simpson, plus a couple from Dunedin.'

'Do you know of anyone who would want to hurt you?' asked the second officer. 'Have you had any threats in recent times, personal or business-related?'

'No! No to both questions.'

'Can we ask what you're doing here in Sydney?'

'I have just signed a deal with Cyber Systems. They will be working with me to develop and manufacture my new chip. We signed the deal this morning.'

Henry went on to explain his technology to the officers. He had no idea who would want to hurt him or Gertrude. He was still shaking his head in bewilderment.

The officers said that they were checking all CCTV cameras at Bankstown Airport and would let him know as soon as they had any new information. He would be required to answer more questions once they were back in New Zealand. The AFP would also be informing the New Zealand federal police of their arrival.

'How are you getting to Mascot Airport, Mr Adams?' asked the first officer.

'Gertrude Simpson, our head of operations, has organised a car to take us to the airport.'

'Fine. We'll have a car follow behind you, to make sure you arrive safely.'

'Thank you, but is that really necessary? Are you really sure that the bomb was meant for us?'

'We can't rule out anything at this moment in time,' said the second officer. 'We did knock on the door of Ms Simpson's room, but there was no answer.'

'No? Oh, she said that she was going to take a bath before the flight. I'll let her know.' Henry said, who was still in shock himself.

'That's fine. But we will need a statement from each of you once you arrive back home. We can't imagine anyone on the plane having a part in this, as they would also have been killed by the bomb, but we can't rule it out either.'

It was all too much for Henry to take in. He informed the AFP officers about the private investigator he'd hired because of the breech in security. Henry gave the investigators the particulars so that they could follow it up.

After the federal police officers left his room, Henry sat back down on his bed and contemplated what he'd just been told.

Who the hell would want to kill me? he thought. Henry decided not to tell Gertrude until they arrived safely back home. He didn't want to alarm her.

Instead, he called his private investigator and informed him of this latest situation. He asked him to run a security check on his work colleagues and run mobile checks over the last week. Henry still couldn't believe one of his employees would orchestrate an act of sabotage. But would a competitor? Either way, Henry needed to know the truth.

★

Chapter Four

Ticket Counter, Sydney Kingsford-Smith International Airport, Mascot
7.22 p.m.

'We've upgraded you and your mother, Ms Donnelly. You're now in seats 17E and F,' said the passenger service agent. 'You're in the front row; in the middle section of business class. There aren't any parents with babies on this flight. No one will be using the bassinets. You'll be much more comfortable there.'

'Oh, that's wonderful. Thank you,' Amy Donnelly replied.

'My pleasure, madam. And don't worry about Heathcliff. He'll be sleeping like a baby by the time the flight takes off.'

'Thank you again.'

'If you go to the service counter at the gate, they'll escort you and your mother on board first.'

'Will do, thanks,' Amy said, as she gathered her paperwork and took her mother's arm.

Amy was amazed. Their trip had become a technical triumph in such a short time. Joanne wanted to go to her friend's funeral in Sydney. Amy had thought that bringing Heathcliff, her mother's guide dog, would be complicated because of Australia's strict quarantine guidelines, but it hadn't been. Customs had confirmed that she wouldn't need to put Heathcliff in quarantine as long as he had a current health certificate. A trip to the vet was all that had been needed before their flight.

Amy had always regarded her mother as one of the bravest women she had ever known, but she knew that Joanne always felt more comfortable when she had Heathcliff by her side.

Having their original return flight cancelled by ANZAL due to technical difficulties had caused her mother some concern. Now, Joanne's only fear was about whether or not Heathcliff would wake up mid-flight. The sedative would only last for five to six hours, but ANZAL had re-assured them that Heathcliff would be given his sedative just before boarding.

With their boarding passes firmly in hand, Amy could finally let her hair down and relax. Maybe even contemplate a drink or two. They had never flown business class before.

She was going to let ANZAL spoil her.

★

The Star Sydney Casino – 80 Pyrmont St, Pyrmont
7.14 p.m.

'*Gankuai*' yelled Lu Ming in Chinese, telling his companion to move quickly.

'*Hǎo ba. Hǎo ba,*' yelled Peng Ming, rolling her eyes and nodding an abrupt okay. As she hurried into the back of the taxi, she realised that they had left their luggage in their suite. There was no time to retrieve it – they should have left yesterday. But Lu had wanted one more day. At thirty-four, and a brilliant mathematician, Lu had finally perfected their signals and strategy at blackjack. At the table, Lu was losing small, while Peng was winning big. They'd lost just enough not to draw attention. However, their strategy had started to unravel, and their luck had finally run out. They had stayed one day too many.

The croupier had been delaying their last hand. The casino was onto them. Lu looked up and saw security guards coming their way from across the large gaming floor. He took his chips and withdrew from the table. He nodded at Peng. As Lu made his way through the casino, Peng excused herself from the table and made her way to the lockers where she retrieved their passports, a backpack and a Coles shopping bag with over $200,000 in cash from their previous winnings.

Peng met her husband at the taxi rank. He yelled again at her to hurry up. Peng jumped into the taxi as it sped off quickly in the direction of the airport. Peng doubted the casino would be kind enough to forward her belongings. She cursed herself at the thought of leaving behind her new Chanel bag and jacket.

'*Shībài zhě*,' Lu said, criticising the casino for being 'sore losers' after he caught his breath.

Peng, at twenty-three, knew what they were doing was dangerous, but she loved the thrill of it. The money wasn't bad either. It was getting harder and harder to beat the house with their state-of-the-art AI monitoring systems. But Lu had found a way. If only he wasn't so greedy. Peng cursed him. They shouldn't have stayed the extra day.

Peng had met Lu at university, he was her maths professor. He had been thrilling to be around at first, but now the novelty was wearing off, fast. He never stopped complaining.

They'd had a run of good luck in Queensland, but Sydney had finally got the better of them. When they arrived at the airport, Lu found them the first available flight out. Lucky for them, flight AN224 was heading to Christchurch, New Zealand. So, they bought two first-class tickets. Lu spent his time before the flight, in the first-class lounge, googling New Zealand casinos, while Peng went on the hunt for a Chanel boutique.

She strolled through the terminal's boutiques, smelt the opulent fragrances of perfumes and soaps, and sampled expensive face creams. Anything to distance herself from her exasperating husband.

Peng wondered how long their ride would continue, believing that two years had been long enough.

★

Pilots Briefing Room, Sydney Kingsford-Smith Airport, Mascot
7.40 p.m.

'Do you have the updated NOTAM?' Captain Flynn asked.

'Yeah, here you are,' First Officer Marcus Whitby replied, as he handed over the notice. 'There's nothing unusual to report. The weather will be fine over the Tasman Sea. At present, the wind is eight knots south at Mascot and currently twelve knots easterly in Christchurch.'

'Thanks, Marcus. What about earthquake activity in New Zealand? Has there been any more in the last six hours?'

'No, everything has been quiet over there. But I'll check hourly during the flight.'

It would be Marcus' responsibility to monitor all correspondence on the Datalink messaging system in the cockpit during the flight. The system allowed pilots to send and receive data between the aircraft and ground crew, airline operations, weather service providers, and Air Traffic Control centres. It was transmitted via the on-board Aircraft Communications Addressing and Reporting System, or ACARS, which conveyed all information via satellite.

'We have a flight crew of eighteen tonight,' Benjamin said. 'I'll go meet them shortly. Once I've introduced myself, I'll do the walk-around.'

'Yes, sir. I'll go over the check lists and make sure nothing else has come in. Then I'll head to the aircraft and start pre-flight checks,' Marcus said.

Benjamin gave his thanks as he got up to leave the briefing room.

Benjamin had only flown with Marcus twice before. They got on well. The last time he'd flown with Marcus he was two weeks shy of getting married. Benjamin knew Marcus' type by reputation – young and ambitious.

Once again, Benjamin started contemplating a career change. He'd thought about it a lot on leave, spending many hours brooding over his options. He still wanted to work in aviation and had therefore considered flight operations, or even air-crash investigation. He needed to get his life back on track. He'd blown it with Elizabeth, but he hoped that one day he would find someone else, just as headstrong and beautiful, to share his life with. He had come to realise that flying wasn't everything in life. It was his passion, but he wanted a personal life too. Flying would have to be relegated to second position if he wanted a second chance at love.

Benjamin was tiring of long-haul trips, but he was still youthful for his age. Tall, with an intelligent, sharply chiselled face, he was still regarded as handsome. His time in the military had taught him discipline, but above all, confidence in himself and his abilities. Surely he still had some abilities in the art of attracting women?

Yet despite all his pondering, all his flirting with the idea of quitting the skies, here he was again – with a chance to fly the A380–800 Airbus. Of all the aircraft on ANZSAL's manifest, Benjamin admired her the most.

Benjamin needed to meet the cabin crew before take-off. He put on his captain's jacket and hat. He picked up his flight bag and left the pilot's briefing room. He felt confident. This short flight to Christchurch and back would be a walk in the park.

★

The Shangri-La Hotel, 176 Cumberland St, Sydney
7.45 p.m.

'How does my hair look?' Millie asked her twin sister vainly, knowing full well it was perfect.

'Fine, as always,' Annie replied, not even looking up at her sister, as she gathered her toiletries from the bathroom. 'Have you finished packing yet?'

'Stop panicking. We have plenty of time before the flight,' Millie replied. 'I can't believe how many fab clothes I've bought in Sydney.'

'Our trip isn't even half over yet. You'll have to buy another suitcase or ship some of it home. And I'm not panicking. I just don't like being rushed.'

'Well, don't worry,' Mille said. 'Have you organised for the car to pick us up in Christchurch? It'll be early when we arrive.'

'Yes.'

'Planes dry out my hair,' Millie said, as she continued to brush her long blonde hair in front of the bathroom mirror.

'It's only a three-and-a-half-hour flight. You'll live,' Annie replied as she walked back into the bathroom. 'You're not wearing that mini skirt and top, are you?'

'Duh! It's Dolce and Gabbana,' her sister said.

'Duh! It's winter in New Zealand. You'll freeze your arse off,' Annie said, walking out of the bathroom, again. Rolling her eyes, Millie admired herself in the mirror for a few more seconds before deciding to wear something a little warmer. But just as fab.

Being twins, they were identical in appearance, but not in personality. At first glance, an admirer would say they were pretty but self-absorbed. Confident but self-centred. But if you looked a little deeper, you would find two intelligent young women living the lifestyle expected of two privileged young socialites from New York.

They could have played another role, but friends and their society expected a lot from them. Maybe it was just simpler to play the game. Or so Millie thought.

Their trip had been a gift from their father for their well-deserved grades after graduating high school. They would be going to different colleges after their breaks. Both sisters knew that it was time to grow apart. Annie was heading to Harvard to study business and economics, while Millie would study fashion, art, and marketing at Cornell. No one could understand the love that Millie had for Annie and vice-versa. Only twins could truly appreciate their connection. Overall, life was carefree for Millie and Annie.

★

Starbucks, Sydney Kingsford-Smith Airport, Mascot
7.50 p.m.

As he slipped into the cabin, he raised his gun to his masculine chest. His own reflection startled him momentarily in the mirror, but he was quick to recover. He paused to admire his sculptured face. He took two more steps into the cabin. His heart was pounding.

She appeared from behind the door. Her gun was pointed at his back . . .

'To kill or not to kill, that is the question,' Pauline muttered to herself. Sitting in the Starbucks as she waited for her flight to be called, Pauline mulled over whether or not she should kill off her protagonist or save him to fight another day.

Pauline Walsh was heading to her sister's place in Dunedin, as she was in desperate need of a confidante and pep talk. Her sister Alice always knew just what to say to her.

Pauline's pessimistic outlook had drawn her to the realisation that her life was in the toilet. At forty, Pauline hated her job, but at least it paid the bills. Her only pleasure was found in her writing. Unfortunately, at the moment, it was only regarded as a hobby, until a publisher or agent said otherwise. Her latest rejection had been yet another proverbial flush down the toilet.

But she wasn't a quitter. Her latest book was set aboard a ship run aground on a coral reef. Crew and passengers fight to stay alive. Only, she didn't have an ending – not yet anyway. What would become of them, or her, for that matter? She hated feeling miserable, and so a trip to see her sister was in order.

Pauline was getting hungry, and lunch had been hours ago. She hoped that they would serve dinner on board. However, since it was a late-night flight, they would probably only serve tea and biscuits. She decided that a muffin was a necessity. With choc chips.

Pauline had been delighted when she'd received a text from ANZAL, rescheduling her previously cancelled flight. She'd packed quickly and headed to the airport before they could change their minds. She'd left behind her hairbrush, toothbrush, dental floss, and pyjamas. But she still had a niggling feeling that something else was missing – something important. Only, she couldn't remember what.

Oh well, she thought. It would come to her eventually. She had her boarding pass and passport – anything else was secondary. As Pauline sat drinking her cold tea, she wondered why life was always so bloody difficult and unfair. One day, she'd write a bestseller and publishers would be knocking at her door, instead of pressing the flush button.

'I think he'll live,' Pauline muttered and smiled to herself, as she continued typing. 'There must always be hope!'

★

Gate 52, Sydney Kingsford-Smith International Airport, Mascot
8.10 p.m.

'Oh, go on, rub my feet, *please*,' Beth begged, her voice straining as she sat uncomfortably on her seat. They were at the gate lounge, waiting for their flight to board.

Angus eyed her with pity.

'All right, then, lift them up,' he said, as Beth quickly took off her shoes and swung her legs on to Angus' lap. They were coming to the end of their holiday. Backpacking had seen them visit Thailand, China, Japan, and Indonesia. Australia and New Zealand were the last legs of their trip.

Beth looked and felt great. She lost weight during their trip and had joked with Angus that when she returned home, she would be able to enter the London Marathon.

Beth was twenty-six and worked as a nurse. She would commence a new posting at Great Ormond Street Children's Hospital upon their return. Angus, twenty-nine, was a sports teacher, but he lived for the weekends when he could go mountain climbing. The pair had now been married for a little over three months. They'd met at an indoor rock-climbing centre. Beth had been struggling up a climbing wall, and to her humiliation, as she'd heaved herself up, she'd accidently passed wind. Just a pop, mind you – but enough of a pop to be heard by the other climbers.

Angus had heroically stepped up and apologised to everyone for his uncontrolled outburst. He'd shown great valour. Unfortunately, Beth couldn't stop giggling and had slipped from the wall and straight into his arms. From that day forward, they'd no secrets between them.

They were married one year later. Angus had referred to Beth from that day on as his little 'poppy'.

They'd had a remarkable holiday, but Beth was starting to feel homesick. They'd been talking about maybe starting a family once they returned home, and Beth didn't know if her edginess was down to her tiredness or the thought of commencing a new chapter in her life. All she knew for sure was that she couldn't do it with any other man.

★

Ticket Counter, Mascot Airport
8.55 p.m.

'Brilliant, thank you,' Victoria Dahl said, as the passenger service agent handed over an economy ticket.

'You're in seat 53K and your flight will be boarding at 9.30 p.m. You better hurry.'

'Thanks. I've only got my overnight bag,' Victoria said, as she picked up her briefcase and luggage bag. She walked quickly towards the customs hall.

Her assignment was last-minute. The federal police had been brought in to investigate a bomb planted on a Learjet bound for Christchurch. The AFP had picked up CCTV footage of a man near the hanger where the Learjet was parked. The police had ruled out a random act of terrorism. They instead believed that it could be a targeted attack, either against Blue Southern Skies or one of their passengers. One set of these passengers were now about to board flight AN224.

Victoria was scheduled to meet her counterparts in New Zealand upon her arrival. The AFP had intercepted communications on an untraceable mobile, and they'd heard the names of 'Mr Wolf' and 'Mr Jackal'. On checking customs video footage, they'd identified a suspect near the Learjet hanger boarding a flight back to Christchurch via another airline two hours earlier. The Christchurch airport police had been notified to detain the suspect on arrival. They would wait for Victoria to arrive before interviewing him. Victoria would then organise his extradition back to Australia.

The New Zealand police would interview the passengers who chartered the Learjet once Victoria arrived in Christchurch.

Victoria doubted that this man had orchestrated the attack. She suspected that he'd simply been hired to plant the bomb. Being a professional, she doubted he would talk, except to ask for a lawyer.

At thirty-five, Victoria Dahl had been in the federal police for over eight years. In that time, she'd seen many things that had made her question whether or not she actually lived in a civilised society. But she believed in the fight – the one for the greater good. It wasn't a cliché to Vicki. She truly wanted to make a difference.

She made her way through the terminal and gate lounge. She needed to read some reports before boarding her flight.

★

VIP Airport Lounge, Sydney International Airport, Mascot
9.12 p.m.

'Ugh, I've told you before, Frank, I won't work with 'im, he's a misogynist pig,' Chyna Day said loudly into her mobile phone as she paced around the room.

After a pause, she went on. 'What about Hugh? … Look! You know, I can't talk right now … Yeah … I'm boarding soon; they changed my flight … Um, it's flight

AN224 … Yeah, I'm still in first … Got to dash. Loves and kisses, see you when I'm back! Ciao!'

★

Constantine Zabinski found the one-way conversation irritating. A three year old Czechoslovakian refugee would have had a better grasp of the English language than this over-rated actress did. He loudly turned the pages of his newspaper in annoyance.

Constantine was heading to New Zealand to oversee the opening of a new restaurant in Christchurch. Twenty years in the military had given him an abundance of skills which his salary didn't commensurate. His passion was cooking, which he had made into a lucrative career after leaving the army and opening his first restaurant in Poland. Now, with two Michelin Stars to his name and eight restaurants around the world, he was an international success.

Constantine was a serious man, but with a great passion for cooking. Only, he chose to play down his celebrity status as a renowned chef. He never liked people knowing his business or being able to read him. He preferred to be a closed book kind of man. His successful restaurants spoke for themselves.

★

A few seats over, Dave and Gladys Honeycombe – from Cornwall, England – sat quietly as they drank their tea. They tried not to gawp at the famous movie star who was pacing the room while talking on her mobile. They felt like trespassers in the VIP lounge.

They'd won their first-class holiday to Australia and New Zealand in a competition. Gladys was itching to take a photo on her own mobile to show her daughters back home. They wouldn't believe her without evidence. But she refrained.

After finishing their Australian leg, their earlier flight had been cancelled due to the earthquakes in Christchurch. Luckily, their hotel concierge had secured them seats on flight AN224, so they wouldn't miss the start of their New Zealand tour, which commenced at 9 a.m. sharp the next morning.

They would be celebrating their twenty-ninth wedding anniversary while in the Bay of Islands, not to mention Gladys' fiftieth birthday, for which she was still in denial. Gladys had done everything humanly possible to avoid the milestone, but alas, there was no stalling it. Dave found her whole reaction hilarious, not that he said so. Especially when Gladys had told him that she was suffering PSTD. He'd chosen prudence over correcting her.

Dave found Australia fascinating and was looking forward to the New Zealand leg of their tour. He had a surprise lined up for Gladys, once they arrived in the Bay of Islands. He watched her now, ogling the actress who paced around the room. For all Gladys' faults, and there were a few, Dave often reminded himself that he was a lucky man.

★

Gate Fifty-Two, Sydney Kingsford-Smith International Airport, Mascot
9.19 p.m.

'Last chance. Who needs to go to the toilet?' Jane Mallard asked, staring down at her three children. They were preoccupied with their iPhones and iPads.

They all shook their heads, vowing that they were all good to go. She couldn't prove it, but she knew that they were lying. They always lied!

They'd been excited about getting on a plane. Hugh and Jane didn't know why they'd bothered booking an entire holiday when they could have just bought airline tickets and flown their children anywhere and back again.

Once on board, Jane could finally relax. Earlier, she had been a woman possessed. Five passports, check. Five boarding passes, check. Five carry-on bags, check. Three children, check. One husband, check. Panadol, check.

Hugh had seemed non-perplexed about the whole exercise. He always did take everything in his stride, which always vexed her.

The return flight was going to go smoothly, unlike their previous departure from Christchurch two weeks ago. Ava had snuck some last-minute things into her backpack, which had caused some concern at the Christchurch customs hall.

Jane desperately needed a drink. She kept imagining a small bottle of red and a delicious cheese board with her name on it. It was going to be her indulgence – *heaven*. She hoped the kids would fall asleep during the flight. Hugh and Jane had purposefully taken them sightseeing all day. Only now, they felt more tired than the kids did.

Nonetheless, Jane was determined to have her cheeseboard and wine before she fell asleep.

Chapter Five

Boarding Flight AN224, Sydney Airport, Mascot
9.20 p.m.

June Wilson graciously welcomed her first-class passengers on board. As this flight's senior flight attendant – or in-flight service manager, as she was now called – she was responsible for all the cabin crew, plus every passenger's comfort, while on board. Tonight, June was responsible for over 480 passengers and seventeen crew members.

At fifty-six, June was well-seasoned. She had seen many changes to in-flight services since she'd begun her career over thirty years ago. June had come to realise that flying was a lifestyle now, not just a service intended to transport people around the globe.

Never would people experience a class system more profound than that of an aircraft. Luxury abounded if you could afford it. Depending on the aircraft's design, first-class passengers of an A380 Airbus could utilise the bar, gym, showers, and conference rooms.

But what never failed to amaze June was the looks on passengers' faces when they first walked onto an

Airbus. Their mouths would drop slightly, and their eyes would light up as they took in the vibrant and warmly lit cabins.

Earlier, June had escorted Joanne and Amy Donnelly to their seats before the rest of the passengers boarded. She had used the lift to take them up to business class. Once they were settled, she'd continued her rounds of both the main and upper decks.

The cabin crew had stowed their overnight bags below in the cabin crew rest compartment, which was located below the main deck. They wouldn't need to use this compartment during the flight, as it was only a medium-haul flight. But for longer trips, such as from Sydney to London, the cabin crew could rest in one of the bunks during the flight.

The flight crew bunks were situated in a small cabin behind the cockpit. But Captain Flynn and First Officer Whitby would not be needing them during this short flight.

As June continued her walk through the economy class cabin on the main deck, the Airbus' soft-lit lights gave a warm opulence to the cabin. The lights blended well with the Egyptian blue seats and carpets. She entered first class and began inspecting every seat, to make sure each pillow was puffed and every designer amenities bag was perfectly placed on each passenger table by their chair. The first-class cabin was complete with decadent wooden panelling and leather alcove seats, which could be converted into beds during long flights. Once June was satisfied that everything was in order, she made her way upstairs. The staircase leading up to business class was lit with a soft blue hue. It always made June feel like she was walking up into a spaceship.

After her walk-through was complete, she descended the spiral staircase at the back of the cabin. It was time to assist with the boarding of economy passengers.

June always enjoyed the serenity of the empty cabins before each flight. Their pristine condition was always gone by the time they landed. The longer the flight, the more dishevelled the cabins would become, with restless passengers anxious to arrive at their destinations.

Whether travelling for business or for pleasure, each passenger always had their own story to tell. June loved chatting to them and hearing their tales. She often thought of writing down a compilation of them as short stories in her retirement. There would probably be many volumes.

★

'Welcome aboard, Mr and Mrs Ming. May I take your coats?' Naomi, one of the first-class attendants, asked.

'Thank you,' Peng replied, as she went to sit in the window seat.

'No, I want the window seat, you know I prefer the window seat,' Lu whined.

'*Yǒu shíhòu nǐ hěn kěbēi*,' Peng said. *You are so pathetic at times*. She turned and sat in the aisle seat instead. Peng had learned that the man she'd married was very pedantic. Brilliant, but pedantic.

Now, as Peng looked across at her husband sitting by the window, she wondered what she had seen in him. She felt that their ride had gone on for long enough.

As Peng fastened her seatbelt, two teenagers walked past. One was talking on her iPhone. American. Peng hoped that they wouldn't be too loud, but she did concede that they had great taste in clothes.

A flight attendant arrived and asked Peng what she would like to drink. As she took her order, Henry Adams and Gertrude Simpson took their seats in 1 and 2A.

★

Henry was glad that his seat was in front of Gertrude's. He valued and respected her as a colleague, but at times he found her overbearing. She hadn't stopped talking in the taxi ride to the airport. Maybe he could pretend to be asleep during the flight. He had much to think about before their arrival in Christchurch.

Henry had been tempted to tell Gertrude about his visit from the federal police in Sydney. But decided not to worry her unnecessarily, until they landed. He knew that the authorities in Christchurch would be waiting to speak to them. He decided to avoid her as much as possible, which was difficult when you're sitting directly in front of them on an aircraft. But Henry thought Gertrude deserved to relax, at least until they arrived in Christchurch.

★

When Dave and Gladys Honeycombe walked into the first-class cabin, their eyes betrayed their awe. They were amazed by the interior. The wood panelling and brown leather seats were ultramodern. They showed their tickets to the flight attendant, Naomi, who escorted them to their seats. They each had their own little compartment, which converted into a bed.

Once Gladys fastened her seatbelt, she took her time checking out the contents of her complimentary amenities bag. Not that she had any intention of using it; she wanted to save it so that she could show her daughters once they returned home. Gladys removed one item at a time and marvelled at what was inside – designer skincare products, eye cream, pillow mist spray, cleanser, and toner. There was also a leather-bound notebook and branded pen. On their long-haul flight to Australia, she had been given pyjamas and slippers, not that she would have dared to wear them in front of everyone.

Gladys asked Dave for his amenities bag, which he dutifully handed over. Inside, she found tissues, a refresher towel, black comb, Lynx body spray, toothbrush and paste kit, razor, shaving foam, lip balm, body lotion, and aftershave. Gladys put everything neatly back into the cases and then discretely placed both inside her handbag.

Now she picked up the menu, which was imprinted with gold leaf. Gladys read through what she was having for dinner and began to regret eating before heading to the airport. The menu offered a choice of succulent blue swimmer crab – with fresh steamed greens and truffle-flavoured jasmine rice – or Wagyu beef served with baby potatoes and hot roast vegetables accompanied by a rich mushroom sauce. For dessert, she had a choice of ginger, apple, and rhubarb pie – with honeycomb ice-cream or clotted cream – or crème brulée with fresh raspberries and blueberries.

She would make herself eat. She wasn't going to miss out on anything. First-class would only come around once in her lifetime. Now was not the time to say, *No, thank you, I'm full.*

★

Constantine Zabinski made himself comfortable as Naomi offered him a pre-flight drink. He was feeling relaxed. That is, until Chyna Day sat down in the seat across from him.

Celebrity or not, he found her annoying. He hoped that she wouldn't be on the phone all through the flight. Apart from her irritating voice, he thought her too skinny. Constantine found women who were all skin and bone unappealing. As a Michelin chef, he believed that food was made to be savoured and indulged. Skinny people had obviously missed the point. He picked up the menu and scrutinized the dishes.

★

'*Danke*,' said Herbert Schwartz as he made himself comfortable in seat 5K, which was at the back of the first-class cabin.

He had been relieved when he'd received confirmation from his hotel concierge that he'd managed to book a seat on flight AN224.

Herbert was back on track. He was expanding his business into the South Pacific, starting with Australia and New Zealand. This week's delay hadn't fazed him. He had plenty of time before a meeting with his lawyers in Christchurch at 11 a.m. tomorrow.

He had brought his skis with him from Germany. He planned to ski at Mount Cook National Park until he'd been informed that the park was closed. While laid over in Australia, he'd headed down to Mount Kosciuszko National Park and taken in some slopes there instead.

At forty-eight, Herbert was still in peak condition. His body was strong and toned. Being unmarried had afforded him the opportunity to show off his sculptured figure to as many women as cared to look – and many did. Herbert was naturally self-assured, thanks to too many years of hard work and discipline. Quitting at anything in life had never been an option for him. Everything he hadn't yet mastered was only a weakness that needed to be beaten.

And there was a lot to master in the meeting tomorrow. Herbert decided to catch a few hours of sleep before his arrival in Christchurch.

★

'I have to go to the toilet, Mum,' Ava Mallard said.

'I asked you before we boarded,' replied her mother.

'I didn't have to go then.'

'Come on, then,' Jane said. Holding her six-year-old daughter's hand. Jane repeatedly apologised to her fellow passengers stowing their bags as she and Ava squeezed past them. It took longer than expected to reach the toilet several rows behind them. She heard Ava continually pleading behind her: 'Hurry, it's coming!'

'Do you want me to come in?'

'*No!* I'm not five anymore.'

'Okay, but don't lock the door.'

'What? What if someone comes in?' Ava questioned, looking mortified at the thought.

'I'm standing right here. Nobody's coming in,' Jane said.

'Fine.' Ava walked in and closed the door behind her.

As Jane stood guard, she thought about how fast her children had grown up. One day soon they wouldn't need her anymore, then what would she do? Her mother had suggested she start a degree or go back to work. Her children had been her life for the past twelve years. Starting a degree and working full-time again was a scary thought. Jane knew that her mother was right, though, even though she would miss those golden years of nurturing.

On the way back, Jane and Ava manoeuvred past more arriving passengers, before returning to their seats in 21E and F. Ava's small hand in hers reassured Jane – Ava would still need her for many years to come. She held onto that thought as tightly as she held her daughter's hand.

When Jane arrived back at her seat, Hugh wasn't there.

'Where's your father?' she asked Felix and Leonor.

'Toilet,' they said together, without looking up from their games.

Once Jane was back in her seat, she pulled out the menu and read her choices for tonight's dinner. Business-class passengers were offered a choice of ocean trout, butter chicken, or a mushroom risotto served with a light salad. For dessert, they had a choice of chocolate gateau or crepes with strawberries and ice-cream. Accompanying their dinner would be an offer of a wide selection of drinks from the airline's cellar.

Jane was finally able to relax. They would be home in under five hours. She was looking forward to her own bed.

★

University professor Windsor Hounslow stumbled with his packages as he hurried towards his departure gate. He had purchased a bottle of whiskey at the duty free earlier on. There were two obnoxious women in front of him; one wanted to buy cigarettes for her dying husband. He had raised his eyes to the sky and thanked God that he'd remained a confirmed bachelor.

He'd also stopped off at the Dymocks bookshop to purchase a couple of novels. As always, time had gotten away from him as he'd indulged in one of his few pleasures – browsing bookshelves.

Now he was running late. He was becoming sweaty and dishevelled as he carried his laptop case under his right armpit and his overnight bag over his left shoulder. While juggling his purchases, he started to wonder if they were such a good idea after all. He was referring to the books, not the GlenDronach Scotch Whiskey. At $260 a bottle, he would cherish it as much as a family heirloom or small child.

Windsor Hounslow finally arrived at the gate. He manoeuvred his parcels around to retrieve his boarding pass, then finally relaxed as he strolled down the gangway and onto his flight.

★

9.37 p.m.

In economy, the attendants welcomed everyone aboard. Being the largest cabin on the aircraft, the vessel was abuzz with people squeezing past each other to find their seats and stow their coats before picking up their headphones and amenities kits. Once seated, the passengers were able to take in the majestic size and ambience of the cabin. They were all silently thinking, *How the hell does this thing get off the ground?*

Dinner tonight was a choice of stir-fried noodles with beef and vegetables in oyster sauce or barramundi in a white wine sauce. A free bottle of wine, beer, or soft drink would accompany dinner, followed by tea or coffee. Drinks and snacks could be accessed from the self-service section during the flight for anyone who was still feeling peckish.

While the flight attendants settled their passengers into their seats, the flight crew were carrying out last minute pre-flight checks in the cockpit.

Chapter Six

Gate 52, Sydney Kingsford-Smith International Airport, Mascot
9.40 p.m.

At the boarding gate, two flight attendants, Charlotte and John, processed the last of the passengers' boarding passes. It was a full flight. Arriving in Christchurch in the early morning, they would only have a short layover. Then they would return to Sydney on AN229, scheduled to leave Christchurch at 9 a.m. tomorrow morning.

'Thank you,' he said as he scanned another boarding pass. 'Thank you.' Since becoming a flight attendant, John's vocabulary consisted of mainly *thank you*, *welcome aboard*, and *tea or coffee, madam?* Apart from the overseas travel, being a flight attendant wasn't as glamourous as he'd thought it would be.

'Thank you, madam.'

As the last of the passengers made their way on board, Charlotte went over to the check-in counter to see how many hadn't arrived yet. Then a woman approached her.

'Could you please confirm if the following passengers boarded this flight?' Victoria Dahl asked, showing Charlotte a list of names and her federal police badge.

Charlotte immediately typed their names into the computer.

'Yes, they have,' she said.

'Thank you.' Victoria started to walk towards the boarding gate, but the flight attendant spoke again.

'Is there something we should know about these passengers before take-off?' Charlotte asked.

'No, they're not a threat. I just needed to confirm that they were on board,' Victoria said, as she pulled out her phone and made one last phone call.

Charlotte checked the flight manifest on the computer, which showed that four passengers had not checked in. There were always stragglers. Charlotte picked up the microphone and made an announcement over the PA system.

'Could Bernard Danbridge, Jasmine Pontrelli, and Yang and Xue Hong make their way to gate fifty-two? Your flight is closing.'

They waited another five minutes as their stragglers arrived, dishevelled and gasping, at the gate. They apologised profusely before making their way down the air bridge, except for Bernard Danbridge, who didn't appear dishevelled in the least and handed over his boarding pass with a smile and in a suave English accent, apologised for being late. Charlotte didn't mind in the least; she'd always loved Colin Firth.

Bertie Danbridge made his way into business class and sat next to a fellow Englishman, who introduced himself as Professor Windsor Hounslow.

★

Pauline Walsh found her seat at the back of the main cabin in economy and made herself comfortable. After fastening her seatbelt, she opened her little amenities kit. It contained a little toothbrush and toothpaste. Handy, considering she'd left hers at home. There was also an eye mask, socks, and ear plugs, although she wouldn't need them as she had plenty of work to keep her busy during the flight. Pauline was at an important scene in her novel.

She was looking forward to dinner – she was starving. She wondered what they would be serving; she'd always loved those cute trays with the little compartments of food. Anything tasted good when you didn't have to cook it yourself.

★

9.55 p.m.

Annabel Jones, who was fidgeting in seat 49A, checked her watch again. It was only ten minutes after the last time she'd checked it. She turned on the airflow and directed it onto her face. She pulled out her bottle of water and took a few large swigs, then placed it back in the pouch of the seat in front of her. Her mouth was dry – a sign she was getting anxious.

Her foot started to tap. She was seated on the portside of the cabin, the second row back from an emergency exit door, near the galley. Looking out the window, she watched as a light drizzle started to fall. She had insisted on a window seat as confined spaces still distressed her. But, at night, there wouldn't be much to see. Annabel kept telling herself that it was only three and a half hours. She sat quietly and closed her eyes, then breathed in for three and out for five, in for three and out for five. This well-practiced technique often calmed her down when she remembered to use it.

Annabel had been excited about the trip. Her organisation, Combat Women Unite, was a great success in Australia. Another charity in New Zealand, which mostly dealt with returned servicemen, wanted to create a similar foundation based on her model. They'd offered her a joint partnership. With more publicity, she might attract even more endorsements back home. She kept imagining all the ex-female veterans she would be able to help.

Being a reporter for the army newspaper, Sergeant Annabel Jones had travelled around the world, documenting the Australian military's activities. Unfortunately, during her tours, she witnessed not just heroic acts but horrific acts of cruelty and depravity. The military's conception that only their serving men suffered PTSD meant that there wasn't much support for female soldiers. Annabel's erratic behaviour had gone undiagnosed for some time. Drinking had helped her to blot out the nightmares until it had become its own problem. Sometimes, she felt like all the happiness had been drained from the world. She would sob for hours.

Finally, she'd sought help, which had drawn her out of her maudlin state. Now a recovering alcoholic, Annabel fought hard to defend and help her fellow female soldiers. By creating Combat Women Unite, she hoped to turn many lives around. This last year, her organisation had picked up momentum. Now, with her new potential alliance with New Zealand, she was taking steps to making it an international organisation. All she needed to do was get through the flight.

One step at a time, she told herself, as she breathed in for three and slowly out for five, waiting for the plane to be pushed back.

As Annabel gazed out her little window, she saw a magnificent full moon appear through the clouds. A female voice came over the intercom.

'Ladies and gentlemen, the captain has instructed that you all fasten your seatbelts. Please make sure that your carry-on luggage has been stowed away for take-off, and that your seatbelts are fastened, your chair is upright, and your folding trays are locked away. If you have any questions during your flight, please do not hesitate to ask one of our in-flight attendants. Thank you.'

Finally, the doors were closed and the captain came on the intercom.

'Ladies and gentlemen, my name is Captain Benjamin Flynn, and I have the honour of flying you to Christchurch tonight aboard our newest ship. We will be flying at a cruise speed of one thousand and fifty kilometres per hour and at a height of 35,000 feet.'

Annabel listened to the confident and reassuring voice. Her gaze was drawn back outside to the full moon. It was smiling down at her. Was it a knowing smile, or was it a malevolent one?

Chapter Seven

Cockpit of Flight AN224
10.02 p.m.

Captain Flynn and First Officer Whitby completed their pre-flight checklist, then Captain Flynn radioed the tractor driver to start pushback. Once complete, the A380-800 commenced its taxi to runway 16R. It was the longest one available; the Airbus needed a runway length of 2900 metres for take-off due to its enormous size.

'Cabin crew, arm doors. Cross-check and report, thank you,' the first officer said.

Once clear of the terminal, Captain Flynn taxied away from the Apron and onto the Taxiway. He and Marcus carried out flight control movements along the way, finally coming to a stop at the holding position. Once Air Traffic Control gave them clearance onto the runway, they manoeuvred the aircraft onto the threshold.

'Flight AN224 cleared for take-off on runway one-six-right, wind one-nine-zero at twelve,' the air traffic controller said.

'Roger 224,' Captain Flynn said as he and Marcus commenced take-off. Benjamin pushed the thrust levers to thirty percent and then paused. The heavy fan blades would take several seconds to accelerate and stabilise to their required setting. With no abnormal activity, the captain released the brakes and advanced the thrust levers.

The plane powered down the runway, her speed increasing with each second. Every person on board felt the force of the four Rolls Royce engines as they were thrust back into their seats. The Airbus lifted off like an eagle in flight and climbed majestically into the night sky.

After climb-out, the landing gear was retracted. Flight AN224 began its slow climb to its allotted height of 35,000 feet. Captain Flynn ordered the flaps retracted in increments until Flaps Zero was attained. Once they reached FL100, they turned off the landing lights and seatbelt sign. The VHF radio was changed to 121.5 MHz, the international distress frequency, so that they could maintain a listening watch.

Once Marcus switched frequencies, he turned on the plane's squawk code. Once their position was identified by ATC, they continued their cruise climb and settled in for the duration.

'I wonder what's for dinner tonight,' Marcus pondered aloud.

'I would have thought you'd have eaten already,' Benjamin replied.

'I was going to make fettuccine boscaiola for Jenny and I, but I was called in, remember?'

Benjamin knew that Marcus had only been married for three months. A pilot's life seemed glamourous to most people, but eventually the novelty would wear off. Long absences didn't always make the heart grow fonder.

God, Benjamin thought. *When did I start being so cynical?*

'How's she taken to being a pilot's wife?' he asked.

'Fine so far. She works from home, so she likes that I'm out of her hair,' Marcus said.

'You'll get along just fine then,' laughed Benjamin. He switched on the PA system. 'Good evening. This is your captain, Benjamin Flynn, speaking. Your first officer for tonight's flight is Marcus Whitby. We've started our cruise climb to 35,000 feet. We have fine weather ahead, so it should be a smooth flight to Christchurch. We'll be arriving on-time at Christchurch airport at 1.25 a.m. Australian time, which will make it 3.25 a.m. New Zealand time, if not a little earlier. Thank you and enjoy your flight.'

Once the captain finished his announcement, the interphone rang. It was June Wilson, asking if they'd like any refreshments or dinner.

'Beef, chicken, or trout?' Marcus asked, turning to Benjamin.

'I'll have the beef,' Benjamin said.

Marcus relayed their orders to June. As always, they ordered something different to each other.

June went to the galley on the upper deck and asked Matilda, a business-class flight attendant, to prepare the pilots' meals and refreshments.

Once the trays were ready, Matilda walked through the lounge and bar area before coming to the first of two cockpit doors. She called the cockpit on the interphone to obtain permission to enter. She was given a code, which released the lock on the first door.

Matilda walked through the passage to the second cockpit door and pressed the chime button. Once Marcus could see on the video monitor that she was alone, he unlocked the second door into the cockpit.

The second cockpit door was bulletproof and could withstand an attack by an assault rifle. The security measures on the A380 Airbuses were state-of-the-art.

Benjamin and Marcus thanked Matilda for their meals. She smiled at them, but before leaving, she looked outside the cockpit window at the magnificent full moon. It always seemed more magnificent at altitude, away from the hustle and bustle of city lights.

★

10.55 p.m.

As Con Pappas rose from his seat, he winced. He excused himself to his wife, Chloe, and told her he was going to the bathroom. He needed to take a tablet. He believed that Chloe still didn't know anything about his condition.

This was their once-in-a-lifetime holiday. After selling their grocery store, Con wanted to take Chloe back to the island of Ios, the Greek island in the Aegean Sea where he'd been born. It was where they'd first met, and where he wanted to die.

He only wished he had taken Chloe back years ago. They could have enjoyed its beauty so much more. Believing in a strong work ethic, Con and Chloe had run their greengrocer business for the entirety of their married lives. They rarely took any time off for themselves. Regretfully, Con hadn't sold the business until after being diagnosed with cancer. Now he was taking Chloe back to Ios, to where it all began, and sadly, where it would all end.

When Con had presented Chloe with the tickets, she'd insisted on stopping off in New Zealand first to visit her sister and family. How could he say no to Chloe? She had been his rock, his Hestia, for forty-seven years. He hoped to God that Chloe would forgive him. He hated keeping secrets from her, but he dreaded all the fuss she would make over him if she knew the truth. It would only make it harder to bear.

Con had decided he wanted to be laid to rest under the warm blue Aegean sky. This was where his ancestors were buried. This was where he wanted to be buried, too.

He smiled kindly at Chloe as he stepped past her and made his way to the bathroom. All around them, the passengers were enjoying the last bites of their meals. The cabin's overhead compartments had now been dimmed to a soft blue light, and many of the passengers were already settled down to sleep.

Chapter Eight

First-Class Cabin
11.15 p.m.

'Would you like another champagne, madam?' Naomi asked Millie Wellington.

'Yes, why not,' she replied, lifting up her glass. As Naomi re-filled it, Millie smiled to herself, contentedly. The legal age in Australia and New Zealand for drinking was eighteen. She hadn't needed her fake ID for the entire holiday. The flight attendant offered her some Koko Black chocolates, and although Millie was tempted, she calculated the calories and regretfully declined. Naomi continued to seat 3K and asked Millie's identical twin if she'd like a drink, too. Annie politely declined. Reclining her seat back into a bed, Annie curled up and tried to get some sleep.

'Hay, miss,' said a voice across the cabin. Naomi turned to see the man in seat 1K waving and clicking his fingers at her. Naomi loved her job, but the one thing she hated with a passion was passengers who clicked their fingers to get her attention. She found it degrading. Naomi walked over to him. He held up his cup.

'I need more coffee,' Lu Ming said.

'Of course, sir, I won't be a moment.' She took his used cup and returned shortly with a fresh one.

Nearby, while Chyna Day was touching up her make-up, Constantine Zabinski was making notes about his dinner. Even though he was a well-respected chef, he also saw himself as a critic. He had created a blog under a pseudonym and wrote on it quite frequently. No one knew who the author really was, but his page had recently been making huge waves in the food scene. Nowadays, his criticisms or compliments could make or break a restaurant, which Constantine secretly enjoyed.

★

Gladys Honeycombe had thoroughly enjoyed her meal, especially as she hadn't had to cook it. Without the slightest hint of shame, she had taken a proud picture of her meal before devouring it. When Charlotte, her flight attendant, cleared away her tray, she was tempted to tell her to give her compliments to the chef, but instead she opened the cabinet beside her and studied the variety of soft drinks, wine, and beer. However, both Gladys and Dave requested another cup of coffee. Gladys was too excited to sleep. They wanted to enjoy every decadent moment. Gladys took out her mobile again and made a short video of the cabin. As she was filming, Chyna Day stood up and stretched before heading to the toilet at the front of the cabin. Gladys couldn't believe she'd actually filmed Chyna Day going for a pee. Her girls wouldn't believe it.

★

Meanwhile, in business class, Clementine were clearing away the last of the dinner trays when one of the call buttons was pressed. She took a note of the seat number – 16K, and walked down the aisle to find out what the passenger needed.

'Yes, madam?' Clementine asked.

'Could I please have another bottle of wine? This one barely wet my whistle,' Lesley said.

'Certainly, madam,' Clementine replied, as she took the empty bottle away.

'Haven't you had enough?' Rose said, leaning forward to speak with her best friend, who was seated in front of her.

'Well, you're the pot calling the kettle black, aren't you?' Lesley quipped, turning around. She knew that Rose had devoured her own small bottle of red.

'I'm still on holiday and will be until I walk through my front door,' Rose reasoned. 'Then it's back to my old hum-drum life.'

'Cheer up, there's always next year,' Lesley said, knowing full well how her friend felt. They weren't getting any younger. Whenever someone reminded her of her age, Lesley would think they were talking about someone else. She didn't feel sixty-one. Lesley laid back and stared out the window. She was staring out at a magnificent full moon while wondering to herself, where had all the time gone?

★

Flight Service Manager June Wilson never stopped patrolling the main and upper decks. Now, as everyone had been dutifully attended to in first class, she started her walk through the most populated area – economy. June was always amazed by how an aeroplane could get so many ethnically and culturally diverse people crammed into such a small space without starting World War III. She put it down to one fact alone: all their fates were out of their hands. They were in it together, whether they liked it or not.

As all of her economy passengers were quietly resting, June headed back upstairs again to continue her walk through business class.

On this particular flight, there was a large medley of international travellers from six continents. There was a group of Swedish university students, Chinese and Japanese tourists, a school troupe from New Zealand returning home, as well as a medley of foreign passengers from England, France, Italy, Syria, and Turkey. However, the majority of passengers were Australian and New Zealanders. June had also noted on the manifest that there were five doctors on board. Statistically, there was always one, and usually a nurse or two.

June had lost count of the many hundreds of kilometres she'd walked around each aircraft over the years. One thing she knew for a fact was that she never tired of it.

★

Con Pappas was restless. He hadn't eaten much and couldn't sleep. He was feeling a little uncomfortable, so he excused himself and took a stroll around the cabin. Chloe watched him as he moved along the aisle. A tear formed, which ran down her face. She quickly wiped it away. She didn't want him to know that she knew. She hated that he was in so much pain. How could Con really think he could keep a secret from her? She found it hard to keep up the pretence. Even while they were packing for their trip.

★

Pappas' Dulwich Hill Residence
Earlier that day …

'Come on, old girl,' Con said lovingly to his wife, Chloe.

'Hold your horses, Con. I'm having trouble closing my case.' Chloe was sitting on her case, in the hope it would miraculously close under her weight.

'The way you've been shopping, old girl, I'll be surprised if you're not over the weight limit.'

'Well, I had to buy something for everyone. I'm sure I've not missed anyone. This koala backpack just won't fit in.'

Con's frail arms came up behind Chloe. He wrapped them around her and kissed her on the head.

'You're the best, you know that?' he whispered.

'You're not so bad yourself,' she said, as she turned around and kissed him on the lips.

'Tell you what, sort out everything that can go by post. Large but lightweight, and I'll ask Maya to post them.'

Chloe quickly sorted out the gifts to be parcelled separately. The taxi would be arriving soon to take them to the airport. They were cutting it fine, so she hurried.

By the time the taxi had arrived to take them to the airport, Con had spoken to his daughter about shipping the remaining gifts via the post.

Now, watching him walk around the cabin, Chloe prayed for him. She hoped they would have enough of time on Ios to say what was needed to be said.

★

A few seats in front of Chloe and Con sat Windsor Hounslow, who was relaxing. He had a speech to give at the university in Christchurch, but he had no need for his laptop. His speech was already written, and with a photographic memory, he didn't need to rehearse it. He laid back and enjoyed his complimentary scotch whiskey while listening to Chopin through his headphones.

★

Meanwhile, down in economy, Beth and Angus McWilliams were resting after their meal. Beth was sleeping with her head on Angus' shoulder. Angus looked at his new wife, sleeping peacefully. He had been overjoyed when Beth had agreed to be his wife. He had counted himself a very lucky man. He watched her sleep as he gently stroked her hair. This was the beginning of their life together. He rested his head back as he imagined himself as a father. A smile slowly spread across his face.

★

The main cabin had settled down. Everyone had eaten and was either reading or had fallen asleep. The passengers allowed the soft vibration of the aircraft to gently rock them to sleep, as the plane travelled at nearly one thousand kilometres an hour.

★

'You have him, that's brilliant,' Victoria Dahl said into her phone. 'Have the arrangements been made with the New Zealand police? … Great, we'll be on the next flight back to Sydney. See you then, Harry.'

ANZAL's new OnAir mobile system allowed Victoria to speak directly to the AFP in Australia on her own mobile. She loved modern technology.

New Zealand customs had detained Terry Burrows. In the morning, they would go in front of a judge and request formally that he be extradited to Australia. Victoria allowed herself a satisfied smile. They'd had a victory.

Yet Terry was only the foot soldier who'd planted the bomb, and who'd been paid to follow orders. They needed to know who'd hired him. He might try a plea bargain, but he would have to know that he now had a price on his head.

That being said, Victoria wondered if he would ever actually see the inside of a prison cell.

Victoria rose from her seat and went to the refreshment self-serve counter.

There were three handsome-looking Swedish men at the counter in their early twenties. They smiled at her. That perked her up. *Those were the days*, she thought. Now, at thirty-five, her priorities had shifted. Her career was too important to her, especially for indulgences like marriage and children. Although, more recently it had been on her mind.

★

Pauline Walsh, stared out into the darkness. She was fed and hydrated, and now she had to excuse herself to her fellow passengers in order to grab her laptop. Once re-seated, Pauline opened it and re-read what she'd written in the café at Sydney airport. As she contemplated her heroine's last move, her computer's battery light flashed.

Pauline pulled out her computer bag from under her legs and rummaged through it for the charger, only to find it wasn't there. Then she remembered what that niggling thing was that she'd left behind. Cursing, Pauline quickly typed out the last few sentences before her computer died.

Once again, she excused herself to replace her laptop in the overhead compartment. Once seated, she fumbled through her handbag for a notebook and pen. All serious writers kept a notebook and pen handy at all times. It was an unspoken code of conduct.

This was not one of those times, however, as she didn't have a pen.

She was tempted to get up and go searching for a pen, but 85B leered at her with steely eyes. Pauline hesitated and decided that it would be best to stay seated. She smiled at the women beside her, and innocently said, 'I forgot my pen.'

The woman leaned down and pulled up her handbag, then retrieved a pen and gave it begrudgingly to Pauline.

Pauline smiled apologetically and started to write long hand. It wasn't long before her hand started to ache. *Who writes long-hand nowadays?* Pauline thought. *Oh, unless you're Jeffrey Archer.*

★

Chapter Nine

Outside of Christchurch, New Zealand
11.30 p.m. (1.30 a.m. NZ time)

The man calling himself Cougar arrived at his destination. He let himself into the house, uninvited. He walked quietly through the place until he found what he was looking for.

Jackal's computer was in his bedroom, tucked inside the second draw of his bedside table. Once Cougar unlocked the computer, he uploaded the incriminating files from his USB flash drive. Then he placed the computer back in the draw, along with an untraceable mobile phone, as instructed.

Walking back through the house, he felt a slight vibration beneath his feet.

'For fuck's sake, not another one,' he said, as he stood still and waited for the tremor to pass.

The ground shook for a further fifteen seconds.

Once the tremor stopped, he exited the house and walked down the street to his car. He didn't notice the two men sitting inside the black SUV stationed across the street. Through tinted windows, the inhabitants of the SUV videoed the man's every move.

By the time Cougar was back in the driver's seat, another mini earthquake had started. This time it lasted twenty-five seconds.

'Don't these fucking things ever stop?' he mumbled, as he started his car and drove away.

The SUV's occupants also waited until the tremor stopped. Then the passenger in the left side seat dialled a number on his mobile.

'We have movement,' he said.

'Find out what he was doing in there,' said the unidentifiable voice on the other end of the phone.

'Will do,' said the agent.

The agents exited their car and entered Jackal's house. It didn't take them long to find the mobile phone and the still-warm laptop. They had no need to follow Cougar. While he was still inside Terry Burrows' house, one of the agents had put a tracker on his car.

Chapter Ten

On board flight AN224, Cockpit
12.40 a.m. (2.40 a.m. NZ time)

An alarm sounded in the cockpit. Marcus turned his attention to the datalink as another message came through.

'Ben, we're getting a report on the datalink,' Marcus said, as he read the bulletin. 'Oh, great! There's been another series of earthquakes around Christchurch. If there are any more within the next hour, Christchurch ATC will close the airport. We may need to transfer to our alternative.'

'Okay. Monitor the situation and advise ANZAL in Sydney. They'll need to co-ordinate the transfers of the passengers or accommodate them until alternative arrangements can be made.'

'They're going to be pissed,' Marcus noted.

'We can't help that. It's Earth at its most temperamental, Marcus. Christchurch are only being cautious. The passengers will understand. But we'll hold off telling them until the last minute, until we know for sure.'

'You're the boss,' Marcus said, glad he wouldn't be the one on the PA announcing the bad news.

Once Marcus had notified Sydney Operations, they went over their pre-landing checks. Marcus also double-checked the coordinates for their alternative airport, Auckland International.

★

AN224 continued towards its destination for the next half an hour, without receiving any more NOTAMs. Christchurch Flight Centre gave Flight AN224 the all-clear to start their descent unless there were any more earthquakes, in which case they would need to cancel their approach and re-route to Auckland.

Marcus requested the ATIS (Automatic Terminal Information Service) for Christchurch and Auckland. Then Captain Flynn commenced their slow descent. At a cruise speed of 1,050 kilometres per hour they would be descending at 2,500 feet per minute. It would take approximately ten minutes to reach flight level 10,000, and by then, they would have slowed their aircraft down to 310 knots.

Once the plane reached 10,000 feet, the seatbelt sign would be turned on and the flight crew could start their pre-landing and descent checks.

As the plane started its descent, some seasoned passengers and flight crew felt the slight change in the engines, signalling that they were commencing their descent.

The flight attendants could always spot the anxious passengers. They would look up at the cabin crew as they walked past them, waiting for a reassuring smile or nod. Some anxious passengers would hold onto their arm rests in anticipation for landing. Some would continually pop their ears, chew gum vigorously, or suck on sweets to help release the pressure in their ears. The cabin crew knew from experience that it only took a gentle smile to reassure most people.

★

Jane placed Ava back in the seat next to hers while Leonor and Felix continued to watch their movies. Embarrassed, Jane helped the flight attendants to clean up her children's mess. Wherever they went, crap always seemed to follow.

Down below, Pauline Walsh handed back the biro to 85B with a thank you. Only, once she'd put her tray table back in the upright position, she realised she had to go to the bathroom. She politely made her excuses to B and C as she squeezed past them again. She didn't have to walk far to the toilet, as it was only a few rows behind her. But when she turned around, there were already two women waiting in line, and Pauline was suddenly busting.

Pauline walked around to the other side of the plane, but that toilet was also occupied, with one waiting. She cursed. Even in mid-air at 35,000 feet, there still weren't enough toilets for women. She couldn't hang on that long, so she headed up to the centre of the cabin and snuck into the handicap toilet. She reassured herself with the fact that she hadn't seen anyone get on board in a wheelchair.

At the front end of economy, Annabel Jones was relieved when the plane started to descend. She made sure that her seatbelt was securely fastened as she tried to relax. *In for three, out for five, in for three, and out for five.*

Annabel's anxiety had prevented her from living a full life. At thirty-eight, she was physically as healthy as she had been when she'd enlisted at eighteen, thanks to her jogging and rowing – which she found to be as therapeutic as they were enjoyable. Looking back, she had no regrets about serving her country. She felt only pride at the opportunity she'd been given. But now, she needed to learn to forgive and live again. Always the fighter, Annabel knew that once she found her confidence again, she could start thinking about marriage and possibly children. This trip was the beginning of a new adventure. *This is just the beginning*, she thought.

At the back of the main deck, Victoria Dahl checked her watch. They were on time. The New Zealand police would be at the airport to meet her. They would escort her to the police station, where Terry Burrows was waiting in a cell to be interviewed. Then, tomorrow, she would be escorted to the courthouse for the extradition hearing. Normally, hearings of this nature were lengthy processes, unless it related to terrorism. Thanks to new Australian and New Zealand treaties, acts of terrorism allowed for hearings and extraditions to be expedited.

★

Upstairs in the lounge, passengers who had been mingling had finally taken their seats for landing. Naomi made sure the bar was cleared and tidy, while Charlotte manoeuvred through first class and made sure all loose items were collected and stowed away in each passenger's compartment.

Gladys and Dave Honeycombe had remained in their seats. They had dozed through most of the flight. Meanwhile, Herbert Schwartz had been reading.

Henry Adams had thought he would have to feign sleep after dinner in order to avoid Gertrude, but luckily, she had spent most of the flight upstairs in the lounge. Henry was tired; mentally and physically. Now that the deal was signed, he wanted to take a break before production started on the chip. He knew he'd be run off his feet over the next few months.

But for the last three hours, Henry had spent his time trying to understand who would want to kill him. His company wasn't the only party to have hired the Learjet, although the Federal Police believed that he was indeed the likely target. It was unfathomable. But the breech in security told him otherwise. *They had to be connected, somehow*, he thought.

Henry still hadn't heard anything back from his private detective. He was also looking into Iceland for him, which had come up during their investigations. Once he knew more, he would present his findings to Gertrude. She'd know what to do. As he reassured himself that all would be well, Gertrude returned from the bar upstairs, followed by two teenage girls.

Millie and Annie Wellington had found their seats and tidied themselves up before landing. Millie pulled out her toiletries bag and touched up her make-up, while Annie flicked through the in-flight magazine to keep her mind off the landing. Take-offs were fine, but landings always made her feel sick. She agreed to go with Annie upstairs to the bar. They had mingled with a couple of first-class passengers. Their favourite actress was also there, talking about her latest movie. As Annie sat back down in her seat, she realised she was homesick. *Everything was changing*, she thought. She would be going home to a new life, new school, and new friends. Millie wouldn't be a part of it. She brushed her maudlin thoughts aside as she fastened her seatbelt for landing.

Chapter Eleven

NGMC, National Geohazards Monitoring Centre, Lower Hutt, Wellington
2.55 a.m. NZ time

Over at GeoNet's headquarters, the alarms sounded for the fourth time that night. Each squall of aftershocks was increasing in size and duration. The senior geologist feared that the South Island was heading for another major earthquake.

'What was the magnitude of the last one?' Oliver asked.

'Six point one,' said his assistant. 'They're increasing.'

'Alert the authorities, if they haven't already latched on,' he replied.

★

03.05 a.m.

Christchurch ATC gave the order to close the airport. All incoming flights were to be diverted. AN224 was less than two hundred miles out; they would have to divert to their alternative airport – Auckland. An updated ATIS was issued, and a priority message sent to all incoming flights.

In the cockpit, Marcus received the latest message from Christchurch, ATC.

'Initiate course change – punch in the coordinates for Auckland,' Captain Flynn instructed. 'Get us up to FL150 on a slow climb and turn.'

'Roger. Changing coordinates,' Marcus replied.

'I better inform the passengers, unless you want to do it,' Benjamin said. He turned and gave Marcus a mischievous look.

'Not on your life,' Marcus replied. Benjamin opened up the mike to the cabins.

'Ladies and gentlemen, this is your captain speaking. I'm afraid I have some bad news. There's been another series of aftershocks in and around Christchurch. The airport authority felt it prudent to close the airport. We have changed course and we'll be landing at Auckland, our alternative airport. I know this is inconvenient. ANZAL will do everything necessary to make sure you arrive in Christchurch as soon as possible. Thank you for your understanding.'

'Not bad,' said Marcus, cupping his hand to his left ear. 'I can't hear anyone screaming back there.'

'Comes with the title, mate.'

★

After listening to the captain's speech, June knew that her flight attendants would be immediately inundated with questions. They knew how to respond, apologise, but not to promise anything.

The cabin, which had been quiet only moments before, erupted into sounds of discontent and annoyance. Passengers fidgeted in their seats. The cabin was now active and restless. Multiple call buttons were pinged, signalling that they needed to speak with the flight attendants. It was now very early in the morning, and no one relished the thought of being stuck at Auckland Airport indefinitely.

June made her way to first class, knowing that they would be the most vocal. Charlotte and Naomi would need her help. Business class would also be very outspoken, with meetings and deadlines too important to miss. Business executives would be crying – delays cost money. This was something that airlines knew all too well.

Herbert Schwartz cursed under his breath. This was not what he'd envisioned. He'd expected the New Zealand leg of his trip to go as smoothly as the Australian one. There was no use complaining to the flight attendants, who had no control over Christchurch ATC or seismic activity. There were already enough people grumbling in first class. He opened the travel magazine in his side compartment and started to search for the article he'd seen earlier about Mount Hutt skiing.

Chapter Twelve

3.10 a.m. NZ time

The latest tremor continued for three powerful minutes. Alarms were ringing throughout the NGMC Centre. The reading showed significant movement along the Alpine Fault line.

Sensors were going off all along the fault line and sister faults.

The Alpine Fault, which lies between the Pacific Plate and the Indo-Australian Plate, shifted more than forty-five millimetres. The displacement was felt along the entire 480-kilometre western coastline of the South Island. The powerful force opened up gas vents, expelling its hot gas into the cold night air and high into the atmosphere. The higher it rose, the more turbulent the air became.

Tremors started out near Arthur's Pass and all the way down to Mount Aspiring National Park. The greatest movement was felt through the Mount Cook National Park, where the dust-filled gas vapours began moving in a westerly direction over the Tasman Sea.

Geologists had no idea of the volume of gas vapour that had been expelled from deep within the Earth over the last week's seismic activity. But this new series of earthquakes had caused more vents to open up, increasing the volume of gas over a wider area.

In the Taranaki Peninsula on the west coast of the North Island of New Zealand a sleeping giant began to stir that afternoon. Mount Taranaki had finally awoken. Previously known as Mount Egmont, Taranaki was known as a stratovolcano. The summit crater was filled with ice and snow and has a lava dome in the centre. Its majestic peak sits 2518 metres in elevation. Major eruptions predominately occur every 500 years, while smaller eruptions occur every ninety years. Its last significant eruption was in 1854. Geologists predicted it was long overdue for another eruption.

As New Zealand fell under the spell of yet another series of earthquakes, volcanic ash began to expel from Mount Taranaki. The increasing expulsion of ash contained tiny glass particles. As the wind changed direction it headed slowly south across the Tasman Sea and down New Zealand's West Coast. Unfortunately, as flight AN224 changed course for Auckland Airport, these gas vapours were now heading in its direct flight path.

As flight AN224 turned north, still low in the sky due to its previous descent towards Christchurch, it flew straight through the invisible gas vapours. The filthy particles of glass and dust were sucked into all four of her Rolls-Royce Trent 900 turbofan engines. The particles began to melt in the jet's engines' heat, fatally damaging the engines' ability to sustain flight. As this continued, the great plane's engines were slowly starved of oxygen and eventually power. They began to choke on the ash particles and gas vapours.

Some of the passengers stopped what they were doing, detecting a slight change in the engines' vibrations. Not everyone noticed it, but the experienced flyers listened as the aircraft's vibration increased.

The cabin crew had flown through turbulence many times before, and always carried on with their work. June was in the galley at the rear of the main cabin when she felt it. She knew what turbulence was – just air pockets and strong winds. But this vibration didn't feel right to her. The plane had a slight shudder to it. June walked to the emergency door on the starboard side of the plane and placed her hands on the emergency door. She rested her head against the oval window to look outside. She was instantly alarmed by what she saw. June stood back and walked to the interphone to dial the cockpit.

'Hello, Officer Whitby. It's June.'

Chapter Thirteen

3.15 p.m. New Zealand time

'It's getting worse,' Marcus said.

'I know, check the instruments. What are the engines saying?' Benjamin asked.

'They're rising. All of them.'

'We may need to land at Christchurch, after all,' Benjamin said.

Their discussion was interrupted by the phone ringing. Marcus picked it up. He listened to what June said and told her to prepare for an emergency landing. Marcus relayed the conversation to Benjamin – that June had seen smoke coming out of the outboard engine on the starboard wing.

'Mayday, Mayday, Mayday, Christchurch Control Centre, this is Flight AN224 requesting an emergency landing,' Benjamin began.

'AN224, state your emergency,' the controller said.

'All four engines are overheating. We have confirmation of smoke coming from engine number four. We won't make Auckland.'

'Understood, Flight 224, squawk emergency code 7700. We will activate emergency services. Be advised that we have received information of widespread seismic activity all along the Alpine Fault. We have experienced continuous and significant earthquakes. Be advised, GNS has just picked up volcanic activity at Mount Taranaki. We will update our NOTAMs and advise all other flights to avoid your airspace.'

'Thank you, Christchurch. Will squawk 7700.'

'Shit, Ben. If that's true about the volcano and seismic activity … God knows what's happening down there,' Marcus said.

'I agree. What's the current wind speed and direction?'

Marcus read back the readings to Benjamin as requested.

'It's possible that we've flown through expelled gas vents or something similar. The wind direction fits. It may explain our engine trouble,' Benjamin said.

'Jesus Christ,' Marcus responded, as he stared out of the cockpit. He didn't know what he was looking for.

'I can't keep this climb up any longer. We'll have to start our descent and reduce speed. Monitor the engines and let me know when the first one reaches fifty percent.'

'Will do.'

'Notify the cabin crew to be seated until landing and make sure everyone else is seated, too. Don't tell them about the engines yet – we may still make it to Christchurch,' Ben instructed.

Marcus made the internal announcement. Then he started on the emergency landing checks. He sent a message to ANZAL operations in Sydney, advising on the status of the plane.

Captain Flynn was deep in concentration. He didn't know if the engines would last all the way to Christchurch or not. He was being optimistic. He thought back to his Air Force days. He'd had one emergency during his years in the Air Force: He'd made it back to base safely, but it was touch-and-go for a while. Benjamin also knew that if he hadn't, he could have simply ejected out of his FA-18 hornet. But that wasn't an option on a plane with nearly 500 people on board.

Benjamin decided to make a straight-in approach on runway 197. He would need to jettison fuel soon.

'Engine four down to fifty-five percent capacity, Ben.'

'Understood.'

Before Marcus could notify Benjamin that engine one was down to fifty percent, engine four exploded.

A thunderous jolt shook the plane. It sent alarms blaring all over the cockpit. Captain Flynn grabbed a tight hold of the control column and turned off the autopilot. He needed to fly manually from now on. He needed to feel the plane as it fought him for every piece of airspace.

The Airbus was now vibrating badly. Within thirty seconds, engine number two – the inboard engine on the port side – caught fire. Benjamin knew at that moment that they were going down.

He knew it was time to speak to the passengers. It was now or never.

The aircraft banked sharply to the right as Captain Flynn tried desperately to keep her straight and level. They had already turned on a south-easterly heading towards Christchurch. But now they were veering away from the airport towards the south-west, and the Mount Cook National Park. Marcus checked the starboard side engines. He could see fire and smoke coming from both of them. Engines two and four were already shut down. Captain Flynn ordered Marcus to shut down the remaining two engines before they exploded as well. Marcus hesitated momentarily as he looked at Benjamin. He knew what that meant, but he obeyed Captain Flynn's orders.

The plane was becoming difficult to manoeuvre. Benjamin could see the damage to the port-side wing through the cockpit window. They couldn't afford another explosion. If the wings broke apart due to flying debris, they'd have no chance.

His mouth dry, Captain Flynn gave the emergency broadcast, updating Christchurch ATC on their situation and quickly relaying their coordinates. Christchurch ATC confirmed their emergency and wished them Godspeed.

Both pilots were rigid as they clung onto their control columns for dear life. As the aircraft headed towards the snow-covered mountain range, a white silhouette could be seen off in the distance. It gradually increased in size. It was Mount Cook, also known as Aoraki.

Marcus felt sick to his stomach. He was looking death straight in the face. He wondered if it would be worse to be ignorant of what was coming, like the passengers behind him were. Marcus started to breathe heavily, but Benjamin stayed focused. He needed a place to land and fast.

Captain Flynn only saw darkness outside the cockpit window below him. There was no freeway he could see to land on; just small patches of lights from little towns below. He couldn't put those tiny towns at risk.

In the cabins behind and below the cockpit, now that the engines had been shut down, the passengers became eerily silent. Minutes before, there had been screaming when they'd seen the starboard engine catch fire. Then, as the aircraft vibrated more violently, passengers on the portside had started yelling when they'd seen one of the portside engines on fire. June had been on the intercom, trying to calm everyone when the oxygen masks fell from the bulkheads above each seat.

Now, panicked eyes darted around the room, looking for reassurance. They gulped the air in fear. They were helpless in their seats.

The flight attendants went through the cabins, helping to secure the oxygen masks, while June kept relaying instructions to the passengers. She was interrupted by the captain.

He spoke calmly and slowly to everyone on board. They were to brace themselves for an emergency landing. They were to follow the instructions given by the flight attendants, without question.

★

After Benjamin finished his announcement, June continued to reassure the passengers. She spoke as calmly as her captain, as she explained what to do during the emergency and afterwards.

June was scared, like everyone else. She had been in two serious situations during her career, but no amount of training could teach you how to cope when faced with them. Fear grips you no matter how experienced you are.

June was grateful that she had a purpose. Both the cabin crew and passengers were relying on her confidence and experience. She composed herself before continuing her broadcast.

Then the plane tilted and dived to the right. She ordered the cabin crew to their seats. Then followed a silence – a deadly silence. The engines had been turned off. The passengers had stopped screaming. The silence was unnatural. June, like many other passengers, started repeating silent prayers in whatever language and to whatever god cared to listen.

*

Shortly before the turbulence started, Pauline Walsh was finishing up in the handicapped toilet. She was zipping up her jeans when the plane started to shake violently. When the starboard engine exploded, Pauline was knocked against the wall of the cubicle. She lost her balance and slipped, hitting her head on the wash basin. She lay unconscious, and unnoticed by her fellow passengers, inside the toilet.

Upstairs in business class, Con and Chloe Pappas held each other tightly and repeated their prayers. Con kept repeating, 'Not like this, not like this.' He kept envisioning his island of Ios. He was afraid that he wouldn't get to see it again.

Jane Mallard made sure that Ava's oxygen mask was on securely. She clung to her daughter tightly. She felt a terrible dread – not for herself, but for her children.

She could see Hugh was holding onto Leonor and Felix's hands.

Rose had outstretched her hand to Lesley, who was in front of her. Lesley's chest hurt. She thought she was having a heart attack. Rose told Lesley that it was only adrenalin pumping through her veins, something she hadn't experienced since the last time she'd had sex – five years ago.

'Hold on, Lesley,' she said to her friend. 'I'll see you when we land.'

Lesley could only turn her head to the left. She was unable to speak.

★

Captain Flynn and First Officer Whitby were working hard to keep the aircraft level. Judging from the pitch of the aircraft, they knew that the starboard wing was damaged. Yet it was still holding together, for now. They needed it to remain that way long enough to get them away from the mountains.

As the engines were no longer providing power, Benjamin turned on the APU – auxiliary power unit – which was located in the tail cone of the plane. Marcus was reading out the emergency procedures when Benjamin realised with stark finality that they wouldn't make it over the mountains. They were losing height rapidly. The airflow over the wings was deteriorating.

He was losing manoeuvrability over the flight controls. He feared that the plane would break up before long. Up ahead, Benjamin recognised the white peak of Aoraki and her smaller surrounding sister peaks. He had limited options. They were descending fast, and they would be extremely lucky to skirt over the top of the mountains.

Aoraki was looming closer by the minute, but there was nowhere else to land.

Benjamin didn't know the last time he had been this scared. He had to make a split-second decision. The realisation of their predicament was inescapable. He was frantically thinking of what he could do. His next decision would be irrevocable. Alarms were blaring all around the cockpit, but as he looked outside the windscreen, he had a sudden thought. He knew the Mount Cook National Park. He'd trekked there on numerous occasions over the years with Elizabeth and the kids. If he could fly in and down one of the valley floors, the heavy winter snow fall would cushion their landing. Glaciers were in abundance in the national park. The valleys that ran alongside Aoraki were over four kilometres wide in some parts and well over twenty-four kilometres in length.

It was insane, but it was better than crashing into the mountains or breaking up in mid-air. He knew he had one option – it was their only option. If he could manoeuvre the plane long enough to line up with either the Hooker or Tasman Valley, they might have a chance. Benjamin's brain was calculating all the risks. He checked their altitude and speed. Then he realised that they were still fuel-heavy. He ordered Marcus to start dumping fuel.

Captain Flynn knew that the snow covering the valley would be as deep as fifty metres. He quickly checked the map. It was decision time.

'Marcus, I've got an idea.' His voice was calm but firm. Yet the alarms kept interrupting his thoughts. He yelled at Marcus, 'Turn those fucking alarms off!'

Marcus turned to his captain. He had been in a daze. He quickly recovered and turned off the alarms. They didn't need the alarms warning of a disaster they already knew was coming.

'Listen, I'm going to try and land down the Tasman Valley. It runs along the Mount Cook ranges. There's heavy snow from the top all the way down for over twenty miles.'

'What, are you fucking crazy?'

'No. It's either that, or we crash into the mountains or break up in flight,' Benjamin yelled. 'Listen, we don't have much time or manoeuvrability. Do everything I say without question! Do you understand?'

'Yes, yes, all right,' Marcus said, fighting against his panic.

Their voices were pitched; their hearts were pounding. Benjamin adjusted himself in his seat. Both pilots did everything they could to control the aircraft. Captain Flynn was yelling orders at Marcus; he needed the navigational map for the region. Marcus brought it up on the navigational computer. He just needed to align the aircraft with the Tasman Valley, which started from the top of Elie de Beaumont and concluded at Tasman Lake.

Their altitude was still dropping fast. He needed to slow the plane down and change the angle of descent, but controlling the aircraft was becoming more and more difficult.

'Config flaps one!' Benjamin said, hoping this would slow their descent and give them more control. His voice sounded loud and strained – with no sirens blaring or engines running, the cockpit had become ghostly quiet.

'Config flaps at one!' repeated Marcus, as he set the flaps to the first of four flap configurations. The plane's descent slowed slightly as it continued to glide silently through the night sky.

★

In the first-class cabin, Millie Wellington was clutching the sides of her seat. She knew that something had happened to the port wing. She was too afraid to look. She pulled down the window visor, then heard some passengers, in economy, screaming that the engine was on fire.

Then she felt the explosion, and everything became a blur. Millie couldn't see her sister, Annie, seated behind her in 3K. She needed her. She wanted her father. All she kept repeating was, 'Please don't let me die,' over and over again.

Dave Honeycombe tried to hold his wife's hand as she outstretched it towards him, but he couldn't keep hold of it.

'Just hang on, Gladie!' he yelled. 'I love you!'

'I love you, too,' she whispered back.

Dave had always thought that marriage would be a compromise. He'd never wanted to give up his wild weekends of hitting London and getting drunk with his friends. But what he'd got in return for marrying Gladys far outweighed what he had missed. Companionship, love, and understanding were emotions he'd never experienced until he'd met Gladys. He thought himself a very lucky man.

In business class, Amy Donnelly was holding her mother's hand tightly. Amy couldn't comprehend the fear that her mother must be facing, not being able to see what was happening in the cabin. Maybe it was a blessing in disguise. Many people had their eyes closed, anyway, choosing darkness. Amy felt that it would be better to see what was coming; to face it head-on. Amy's thoughts then went to Heathcliff, down below. She hoped he was still sleeping peacefully.

Jane Mallard was still holding Ava tightly, stroking her hair and repeating over and over, 'Shush, it's going to be okay, it's going to be okay. If she lost her children, she wouldn't be able to go on.

Con Pappas was holding Chloe's hand. He kept thinking, *Me, not her.* Meanwhile, Chloe's thoughts were strangely focused on the gifts she'd bought. How would they know what gifts belonged to whom? She hadn't put labels on anything. Then she remembered, she hadn't bought her sister's grandson, Bailey, anything yet! She felt terrible about that; he would feel left out.

In the economy cabin, Beth was holding onto Angus' arm as she cupped her head on his shoulder. She heard him softly repeat, 'I love you. It's going to be all right.'

Annabel clung to her pillow. Tears flowed down her cheeks. She felt so helpless. She had forgotten about her in-for-three, out-for-five breathing routine. One fear was now replaced by another.

The flight attendants were upstairs in their flight seats in between business class and the galley. They didn't really know each other, but they held each other's hands tightly all the same, each rigid with fear. They couldn't move even if they wanted to. Their simulated training had never prepared them for this. Nothing could've prepared them for this.

★

The cockpit was pulsing with energy as both pilots fought feverishly to control the aircraft as the Airbus experienced more vibrations and control fluctuations. But the aircraft held together.

Captain Flynn knew that if he could just get her down on the valley floor, they'd have a fighting chance. But he also knew that when they landed, they would slide and skid along the snow and ice, uncontrollably. They could flip over, or crash into the sides of the valley wall. He would have no control once they landed. Then his mind drifted to avalanches and seismic activity …

Stop, he thought. He had to rid his mind of all the negative thoughts, focus on the here and now.

Marcus changed the flap setting to configuration two. They felt another jolt as the aircraft slowed even further. The vibrations increased. But the left wing was still holding together. Benjamin prayed it would stay that way until they were down.

He ordered configuration three flaps, although the plane fought them every second of flight. It took all of Benjamin and Marcus' strength to handle the aircraft.

'She's up ahead!' Benjamin yelled.

'Fuck, she's big!' Marcus screamed.

'Steady, keep her steady!

'I'm trying!'

Benjamin was rigid in his captain's chair as the plane flew closer to the foreboding peak of Elie de Beaumont. As it flew overhead of its majestic peak, Flight 224 skimmed past its top with only twenty metres of depth to spare. The force of the aircraft caused the peak, covered in snow, to break away.

Benjamin quickly flicked the interphone on and yelled, '*Brace, brace, brace!*'

He gripped tightly onto the control column as if his life depended on it – which, maybe, it did. His heart was beating out of his chest. Fear gripped every part of his hardened body as he saw what was about to happen. His thoughts flashed momentarily to his children, but he didn't have the luxury to reminisce. He had to act, fast.

Captain Benjamin Flynn pitched the nose down. The plane descended between the surrounding peaks of Mt Walter, Mt Green, and Mt Darwin. He heard a terrible noise and knew that part of the left wing had just broken away. The plane turned sharply on its side, then hit the surface of the valley floor hard. Cushioned by the virgin snow-covered floor, which exploded all around the plane, it continued its long descent down the Tasman Valley, skidding and sliding, bumping, and jolting over the snow and ice as it began its journey down the valley floor.

★

The aircraft's speed increased as the valley's angle of descent steepened. As it did, the plane started to swerve. It skidded over to the left side of the valley wall and hit a large piece of solid ice. What was left of the left wing was completely destroyed. Fuel spewed out of the mangled wing, leaving a trail of fuel behind them in the snow. Fragments of the wing were strewn in every direction.

The starboard wing had finally broken apart. As the fragments ripped away from the wing, they hit the fuselage and ripped open a gaping hole in the roof at the back of the plane, killing a number of passengers instantly. Cold air swept through the upper cabin. The freezing air caused even more panic inside the plane. Paper, food items, and drinks were thrown everywhere, hitting passengers. The flotsam looked like it was trapped inside a mini tornado. The sounds were tremendous, with screeching metal and now the blistering cold night air.

The passengers still had their oxygen masks on, taking giant gulps of air like their lives depended on it. All waiting for that inevitable crash and explosion.

Outside the aircraft, ice and snow churned up around the Airbus as it skidded its way down the valley. The virgin snow, broken apart, started moving down the valley behind the aircraft. Cracks in the ice appeared as it was violently awoken from a winter's sleep. The elevators were finally ripped apart, sending more fuel out into the cold night air.

Passengers were tossed around in their seats, their heads knocked from side to side. Some people had leant forward and gripped the seat in front, while others bent down and covered their faces with a pillow or blanket. Some threw themselves back into their seats, stiff and rigid, their knuckles white as they gripped the armrests. The soft, calm warmth that had emanated from the cabin earlier that night was now gone. The only lights still working were the emergency ones along the floor and above the overhead compartments. They wouldn't last long if the axillary power failed.

Passengers braced with the anticipation of death, but it still wouldn't come. Some of the window-seat passengers, whose shades weren't already pulled down, could see a white powdery substance flying around their windows. The plane was still moving fast, but it hadn't crashed or exploded. They knew they were on the ground. Why weren't they stopping?

Another sharp jolt propelled the plane around as it hit the side of the valley wall again. Finally, as the valley floor started to level out, it also slowed the aircraft's speed. The jolts and vibrations slowly diminished as the plane finally came to a rest.

Steam, smoke, and periodic sounds of creaking metal was all that could be heard and seen in the cold night air. Those inside the plane remained hideously silent.

★

Seismic activity in the Mount Cook National Park had violently shaken awake the great mounts like a child's rattle. The mountains had been fractured by the violent displacement. Rock and ice were dislodged, and it wouldn't take much more seismic activity for them to break away and come tumbling down into the valley below. Warm air from expelled vents was still rising, while cold air descended from higher altitudes, causing turbulent conditions overhead. Soon the snow would start to melt in the superheated atmosphere, making the terrain even more perilous as millions of tonnes of glacial ice and snow started to funnel their way down into the valley. Amongst this chaos, AN224 had quietly come to rest – broken but with its body intact – on top of forty feet of ice and snow in the Tasman Valley.

The plane was approximately ten kilometres from its initial brush with Mount Elie de Beaumont, resting at an altitude that was still over 5,000 feet up in the valley. Dust particles were falling onto the pillowy white snow as gas vents continued to spew forth their congested secretion into the night air.

For the shocked and silent passengers inside AN224 – those who had survived the crash – time was of the essence. The mountains around them continued to tremble under the weight of the latest Alpine Fault displacement.

★

The Māori name for Mount Cook is Aoraki – a word that means 'cloud piercer'. It rested at a staggering height of 12,316 feet. It was surrounded by nineteen other peaks with elevations of over 10,000 feet.

Its alpine beauty was unquestionable, but it was also an unforgiving mountain range of ice and rock. The weather could change rapidly, bringing with it below-freezing temperatures. With many glacial lakes, ice-carved fiords, sinkholes, fissures, crevasses, and underground streams, the Mount Cook National Park hid a dangerous terrain.

About eighty million years ago, Gondwanaland broke apart. This was a subcontinent made up of New Zealand, Australia, Antarctica, Africa, and India). It separated New Zealand from Australia and created the Tasman Sea. Then, around twenty-five million years ago, New Zealand split in two. This was caused by the Alpine Fault. New Zealand, which was mainly underwater, lay across two major plates: the Pacific Plate and the Indo-Australian Plate. As these plates moved, they collided with each other, pushing the land up and creating Mount Cook and the surrounding mountain range.

The Pacific Plate continues to move down below the Indo-Australian Plate in the North Island at a rate of fifty millimetres per year, and at thirty millimetres per year in the South Island. In the Mount Cook National Park, these plates now move past each other at a rate of forty-five millimetres per year, when a build-up of pressure develops during sudden movements, it causes powerful earthquakes.

Aoraki lies south-east of the main divide, with the Tasman Glacier to its east and the Hooker Glacier to its southwest. After a massive rock and ice avalanche in 1991, Aoraki's height was reduced by thirty feet.

Over these millions of years, it is estimated that approximately twenty-five kilometres of uplifts have occurred at Aoraki, but that erosion has kept up with the rising plateau. If it weren't for the elements, in three million years, Aoraki would be five times its present height, or twice the height of Mt Everest.

Chapter Fourteen

3.30 a.m. NZ time

Captain Flynn regained consciousness. The aircraft had stopped. He removed his oxygen mask and turned to Marcus, who was still unconscious. Benjamin unfastened his seatbelt and leaned over to Marcus and checked his pulse. There was blood on the right side of Marcus' head. Benjamin could see a gash on his temple, but he couldn't see any other visible injuries, so he removed Marcus' mask.

'Hey, Marcus, wake up. Come on, mate,' he said, gently tapping the side of Marcus' face. Benjamin saw that his hand was shaking. He noticed that the windscreen was fractured, but it hadn't imploded on them. Benjamin squeezed his co-pilot's hand tightly and gave it a shake.

Marcus started to stir. He was momentarily dazed. Benjamin gave him a moment while he pushed back his chair and climbed out of the captain's chair. He needed to use the satellite phone and let the authorities know their exact location. He had a direct line to operations in Australia, so he called them first. Once he got through to the operations manager, Margaret Tennyson, he told her their situation and coordinates. After a moment's delay, which was due to Margaret's relief, she said that she would co-ordinate with the New Zealand emergency services immediately.

'What's your altitude?'

'I'm not sure yet. We could be as high as 7,000 feet, maybe more. We came down the Tasman Valley. I'll have to check outside to get an idea of where we are.'

'I'll need to know how many are dead and how many are needing medical attention,' remarked Margaret gravely.

'I'm about to head into the passenger cabins now. I'll call you back with details soon. I don't know the condition of the plane yet, either. Just get those emergency services here as soon as possible.'

'I will. Keep that phone close. I'll be in touch shortly.'

Margaret was relieved beyond words. When she heard that they were going down, her heart stopped beating. A dreadful feeling had engulfed her when she'd realised that she was about to lose over 500 passengers and crew, not to mention a brand-new Airbus.

She'd been numb until she'd received Benjamin's call. Margaret had to compose-herself – she could only imagine what Captain Flynn must have just gone through.

Benjamin needed to check on his passengers and crew. He grabbed a torch as he left the cockpit. He unlocked the first cockpit door, then put his briefcase against it so that he wouldn't be locked out. He didn't know how long the auxiliary power would last.

When Benjamin emerged through the second cockpit door, the frigid air caught him off guard. He entered into the lounge area. Apart from the flying debris, which had settled on the ground, the room was empty. He walked towards the curtain, which separated the lounge from the business class section, and pulled the curtain aside.

It was vastly changed from when he'd seen it last. Passengers were still strapped in their seats with their oxygen masks still covering their faces. Some were stirring, while others remained deadly still. Luggage and debris was everywhere, as was blood.

Benjamin needed to locate the source of the cold air. Otherwise, they wouldn't survive long exposed to the elements. There had to be a tear in the fuselage somewhere. He had to wade through the rubbish, careful of where he was stepping. He checked some of the passengers in the aisle seats as he did so. An elderly gentleman in seat 13F started to stir and moan. He reached up into the overhead compartment and retrieved a blanket and pillow and covered him from the cold. All of the passengers would need attention. He needed to find June Wilson and get the cabin crew organised – those that weren't injured or dead.

As he walked towards the galley, food and rubbish was scattered everywhere. He checked on the flight attendants.

They had been knocked around badly in their seats. They were unconscious but alive. The crew would have to prioritise the injured. *God*, he thought. *With a full flight, there could be hundreds.*

Benjamin headed to the back of the cabin. As he walked into the premium economy section, he saw a gaping tear in the fuselage. Snow was drifting in with the cold, frigid air.

While Benjamin was assessing the damage, he started to hear moans coming from around the cabin. He needed to get down to the main deck and assess the situation there. The surviving passengers would be in a state of shock, but that would eventually wear off, and then they would start screaming and panicking. He needed them to remain calm. Another priority was to go outside and assess the plane and ascertain their location down the valley. He hoped that the plane was dug deep enough into the snow to prevent them from sliding further down the valley. Especially if there were any more tremors. They would need to evacuate at daylight; he knew it would be too dangerous at night.

He checked his watch. It was three 3.35 a.m. It wouldn't be light for another two or three hours.

Up ahead he saw June Wilson, taking care of a passenger. She appeared unharmed. He had flown with June for many years, and this was the first time he had ever seen her dishevelled. Technically, June would have said she was out of uniform. Benjamin was unsure why he thought of that, but somehow it made him smile. He called to her as he approached.

June turned when she heard Captain Flynn call her name. Relief instantly spread across her face. She met him halfway and threw her arms around him, tightly.

'Oh, thank God,' she said, as she pulled herself away.

'Are you hurt?' Benjamin asked. June replied in the negative.

'I need to let the emergency services know how many are dead, injured, or missing. I need you to gather all the uninjured cabin crew and start a rollcall. If there are any doctors or nurses on board, go to them first and get them up and prioritising the injured.'

'Yes, Captain.'

'We'll need to set up a triage and move the dead to the back of the plane. Keep them away from the survivors. We can move the seriously injured into first class, as their seats recline into beds. The moderately injured can go into business. Do you understand me, June?'

'Yes, Captain. What the hell happened?'

'I'm not entirely sure. There's been more earthquakes and seismic activity in the last few hours. It's possible that we flew through escaping gas vents or something to that effect. If particles were caught up in our engines, it could explain them all burning out at the same time. Last I heard, New Zealand is experiencing another round of devastating earthquakes, just as severe as the ones last week.'

'Thank you for being honest, Captain. The passengers are going to want answers. Where are we, by the way?'

'We landed down the Tasman Valley near the base of Mount Cook. We'll need to evacuate as soon as it's light,' Benjamin said. 'But no one must go outside.'

'Yes, of course. I'll organise the cabin crew and medical help.'

'Try and get some of the uninjured passengers to help as well.'

'Yes, Captain.'

'It'll be all right,' the captain said, as he put his arm around her shoulder. 'I need to go outside and inspect the plane and figure out exactly where we are. I'll have to open one of the exit doors. It'll get even colder in here. So, make sure everyone has a blanket. If they don't have their coats with them.'

'Yes, Captain. I'll organise it straight away.'

'Thank you, June, and please call me Ben.'

'Yes, sir.'

Chapter Fifteen

Margaret Tennyson stood speechless. She'd lost a plane. A brand-new A380 Airbus. She felt sick. The number 500 kept flashing in her mind.

Margaret quickly dialled the number for Christchurch Air Traffic Control and relayed the message that Captain Flynn had given her. She requested that a mountain search-and-rescue be initiated. They reassured her that the Rescue Co-ordination Centre had already been notified, but that they wouldn't be able to start actual rescue operations until daylight. They had also notified the Ministry of Civil Defence and Emergency. The strained voice on the other end of the line reiterated that the earthquakes had caused a lot of damage throughout the South Island. Thousands of people were calling emergency services for help. The crash would be a priority, but as rescue resources were stretched to their limits, they would be co-ordinating directly with the Mount Cook Rescue.

Margaret thanked them. Her next call was to Mount Cook Rescue. They had their own helicopter and would co-ordinate with the army for further assistance.

Margaret notified the board of ANZAL. They would be meeting within the next few hours to discuss the situation. The operations centre at Mascot was about to be rudely awakened. Margaret knew that she was going to have a long night and day ahead of her.

Nonetheless, so would everyone on board of AN224. Her shift wouldn't finish until every man, woman, and child was rescued off that mountain. She checked her watch: 1.40 a.m. AEST, and 3.40 a.m. NZ time. She wondered how long it would be before the blame game started.

'Fuck, what a mess,' Margaret said to herself, before she re-dialled the satellite phone.

'Captain Flynn, it's Margaret Tennyson from operations.'

'Yes, go ahead.'

'I've given your phone number to Mount Cook search and rescue. They'll co-ordinate rescue operations with you. They said that the army has been called in to help. They won't be able to start rescue operations until first light. I'm sorry, but they said that with all the earthquake activity, it's too unstable to attempt any kind of helicopter landing until they've surveyed the area, which won't happen until daylight.'

'Yes, I thought the same thing. We have a couple of doctors on board. We'll need the most seriously injured evacuated first. They'll need to be air-lifted. But if they can drop off some medical supplies in the meantime, that would go a long way to saving lives up here.'

'Okay, I'm on it, Captain. You'll be hearing from Mount Cook rescue services soon. Good luck, Benjamin,' Margaret said. 'I'm here if you need anything.'

'Thank you,' he replied, before disconnecting the line.

Margaret knew that he would need all the luck he could get over the next few months. *It was going to be messy*, she thought, as she dialled another number. *At least Captain Flynn was alive to defend himself.*

As Benjamin put the phone back in his jacket pocket, he walked out of the first-class cabin and continued through into economy. The main deck was the most populated. The passengers were awake, crying, and calling for help. But some remained coldly silent. Benjamin hoped that they were just in shock, but he knew that there were dead amongst them, trapped in their seats.

Up ahead, Benjamin could see some passengers near an emergency door. They were trying to open it. He called out to them to stop. As he arrived near the door, he had to repeat himself.

'Ladies and gentlemen, can I have your attention please,' he said over raised voices. Passengers stopped what they were doing to listen to him.

'We've landed down the Tasman Valley. Please do not open the doors. We're high up in the mountains. You'll freeze to death if you go outside dressed as you are. There's heavy snow and ice all around the aircraft which has now become unstable. Help is on the way. I've spoken to operations, who are co-ordinating with the local search and rescue units. We need to stay inside, keep warm, and look after the injured. Once the sun rises, we can start evacuating. The cabin crew will need your help with the injured. Can you please help them?'

The passengers responded with nods of agreement as they walked back to their seats, relieved that help was on the way.

Benjamin asked a passenger seated near the door to make sure no one tried to open it again. He nodded in agreement. However, Benjamin realised that he would have to ask the same request of other passengers seated near the rest of the emergency doors. He made his way down to the next exit, and so on. As he walked down the aisle, passengers were grabbing his arms, throwing question after question at him. He tried to answer them calmly. They deserved the truth – no secrets and no unrealistic promises. He could see how afraid they were. But he needed to get outside and assess their situation.

However, Benjamin's number one priority was to remove the dead passengers from the living as quickly as possible. It would be too much to bear for them to remain alongside the living.

Guilt started to rear its ugly head. Benjamin started to wonder if he could have done anything differently. Should he have changed to their alternative airport earlier? Did fuel costs and delays have any bearing on his decision? Benjamin had to shake the negative thoughts from his mind. There would be time for recriminations once they were rescued.

He couldn't indulge in self-doubt; his passengers and crew needed him. He headed back to the cockpit to check on Marcus and retrieve his coat and gloves. Then he would have to go outside and examine the aircraft and their situation. As he climbed the staircase, Benjamin pondered whether he would react the same way again, under similar circumstances. There was only one answer that came to him: yes.

When Benjamin reached the top of the staircase, he heard a distant rumbling sound. He held onto the railing and felt its vibration. He knew that ice and snow was breaking up high in the mountains around them. He didn't want to think of what would happen if there was an avalanche; it could consume the entire plane, or thrust the plane down the valley, crushing it beneath its weight.

As Benjamin arrived at the first cockpit door, Marcus came out, holding a handkerchief to his head.

'I don't know how you did it, but we're alive, thanks to you.' Marcus shook Benjamin's hand.

'Thank you,' Benjamin said, feeling embarrassed at the gratitude. 'But we're not out of the woods yet. Rescue services won't be here until daylight. I need you to help June Wilson co-ordinate the dead and injured. I'm going outside to inspect the plane.'

'Will do,' Marcus said, as he buttoned up his jacket and headed off in search of June.

Benjamin gathered up his scarf, coat, and gloves before heading outside.

★

03.45 a.m. NZ time

Jane Mallard hadn't woken up. She was still clutching Ava in her arms. Hugh Mallard was helping his son, Felix, who was complaining of pain in his chest. Leonor appeared unharmed. Ava had been trying to wake her mum and was crying under her mother's tight grip. A woman, who was seated in front of them, had come over to help. She introduced herself as Dr Ruby Singh. Retrieving her medical bag from the overhead compartment, she examined Jane Mallard. Once she finished her examination, she told Hugh that she believed his wife may have a concussion. She couldn't rule out bleeding on the brain, either.

'I can't see any other injuries. We'll need her to wake up before we can assess her condition fully. She may even have internal bleeding. Your youngest daughter appears unharmed, though.'

'Thank you,' Hugh said. He couldn't stop shaking. He didn't know what to do. 'My son is having trouble breathing. He said his chest hurts.'

Dr Singh went over to Felix and examined him. After listening to his chest, she said,

'He has a collapsed lung. I need to relieve the pressure.'

'Oh, fuck … Please help him!' Hugh said. His family was breaking apart all around him and he didn't know what to do.

'I have to insert a tube in between his ribs to expel excess air,' Ruby said, as she undid Felix's shirt and removed a long chest tube from her bag. Hugh watched as Dr Singh inserted the tube into Felix's chest. As she removed her finger from the top of the tube, Hugh thought he heard the air expel from his son's chest. Then he saw his son respond as his breathing improved.

That was when Hugh finally started to cry. His family was hurt, and he felt useless to save them.

'Thank you, thank you so much,' he said, as he bent down and stroked his son's hair and kissed him on the forehead.

Dr Singh picked up her bag and continued on to the next person calling for help.

Further down the aircraft, Con and Chloe Pappas were still buckled in their seats. Con was in pain, but not from any injury caused by the crash. He needed his medication. As he got up from his seat, he winced again. Chloe couldn't bear it any longer. She wished he'd been honest with her. He found his bag on the floor amongst a number of overnight bags, which had been thrown out of the overhead compartments. He placed his bag on his lap, then held Chloe's hand, as he saw that she was crying.

'It's okay. We made it. We'll get out of here, you'll see.'

But that wasn't why she was crying. All she could think about was returning home to her children and grandchildren, without Con. Going back to the way things were. She knew her life was never going to be the same again, though.

★

'Wake up, will you?' Lesley said, slapping Rose across the face. Lesley had woken up in pain, but Rose was still unconscious. However, the slap stunned her best friend awake, and she was now coming around. Relief was clear on Lesley's face. She started to laugh and cry all at the same time.

'What the fuck happened?' Rose asked, a little dazed.

'We crashed, you idiot,' Lesley replied. 'Are you hurt?'

Rose started to feel all around her body. With a deep sigh, she said, 'No.' Looking at Lesley, she could see that the side of Lesley's face was bruised.

'That's grounds for divorce,' Rose said, pointing at Lesley's face. Lesley winced when she put her hand on her face.

'Don't make me laugh, it hurts,' she said, trying to stifle a cough. Lesley sat back down in her own seat, as she felt dizzy. Help would come. They were alive, that's all that mattered. Their injuries were nothing compared to others around them. As Lesley laid back, she could hear a child crying for her mother. She closed her eyes and said a silent prayer of thanks. She was grateful that her children and grandchildren weren't on board.

Lesley stifled another cough, and as she did, she grimaced with pain.

★

03.50 a.m. NZ time

Benjamin Flynn made his way to the back of the airplane. The carnage in premium economy was unbearable to witness. He had to squeeze past people in the aisles, who were tending to the injured. Some crew and passengers had started moving the dead to the back of the plane and the injured forward. As he walked into the galley at the rear of the plane, he saw that someone had placed a blanket over the dead body of a crew member, still in her seat. There was blood everywhere, getting soaked up by the snow, which had fallen into the plane through the ripped fuselage in the ceiling above him. The red snow appeared more surreal to him at the very moment than everything else around him. He needed to focus. Benjamin raised his torch and examined the hole in the ceiling. The wind was howling outside, blasting snow into the cabin.

Passengers had wrapped blankets around themselves and were wearing their coats, but he knew that it wouldn't be enough. He would have to transfer as many passengers as possible to the lower cabin, where it would be warmer.

★

June Wilson was as good as her word. She had mustered the cabin crew together in the galley on the lower deck behind first class. Of the eighteen crew members aboard flight AN224, four were dead and three too injured to assist. The remaining cabin crew were eager to get to work. They were shaken, but glad to be alive, June being one of them.

'Clementine and Yen, I need you to quickly make your way through the upper deck. Sarah and Franny, main deck. Beside passengers' names, I need you to mark off everyone on board, and whether they're alive, "A", injured, "I", or dead, "D". And if they're missing, an "M". I need this done as soon as possible. The captain needs to let the emergency services know how many people are alive and/or injured. It will be hard, as some people are moving about. Just ask them their name if they pass you.'

'Yes, June,' they said in unison, as June handed them two copies of the passenger manifest.

'I only have two lists. So here,' June said, as she handed some paper and pens to the other cabin crew. 'I'll need you to write down the seat numbers and names yourselves.'

June turned to John, another flight attendant. 'Now, I need you and Toby to locate the doctors on board.' June handed over a hand-written list of their names and seat numbers. 'I don't know what type of doctors they are, but most would have some kind of medical training. Go up and down the aisles asking if there are any nurses or medics. They're probably already helping the injured, but we need to organise the injured in one part of the plane, where they can be prioritised and treated. So, I'll need you to start relocating passengers in first and business class who aren't injured down into economy.'

'What about the dead? There's quite a few,' Charlotte said, who was still shaking. She could feel that the back of her neck was stiff with tension. She was trying to calm herself down by taking deep breaths, but it wasn't working.

'We've started relocating them to the back of the plane,' continued June. 'Passengers will need to be confirmed dead before we relocate them. Although, some will be obvious. Some passengers have lost loved ones – be respectful and patient with them when you do this.'

'I don't know if I can do that,' Naomi said, trembling.

'You won't need to move them yourself. I've organised for some of the male passengers to help John and Toby carry the dead,' June said. 'When you've finished, help with the injured.'

'Okay, I can do it,' Toby said.

'Me too,' John said. They headed off.

'Make sure that all passengers are kept warm. It's going to get very cold in here. We could be here awhile,' June said.

Her flight attendants responded with nods of agreement.

'Right. Lawrence and Naomi, help move the passengers in first class. I'm about to check on Matilda and Michael and see how badly they're hurt.' June organised the remaining flight attendants to assist in the various cabins.

June could see that her crew were shell-shocked. 'Do as the doctors ask. I've put the first-aid bags and defibrillator in the first-class cabin. Remember your training, and we'll get through this. I'm very proud of you all.'

★

Benjamin wrapped himself up tight against the freezing cold. When he opened the emergency door in the first-class cabin, a gust of cold wind slapped him across the face. He'd asked a passenger who'd introduced himself as Herbert Schwartz to close the door behind him, but to wait there for him to return.

The snow was only a metre below the emergency door. Benjamin retrieved a piece of luggage that was strewn on the floor near him. He dropped it onto the snow. It didn't sink too deep, so he climbed down out of the aircraft.

Benjamin trod carefully. He could only estimate how deep it was. With all the displaced snow, it could be double what he thought, or deceptively less. He didn't want to think about possible crevices and ice caves beneath them.

Benjamin was grateful to the full moon for providing some light. Its silhouette against the mountains and glaciers was insidiously beautiful. He could feel the looming presence of Mount Cook off in the distance.

On the opposite side of the valley, he could hear the fracturing of glaciers and ice movements. The sounds echoed in the early morning air. Benjamin felt intensely small. Even the impressive size of the Airbus was timid in comparison to the resplendent presence of the mountains that surrounded them.

Benjamin walked through the snow towards the back of the plane. Here, he was able to inspect the damage more closely. He could also smell fuel. He hoped there wasn't too much around the aircraft; it would only take one spark to set it off.

The plane's wings, elevators, and ailerons were completely destroyed, but her body was intact. Benjamin could see that the fuselage was torn in certain sections. Dented, battered, and bruised, she precariously held it together.

Benjamin looked up the valley. He knew that the plane had disturbed millions of tonnes of snow and ice – as high up as Anna Glacier – on their descent. He wondered how long they would have before the bulk of it started to move down the valley. When the sun rose in the morning, it would bring new challenges with it. He realised that he would have to get on the roof of the aircraft for a better indication of their location. He would have to climb through the ripped hole in the roof at the back of the aircraft. Once daylight arrived, they would be better equipped to judge how best to evacuate.

As he made his way back to the door, Benjamin felt the ground beneath him rumble. If felt like a jet plane landing. He waited until it passed. He listened as the mountains moaned with discontent – the pressure was again building up beneath them. He put his hand on the fuselage and thought, *Please, just hold together until we're rescued.* Then he banged on the door to be let back in.

Herbert pulled open the door and offered his hand. Once he'd helped Benjamin back inside, they both heard ice breaking apart, off in the distance. Herbert knew what that meant. A skier all his life, he understood their predicament. Benjamin closed the door.

'Thank you,' Benjamin said.

'You're welcome,' Herbert replied. 'How unstable is the snow out there?'

'I'm not entirely sure. We're wedged in, though. But if there are any more earthquakes, we might slide further down the valley.'

'*Danke, Kapitan,*' Herbert said.

'Will you help me? I need to climb through the ceiling on the upper deck and onto the roof. I'll need a hand getting out and back in again.'

'Of course,' Herbert said, as both men made their way up the staircase and along the aisle to the back of the plane. Herbert thought about his skis below in the luggage compartment. His ski suit was also in his suitcase.

He wondered if he could ski down the mountain. He didn't want to be trapped inside this tube if there was an avalanche, or if the plane slid further down the valley.

★

'Please, Amy, ask,' Joanne said to her daughter imploringly.

'Okay, Mum. I'll ask. But the flight attendants are far too busy with the injured. They won't have time to go below and check on Heathcliff.' Amy was glad that her mother couldn't see the carnage around them.

Amy needed to help the other passengers, but she didn't want to leave her mother. She didn't believe her shoulder was dislocated, although there may be a fracture.

As if she knew what her daughter was thinking, Joanne replied, 'I can hear their pain, Amy. Their cries and screams. I can smell the blood. You're a paediatrician, you need to help the injured. But please have someone check on Heathcliff. He could be dead or injured. He's been my eyes and companion for years. I don't want him to suffer.'

'I'll ask a flight attendant when one passes. Now, are you sure you're not hurt?'

'No, I'm okay, sweetheart. What about you? Please don't lie to me.'

'I hurt my shoulder, but I don't think it's broken or dislocated.'

'Thank God for that,' Joanne whispered.

'If you're sure you're okay, I'll go and help the injured.'

'I'm all right. Please don't worry about me,' her mother said, who was filled with relief that her daughter was not seriously hurt.

Chapter Sixteen

'Annie, please wake up. Please wake up,' Millie repeated, but her pleas had gone unanswered. Annie was badly hurt. There was blood everywhere. Millie looked around the room for help. It was mayhem in first class, and she could hear yelling from a man a few seats in front of her.

'Please, someone help me,' she yelled. But everyone was too preoccupied with their own injuries. Finally, a flight attendant came in and Millie called her over.

Charlotte raced over to the young woman. She remembered they were identical twins.

'You have to help her,' Millie pleaded. 'I can't wake her.'

Charlotte checked her pulse. There was a faint beat.

'I won't be a moment. I have to get a doctor,' Charlotte said. But Millie grabbed her, pleading with her not to leave. Charlotte reassured her that she would be right back with help.

'Just keep talking to her. I'm sure she'll hear you. Stay calm, I won't be long.'

Nearby, Lu Ming was screaming as he gripped his leg. Peng could see bone sticking out of it – it was disgusting. She thought she was going to be sick. She hadn't realised the extent of her own injuries. Before Peng could get the flight attendant's attention, she had run from the cabin to get help for one of the twin sisters she saw come aboard. Peng tried to calm her husband by putting her hand on his head, but he swore even louder. She looked over at the twin, trying to wake her sister. A sense of dread washed over her. She felt for the girl. Her thoughts were brought back to Lu, as he swore again.

Charlotte eventually returned with a doctor. He began assessing the injured in the first-class cabin, he asked Charlotte to help transfer the non-injured to the other cabin as they needed the seats. After looking at Lu Ming's leg, he examined Peng. Once her shoulder was bandaged, he asked her to go up to business class. She was happy to oblige.

★

… ten minutes earlier in the first-class cabin, Flight AN224

Henry Adams counted himself lucky to have survived uninjured. He couldn't believe what had happened. Once the initial shock wore off, he took in his surroundings, but it was all too surreal. He thanked whatever god was watching over him. He wasn't a religious man – as a scientist, he'd always dealt in facts alone. Beliefs were luxuries he'd had no time for, until now.

He looked through his portal window. He saw only darkness, but he could make out snow flurries dancing outside his window. He could hear the howling wind also. It made him shiver.

The once-pristine cabin was now a mess of papers and personal belongings. He saw blood splattering around the cabin. When Henry got out of his chair and turned to Gertrude, her body was at an awkward angle, and she wasn't moving. He leaned over her and checked her pulse. Her head bobbed in his hands, which were now covered in her blood. He quickly pulled away.

Cursing himself for acting like a coward, he re-checked her pulse again. It was there, then he remembered, head injuries also bled a lot, they weren't always as bad as they looked. Henry straightened Gertrude up in her chair. He looked around for a flight attendant, but there wasn't one in the room. He pulled a blanket out of the drawer to keep her warm. It was getting colder. He had to find someone to help Gertrude.

Henry heard someone yelling. He turned to see a man across the cabin screaming at his wife. He was clutching his leg. He saw one of the young girls lying lifeless in her seat, while the other was trying to wake her. He was normally a detached man, not prone to rash judgements or emotional outbursts. But seeing the carnage around him, he felt a surge of panic for everyone. He didn't know what to do. He wasn't a doctor or a medic. He felt momentarily useless. Other passengers in the cabin were moving, but some were hideously still.

Henry had known since childhood that he was in that one percentile of the most highly intelligent people in the world. But he knew nothing about first aid. He looked across the cabin and saw a middle-aged couple holding each other. The woman had blood running down her face. She was badly bruised. Her husband was stroking her head, comforting her.

Another woman he recognised from the television was trying to use her mobile. Her hands were shaking.

He asked her if she was all right. Chyna Day looked up at Henry and said, 'I can't get my phone to work.'

'You've probably got it on flight mode still,' he said, trying to re-assure her. It was the first thing that popped into his head.

'Oh, yeah,' she replied dazedly. She appeared to be in shock. She tried to press the apps on her mobile but couldn't get past the settings tab. Henry could see that she was shaking, although she didn't look injured. He saw a man kissing his wife's cheek. They were all afraid – not for themselves, but for their loved ones. For a fleeting moment, Henry felt very alone.

He shook the thought away. No time for self-pity.

Henry needed to help. He went over to the man across from him. But when he tried to help him, the man only screamed in pain. His wife just looked at Henry and shook her head, signalling for him to keep well clear. Henry decided that it was better that he go in search of a cabin crew attendant. He was about to leave when Charlotte returned with a doctor. The female doctor immediately started to assess the injured in the room. Henry decided that he would be more useful in one of the other cabins. After speaking with the doctor about Gertrude, he headed into economy to offer his assistance.

When Henry arrived in the economy section of the cabin, he wasn't prepared for the scene that lay before him. He stifled a gasp, then managed to squeeze past some passengers in the aisle as he made his way to the flight attendant who was giving orders to her cabin crew.

'Hi,' he said, touching June's arm.

'Can I help you?' she asked, turning to him.

'I was hoping that I could help you. I'm not hurt. Can I help in any way?'

'Thank you, yes you can. We need to move the dead bodies to the back of the plane and move the injured into first and business. They will be more comfortable there.'

Henry instantly regretted asking. Moving dead bodies wasn't what he'd had in mind when he'd offered. But he couldn't say no. Not when he saw other male passengers doing it.

'Of course I can,' he said sincerely.

June patted him on the arm and thanked him. She pointed to another flight attendant and said, 'John is co-ordinating the relocation of the bodies. Please go to him.'

Henry nodded and headed off in his direction. The cabin was still fairly dark and cold. The emergency lighting was barely adequate; he wondered how long it would last.

★

After Henry had placed another passenger in an empty seat and covered her with a blanket, he headed back up the aisle. As he did, he came across a woman straining in her seat. Her legs were trapped. The fuselage had caved in beside her and the seat in front was wedged back, trapping her legs. She was trying to move the seat forward but was having no luck.

'Hang on, okay,' Henry said. 'I'll find something to use as a lever to pull the chair back.'

'Thank you,' Victoria said through gritted teeth. The pain was becoming unbearable – she had only just regained consciousness, but then the pain had set in; more so when she tried to move.

When the plane hit the ground, Victoria had thought she was going to die. The wing had broken apart and hit the fuselage right outside her window. It had decompressed like a tin can.

That was when her leg had become trapped, and pain had shot through her body. She'd said a thousand *thank-you*s since she'd awakened, but now the pain was overbearing.

Henry looked around for something to use. Unfortunately, an A380 Airbus didn't have many tools available for such a thing. He would have to find the flight crew. If there were tools on board, they'd know where they were kept.

'Hold tight. I'll be back in a minute,' he said, regretting the remark when she stared up blankly at him. He smiled apologetically at her, then quickly left in search of the captain.

★

Annabel kept repeating her times tables. She had gone through all the basics, two to twelve, three times since the crash. She couldn't stop shaking. She needed fresh air. She needed to get out of the plane. But her legs wouldn't move.

'Are you hurt, madam?' Sarah enquired.

'Sorry, what did you say?' Annabel asked, as she looked up at the flight attendant.

'Are you hurt?'

At that moment, Annabel realised that she wasn't. Her heart was pounding, but that was normal under the circumstances.

'No, I don't think so.'

'That's great. Do you have any medical training?'

'Only a little. When I was in the army.'

'Brilliant. Would you please help the doctors and nurses? They'll need all the help they can get.'

'I … I don't know if I can move,' Annabel said.

'I know that you're scared − we all are. But if you're working, there's no time to think about the fear, is there? Remember, you're one of the lucky ones.'

'Yes, of course,' Annabel said, realising that the attendant was right. She felt instantly ashamed of her behaviour. Annabel unfastened her seatbelt and stood up, then took a deep breath, which she let out slowly. She read the name on the attendant's jacket.

'Who should I report to, Sarah?'

Sarah pointed Annabel in the direction of June Wilson. She took another deep breath and headed off towards the mature flight attendant giving the orders.

★

As Benjamin climbed onto the roof of the A380 Airbus, he was hit more vigorously by the cold wind funnelling its way down the valley. He pleaded for the sun to come up. Shining the torch didn't get him very far, but the light from the full moon showed their partial descent down the valley. He could see the imprint that the plane's body had made. But what frightened him more was the volume of snow and ice behind them. It would eventually start its journey down the valley. He turned around and squeezed his eyes together to see down the valley, as the strong wind blew snow flurries everywhere. But what caught his eye was the impressive mountain looming above him, known as Aoraki. Its height was imposing. He saw all he needed to before climbing back into the aircraft.

Herbert helped Benjamin back in. Stamping his feet to warm them up, Benjamin thanked Herbert, then headed back towards the cockpit, leaving Herbert to his thoughts.

Benjamin pulled out the satellite phone and dialled operations to give them the grave news.

★

'Excuse me, Captain,' Henry said, when he sighted the pilot walking down the aisle.

'Yes, how can I help you?' he asked.

'My name is Henry Adams. I need a toolkit, as a woman is trapped in her seat. If I can unscrew the bolts, I can remove the seat in front that's pressing against her legs.'

'Yes, of course. Follow me,' Benjamin said. He led Henry back to the cockpit.

The journey to the cockpit took longer than expected. They had to make way for injured and dead passengers who were still being relocated. Benjamin had to put the images out of his mind – he would mourn the dead later. For now, his priority was saving the living. But the constant scene was proving it difficult.

Benjamin gave Henry his GA toolkit. He offered to go back and help Henry, but on their way back through economy, Benjamin saw a woman struggling to support an injured man to business class. The two men parted as Benjamin jumped in to help, placing the passenger's arm across his back and helping him to his new seat.

'Thank you,' Annabel said, after reclining the man in the business class chair.

'No, thank you,' Benjamin responded.

Annabel could see the strain on the captain's face. She recognised emotional trauma all too well. She couldn't imagine what he must be going through after such an event. All she could offer him was a sincere smile. She stood up and told the passenger that she'd be back with some water and pain medication. Benjamin was left to his thoughts. He made sure that the man was comfortable and headed back to the cockpit to make his phone call.

★

Henry finally returned to Victoria with the toolkit. She was relieved; she'd doubted whether he'd come back. But he had, and he'd brought another passenger with him. Her spirits lifted as they began to unscrew the reclined chair in front of her. She could feel cold air coming in from beside her, where there was a large crack in the fuselage by her right leg.

★

'Help, let me out! Can anyone hear me? H.E.L.P!' Pauline yelled as she banged on the toilet door. Finally, someone opened it.

'Oh, thank Christ, what the fuck happened? Did we hit turbulence?'

Angus McWilliams smiled at her and said, 'Well, I've got some good news and some bad news for you.' He stood aside to let Pauline out of the toilet. When Pauline exited the cubicle, she was a little unstable, and couldn't comprehend what she was looking at. The pristine cabin was unrecognisable. People were carrying other people.

The floor and walls were strewn with rubbish, bags, and debris. She could see blood on the floor and on the seats where passengers had been seated only moments before.

'The bad news is that we crash-landed. The good news is that you survived.'

Angus saw bruising and blood on the side of Pauline's head.

'You better have a doctor look at that,' he said, turning her head to the side. Pauline felt a pang as he touched her. 'How many fingers am I holding up?' He showed Pauline four digits.

'Four?'

'Good. Head up to business class and the doctors there will assess you.'

'Yes, okay. Thank you,' Pauline said, as she slowly made her way back to her seat, now occupied by a deadly still figure whose body was covered with a blanket.

Pauline felt the lump on the side of her head throb. She realised for the first time how lucky she was to be alive.

A flight attendant offered to escort Pauline into business class, but she told them she could manage. The flight attendant instructed her not to go up the back staircase due to all the damage, and to instead use the main staircase at the front of the plane.

Pauline wanted to retrieve her handbag and laptop first before heading upstairs. Once she found them amongst the jetsam, Pauline made her way through the cabin, past the galley, and into the first-class cabin.

Hours earlier, she had wondered what it was like to travel first class, but what she saw turned her stomach. She made her way up the staircase, wondering how business class had fared. She found a seat in row 27, against the aisle on the starboard side. There was a woman already resting in the chair beside her. She was bruised and her make-up was smeared across her face. She also had a sling across her arm.

Pauline sat down and put her seatbelt on. She was unsure why she did it, but she felt safer buckling up all the same.

'Hi, I'm Pauline,' she said.

'Peng,' the other woman said.

'Slight concussion,' she said. 'How about you?'

'Black eye, possible fractured shoulder blade, and my lipstick has smudged all over my face, hasn't' it?' she said, looking at Pauline for reassurance.

'Yep.' Pauline reached into her handbag and pulled out a wet wipe from dinner. 'Unused,' she said, as she unwrapped it and offered it to Peng.

'I hate throwing anything away.'

'So will I in future,' Peng said, smiling as she accepted the wet wipe to clean her face.

Chapter Seventeen

Mount Cook Rescue, Mount Cook Village
4.10 a.m.

'Thanks everyone for getting here so quickly. I know it's early,' Linus O'Rourke said, acknowledging Michael Porter, Olivia Quinn, and Zeke Goldsmith. The remainder of the rescue team would be arriving shortly. Sunny was prepping the EC145 rescue chopper for flight.

'What's the emergency? Do we have stranded skiers?' Olivia asked, stamping her feet to fend off the cold.

'No, it's more serious than that. An ANZAL flight crash-landed up in the Tasman Valley just under an hour ago.'

'Holy shit,' Zeke said. 'How many passengers were on board?'

'About 500.'

'Oh my God,' Olivia said, sitting down in a chair.

'One of the local charter companies has given us the use of their chopper to help ferry out passengers once it's light. They're not equipped to handle anything serious, but the chopper can hold up to six people. In the meantime, I've instructed our rescue chopper to head up the valley and locate the aircraft. It'll drop buoys to pinpoint their exact location. As you've all felt, in the last couple of hours a number of earthquakes have caused considerable movement in the park. The NGMC believe that it's far from over. The captain has said that he heard a lot of breaking ice around them. So, you can understand the seriousness of their situation.'

'So, we can expect more earthquakes and avalanches before this is over?' Michael said.

'Precisely why we need to tread carefully,' replied Linus.

'Do we know how many have survived?' Olivia asked.

'We'll be given a passenger list shortly of the injured and dead. Then we can ascertain how many need rescuing. As you can appreciate, we'll have to leave the dead where they are for now. Our priority will be the living, only. The most seriously injured will be evacuated first, then the rest of the injured and the women and children. Then we'll bring up the rear with the remaining men. I've also been informed that the Army is arriving soon. They'll set up a MASH unit and triage on the outskirts of the village. They can stabilise the worst cases before transferring them to hospitals. In the meantime, get your gear ready.'

Linus watched his team as they readied themselves. There was no hesitation on their part. They knew the risks and were still prepared to go. He was proud of every one of them. It was going to be a mammoth task, but they would get it done.

The Rescue Co-ordination Centre asked Linus to liaise with the Army. He was told that a Major Wilkinson would be arriving soon, along with his medical unit. The major would be responsible for the passengers once they were on the ground. But Linus was in charge of the overall rescue and evacuation. The distance to Tasman Lake from Mount Cook Village was approximately ten kilometres, and the massive lake resided at the lower end of the Tasman Valley. If large volumes of ice and snow started collapsing down the valley walls, it would eventually end up in Tasman Lake. The lake would grow rapidly in size. They might not be able to go around the lake and going across it would be just as dangerous.

Linus made himself a cup of coffee and sat quietly as he thought about their options. They would have to fly all the passengers out directly from the crash site down to the village. It was further away, so it would take longer, but evacuating them to the lower end of the valley could still be risky. Linus didn't have the luxury of relying on unpredictability.

★

'Come on, old girl. Try and drink something,' Con said as he offered Chloe some water. She wasn't looking very good. A flight attendant told Con that the doctor would be with him soon. But it seemed like it had been hours. Finally, a nurse arrived, who introduced herself as Beth McWilliams. She examined Chloe.

'I believe she is suffering from shock. I can't see any major injuries. I'll get the doctor to come over. She may have a chest injury, since her breathing is shallow.'

'Thank you. Please ask the doctor to come soon. She's my Chloe.'

Beth put her hand on his shoulder for support. She understood him all too well. She hurried off to get the doctor. Tears were welling up in her eyes as she found a doctor assisting another patient.

'Doctor, I have a woman who I believe is possibly in shock, but I'm concerned about her breathing. I'm worried she may have had a heart attack. Can you please check on her?'

The doctor said he would come straight over. He gathered his medical bag and followed Beth back to Con and Chloe. The doctor was frustrated. With only his medical bag and one of the aircraft's first-aid kits, he was limited in his ability to help the passengers.

When he checked on the old woman, he confirmed that she was in shock. There were many passengers who had the same symptoms as Chloe. There wasn't anything he could offer her; she hadn't suffered a heart attack. But if she did, all he could offer her was aspirin. It would help reduce the risk of a further heart attack or stroke. He told Con to keep her comfortable and continue talking to her. Hearing his voice would comfort her.

Con diligently stroked Chloe's hair as he told her how much he loved her. He had momentarily forgot about his own pain.

★

'I'm not leaving her,' Millie said, defiantly. Dr Munir Uzer was examining Annie. He stipulated that she wasn't to be moved under any circumstances.

'She has a piece of metal through her side and back. We can't remove it, or she'll bleed out. She's already lost a lot of blood,' Munir said to Charlotte.

'Are you even a real doctor?' Millie yelled. Her disrespectful tone caused some of the passengers to stare at her. Dr Uzer's accented English was due to him being born in Turkey and immigrating to Australia as a teenager. Now, at twenty-eight, he was a qualified surgeon, graduating second in his year at Sydney University. He allowed the slight to pass unanswered. She was no different than most. But he put her manner down to the stress of her sister.

Once Millie calmed down, she realised her offence. 'Sorry, I'm sorry. My mouth is bigger than my manners. Please help her. You can take my blood, anything you need. We must be the same blood type.'

'I'll monitor her. If her blood pressure drops any more, then yes, I'll need to perform a blood transfusion,' Munir said.

Munir was grateful to the flight attendant who'd given him a first-aid bag. He hadn't brought his medical bag with him.

'I've been told that the most serious cases will be evacuated first. That will be your sister,' said Dr Uzer. 'But we need to stabilise her first.'

Dr Uzer applied padding carefully around the piece of metal in Annie's side and back. He made her as comfortable as possible, then stood up to help another passenger who had just been carried into the first-class cabin.

'Thank you,' Millie sighed. Munir nodded at her and walked off.

Millie looked at her mirror image lying on the bed. She couldn't comprehend Annie dying. They were one and the same, even long after their mother had stopped dressing them identically. Millie played the socialite, as her friends expected her to, while Annie was far more introverted and independent. She never cared what anyone thought.

Millie wanted her father here. He would know what to do. He would make it all right. Fear gripped at her chest and wouldn't let go. She believed it was the same pain Annie was experiencing.

'If you want to stay in first class with your sister, you'll need to help,' Charlotte said. As she covered Annie with a blanket, she said softly to Millie, 'Do you understand? I know it's hard, but other passengers need help also. There's limited room in here.'

'Yes, yes, I'll help. Just tell me what to do. I can't leave my sister.'

'Okay. Please help the nurse with the young lady in seat 3A. She has large gashes along her arm and forehead. Help her with the bandages.'

Millie hated leaving her sister's side even for a minute, but she had to help in order to stay. Annie was still unconscious. It was a blessing, as she would be in a great deal of pain. Yet Millie still wanted her sister to wake up.

Charlotte took her over to help Sally Keogh, an RN from Auckland. Then she went to check on Dave Honeycombe. The doctor had put a makeshift sling around his right arm and shoulder. It was dislocated, but a doctor had put it back in place. All flight attendants had first-aid training, but nothing prepared them for the volume and gravity of the injuries on board. They were glad to have so many doctors.

Charlotte politely asked Dave and Gladys Honeycombe to relocate to business class. They needed their seats for the more seriously injured. They graciously agreed and collected their belongings before they walked upstairs to the business class section to find two spare seats.

They actually preferred it upstairs. The gravity of their situation wasn't as surreal away from the critically injured. Seeing the doctors make life and death decisions wasn't something they were used to. When Gladys found two seats in business class, she sat down and glanced out the window. She heard the howling of the wind and saw the darkness that leered back at them. She pulled the shutter down and wrapped the blanket around her, then snuggled into Dave's good shoulder. She felt Dave's hand on hers and was relieved that his injuries weren't as bad as some.

Gladys realised that Dave would be evacuated before her. That thought frightened her more than the sounds coming from outside. She didn't want to be left up here alone.

★

'Excuse me, Miss Day, can you please move into economy? We need your seat for an injured passenger,' Charlotte asked, politely.

'What am I supposed to do in there?' Chyna replied. She was reclined in her first-class seat.

'Maybe you can help with some of the frightened passengers?'

'*I'm* frightened.'

'We need your seat. Once the injured have been evacuated, you can come back in.'

'Great. Fine, then,' Chyna said with annoyance. 'Oh, and my phone doesn't work.' She waved it in Charlotte's face.

'You can make a complaint to New Zealand Telecom when you're off the plane,' Charlotte said.

'Was that meant to be funny?'

'I hope so. You're lucky you're not hurt. We have many dead. Now please, Miss Day, if you'll head into economy.'

Chyna rose indignantly and left with her handbag and makeup case.

In the seat behind, Constantine Zabinski didn't need any persuasion. He was a little bruised but unharmed. He just looked at Charlotte when she approached him and said, 'Just as long as I don't have to sit next to her …'

Charlotte smiled and thanked him as two more seriously injured people were carried into first class.

★

Every passenger reacted differently to their predicament. Some were helping to relocate the dead, while others were handing out drinks and warm clothing and blankets. Some cleared away the debris strewn over the cabin floor. Some stayed in the seats, subdued and sobbing silently, while others were pumped with adrenalin, pacing the corridors.

One indignant passenger was not happy about being relocated to economy and was taking it out on a male flight attendant. 'I've paid for this seat,' he said to John, who was now assigned to the business class cabin. John, who was a gentle soul and always spoke in a polite, soft voice, was straining under the pressure. His career choice suited him – he was always willing to help others. Only, this passenger was making it difficult for him to love it as much as he usually did.

'I appreciate that, sir, but we're moving all of the less seriously injured passengers to business class. That way, they can be monitored and evacuated first.'

'Can't you move other people first?' asked Sir Roger.

'We have, sir,' he said, smiling through gritted teeth as he lifted his arm up to show the passenger which direction he needed to move in.

'You'll be in for a massive lawsuit,' said the passenger, as he reluctantly got up and collected his holdall.

'Where am I supposed to go now?' he said to a flight attendant.

She turned to him and said, 'There're seats in economy. Please go downstairs. It'll be warmer down there for you.'

He walked with a belligerent gait through the bar area and down the staircase, mumbling under his breath again about the massive lawsuit he would instigate on behalf of every passenger on board. He loathed the idea of sitting next to a complete stranger. They'd probably want to hold hands. Or worse, pray together. He shivered again, but not from the cold.

Windsor Hounslow hadn't needed any persuasion. He had collected his belongings, including his Glendronach Scotch Whiskey and headed down to the main deck when first instructed to move. Once he found a seat, his thoughts had been about his will. Or lack thereof. He had always thought he would have plenty of time to write one. Now, it was all he could think about. Not married, and no children, that he knew of, he knew everything would go to his sister. But without a will, the whole ordeal would be a lot more difficult and time consuming.

His thoughts were interrupted by yet another aftershock. The tremor shook the plane like a tin can. The snow beneath them started to shift under the movement, and passengers started to scream. They clung to anything they could as the plane started to slide over the snow. The rumbling movement felt like the Underground in a London Tube station, as a train passed by.

When the plane finally came to a rest, it had tilted by about five degrees to starboard. As they acclimatised themselves to this new change, the passengers began to notice a terrifying sound coming from outside the aircraft. It was a blistering, cracking sound, as if the mountains around them were screeching in pain. The sound echoed down the valley and through the cold and windy night air. The passengers and crew held their breaths until it had subsided, and a stark awareness hit many that the danger still wasn't over and wouldn't be until they were out of the plane.

A thunderous clap sounded in the distance as an avalanche began to fall just below Elie de Beaumont. It would be the first of many.

Flight AN224 was now resting on the eastern side of the Tasman Valley. As the avalanche travelled down the valley, bypassing the Airbus by a few hundred feet, its thunderous vibrations shook the plane. Everyone held their breath until the vibrations and noises abated.

★

Captain Flynn raced back to the cockpit. Once inside, he strained to see the avalanche through the cracked cockpit window. He pulled out his satellite phone and dialled the number he'd been given.

'Hello,' said the voice.

'Who am I talking to?' Benjamin asked.

'My name is Linus O'Rourke. I'm heading up the rescue.'

'This is Captain Benjamin Flynn. Did you just feel that earthquake?'

'Yes, and I'm afraid there'll be more aftershocks to come. Has your situation changed?'

'Yes. We just slid further down the valley, about twenty or so metres. Then we heard a God-awful sound. I think it was an avalanche – off in the distance. If an avalanche occurs close to our plane, it will completely engulf us.'

'I understand. We'll head up the mountain shortly. Our EC145 rescue helicopter has been prepped. It's search only, I'm afraid. It will pinpoint your position, and once it's light, we'll start rescue ops. Just keep everyone inside.'

'I will. Let's hope we're still here by morning,' Benjamin said sarcastically.

'Have you finished with the passenger list yet? We need to know how many will need stretchers and how many can walk out. The chopper can hold six passengers plus crew. The army will be supplying a Chinook and we've been offered a second EC145 to help assist. The South Island's been badly hit, so rescue services are stretched thin, as you can appreciate.'

'I understand, but I need to get the injured to help quickly. The hourglass is running out,' Benjamin said.

'I know. But moving across unstable snow and ice will be dangerous for everyone, especially when using choppers, Captain. Once I'm up there, I can assess the terrain.'

'I appreciate that, Linus – I was worried about that myself. The choppers themselves could cause more avalanches.'

'Are you near the valley wall?' Linus asked.

'Yes. I think we're pretty close, which is why I'm worried.'

'I'm not sure how long it'll take to evacuate everyone. It depends on whether people can walk or need to be carried or winched into the choppers.'

'I understand,' Benjamin said, his anxiety increasing.

'Thank you, Captain. I'll be in touch as soon as we're airborne.'

'Thank you, and please call me Ben.'

'Will do.'

'There's one more thing. Can you air-drop medical supplies once it's light? We have doctors and nurses up here, but they need more medical supplies.'

'Yes, that won't be a problem. Just let me know what you need.'

'I'll get back to you shortly. Thank you, Linus.'

'Good luck, Ben,' Linus said, as he rung off.

Benjamin left the cockpit and went looking for June. He found her in economy, being her usual efficient self. He asked her to get a list from the doctors of what medical supplies they needed.

June immediately pulled out her notebook and pen and headed off to the first-class cabin in search of Dr Philippa Carlson who was the senior doctor on board and was in overall charge of the injured.

★

Windsor Hounslow, now relegated to economy, was cuddling his bottle of Glendronach Scotch Whiskey when he saw a middle-aged – but not unattractive – flight attendant buzz past. He was warm and safe, and so was his whiskey, and that's all that mattered. He had come close to opening it a few times, wondering if it was a 'now or never' situation, when a gruff-looking man passed him. He looked down at Windsor's bottle of Glendronach and abruptly sat down beside him. He stuck out his hand and said, 'Sir Roger Standish. Nice to meet you. Now, are you going to open that bloody thing or not?'

★

'I need to take a look, please. Remove your hand,' said Dr Philippa Carlson, trying to help the young woman.

The young woman was being difficult. Her companion had suffered a broken collarbone but was now resting back in her seat upstairs. The girl spoke German, but their English wasn't too bad. She understood what the doctor was asking but didn't want to face the truth.

Millie Wellington came over to help Dr Carlson remove the young woman's hand. The gash across her face was substantial, but not life-threatening.

'It isn't that bad. You'll need cosmetic surgery, but you'll recover,' Dr Carlson said, trying to calm the young woman.

'*Ich bin ein modell*,' the woman said through tears.

'I'm sorry. I don't speak German,' she replied.

'I'm a model!' she replied, trying to look away from the doctor.

'I'm so sorry. But you know, surgeons can do amazing things with facial injuries these days. Try to be positive – you're luckier than most,' Dr Carlson said, sounding firm but reassuring.

'How so?' she asked sarcastically.

'You could have lost your eye,' Dr Carlson replied. The model's face turned ashen. She hadn't realised through all the blood and pain that the potential scar could have been a missing eye.

Dr Carlson gave the young model some painkillers, then bandaged the right side of her face. Then the model turned away to look out of the cracked window.

As Millie stood up, Philippa whispered to Millie, 'We'll have to move her. We need the seat.'

'Yes, all right. I'll escort her back to her friend. She'll be more comfortable there.'

Millie escorted the young German model upstairs into business class and sat her beside her friend.

As Dr Philippa Carlson turned to help her next patient, Dr Munir Uzer came up to her.

'I'm concerned about the young lady over here,' he said, pointing towards Annie Wellington. 'She has a sharp piece of metal lodged in her back. She was stable, but after that last tremor, her wound has reopened and she's bleeding profusely. I'm not quite sure what to do. Her blood pressure is dropping. If I remove the fragment, she'll bleed even more. I don't know whether we can suture the wound under these conditions. God knows how much internal bleeding is going on in there.'

'Where exactly is the shrapnel located?' Dr Carlson asked.

'The mid-left side, right of the lumbus,' Munir said. Dr Carlson went straight over to Annie Wellington and examined her.

'Her blood pressure is very low. She'll need a blood transfusion before we attempt to remove the piece of shrapnel. If she is bleeding internally, we'll need to find it and fix it before she is moved. There'll be a medical drop as soon as it's light. They'll have plasma and everything else we need to stabilise her before she's air-lifted to a trauma centre.'

'Her sister, Millie, has agreed to donate blood. They're twins, so it's highly likely they'll have the same blood type,' Munir said.

'Okay. Give her a blood transfusion. Do you have what you need?' Philippa asked.

'No,' Munir said, feeling embarrassed. 'I was heading to New Zealand on holiday. I didn't bring my medical bag.'

He remembered something that his lecturer had said in his first year – 'A doctor is never off duty.' He made himself a promise to never go anywhere without his medical bag again.

Dr Carlson smiled at him and handed him her bag. 'Take whatever you need.'

Munir went in search of Millie. He found her in business class. He explained what he needed to do. She didn't protest. Instead, she simply rolled up her sleeve and outstretched her arm.

'Take whatever you need, Doctor.'

Once back in the first-class cabin, Munir set up the transfusion. He heard Millie whispering under her breath. 'Please don't let her die.' He didn't know if it was said directly for him, or for God.

Dr Carlson had been on her way to Christchurch to give a series of lectures. She was a key speaker, specialising in Vascular Surgery, and she was one of the most experienced surgeons in Sydney. At forty-three, she had only just discovered that she was one month pregnant. Married for twenty years she never gave a lot of thought about being a mother. Work had always monopolised her time, but now, Philippa was starting to warm to the idea of being a mother. She agreed to give the lectures as she decided to take a sabbatical for the next few years.

As Philippa went from patient to patient, she tried to forget about her own fears for her unborn baby. She knew that this pregnancy might be her last and only chance. Aboard flight AN224 she was the senior doctor. The remaining doctors, nurses and flight crew looked to her for guidance. Her ten years in emergency would be put to the test over the next few hours.

Chapter Eighteen

The sun was due to rise in less than an hour. Passengers were still using their mobile flashlights to manoeuvre around the cabin. The emergency lighting, which pulsed from above the overhead compartment and along the floor, was fading. Captain Flynn knew that it wouldn't last much longer.

As Benjamin walked through each cabin, he noticed a new calmness settling in. Maybe it was the onset of daylight that was lifting everyone's spirits.

He'd flown passengers all around the world, always with their lives in his hands. To them, he was only ever a voice that occasionally came over the intercom. Now, as he looked down at them, he regarded them in an entirely new light. It was more personal now.

Upstairs, he found Marcus talking to some of the passengers. It grew colder the further aft he walked. Snow was still falling in through the ripped fuselage, and the dead, at the back of the premium-economy cabin, lay still and cold under their blankets. This area was now being referred to as 'the morgue.'

Benjamin needed to cover the hole up somehow. The thought of bringing luggage up from below flittered through his mind, but he brushed it away just as quickly. Any tremors would topple the luggage over. Instead, he needed a large tarpaulin. Benjamin pulled out his satellite phone and dialled Linus at the rescue co-ordination centre.

'Hi, can you bring up a large tarpaulin? It will help keep the snow out. The upper deck is freezing. About three-by-ten metres will do it.'

'Will do, leave it with me. We have your medical supplies, too – they'll be air-dropped when the chopper flies up in about half an hour.'

'Thanks, Linus.'

'Once evacuation starts, we'll need to know where you'll be evacuating the passengers from. What's the distance to the ground from the upper deck?'

'It's too high. We'll have to evacuate from the main deck. I'll check each emergency door for the safest evacuation point,' Benjamin said. 'The injured will need to go out that way.' '

'Okay. We'll assess that once we know what we're looking at,' Linus said.

'Thanks, talk soon,' Benjamin said, and he hung up.

Benjamin started the journey back to the cockpit. As he was walking back through business class, a woman in her thirties approached him and touched his arm.

'Please, Captain, can you help us?' Amy said.

'What do you need?'

'My mother's guide dog, Heathcliff, is below in the storage compartment. He would have woken up by now. He could be hurt or dead. But we need to know. Please can you send someone down there and check? I would go, but I'm a doctor and I'm needed up here. We can't bear the thought of him in pain and afraid. He'll be no trouble. He'll simply stay by my mother's side.'

Benjamin looked at Amy's mother. He hadn't realised that she was blind in the half dozen times he'd walked past her since the crash. *Brave woman*, he thought, *going through this harrowing ordeal in darkness.*

There wasn't much he could do until the first airdrop except to check the emergency doors. June Wilson had the first-class cabin under control. Benjamin was sure she had been a sergeant major in a previous life. The doctors and nurses were organised, and so he offered to go himself.

'Oh, thank you,' Joanne said, speaking for the first time. She looked up in the direction of his voice.

As he walked back towards the staircase, he called for Marcus to follow him.

'I might need your help, mate. We need to go down into the luggage compartment. We have a small rescue to perform.'

'Sure. Who're we rescuing?' Marcus asked.

'Heathcliff.'

'Okay. Who else, Catherine Earnshaw?'

'Funny guy. A passenger's guide dog, actually. He'd be awake by now. They're concerned that he might be injured.'

'No problem. Listen, some of the passengers were talking earlier,' continued Marcus, with a little more seriousness in his tone. 'They want to leave once the sun comes up. They believe they can climb down the valley once it's light.'

'That's absurd.' Benjamin stopped and turned to Marcus. 'I hope you told them that it's far too dangerous. We don't know how deep the snow is out there, not to mention sink holes, crevices, and potential avalanches they could encounter.'

'They're scared. Some of them will be amongst the last ones off.'

'I know they're afraid. So am I, Marcus. But we're safer in here.'

'Yeah, that's what I thought,' Marcus said, walking ahead of Benjamin so that his captain couldn't see the insecurity on his face. He'd thought it was a good idea at the time. Marcus knew the risks of leaving, but he'd believed there were greater risks in staying. He felt as though he were trapped inside a tomb, waiting for a bomb to go off. He hated that feeling of helplessness.

Marcus and Benjamin arrived at the access panel and climbed down into the cargo bay. The place was a mess, with luggage and cargo strewn everywhere. It was bitter cold in the compartment. Snow had fallen through in some places.

'Shit,' Benjamin said. 'The belly's been breached, too.' He pointed to the fuselage on the portside. He was now concerned that the breach would weaken the fuselage and cause the bulkhead to cave in.

Then they heard whimpering. They made their way toward the sound, shifting luggage out of their way as they trod knee-deep through the mess. They finally arrived at an upturned cage. Benjamin and Marcus hauled the huge cage back upright, and then Benjamin bent down and unfastened the latch.

'Come on, boy, come on,' he said, trying to coax the frightened dog out.

Heathcliff stood up and staggered – still half-drugged – out of the cage. He came up to Benjamin and licked his face in gratitude. Benjamin patted him and rubbed his beautiful winter coat.

'Come on, Heathcliff. You'll be safer upstairs with your owner.'

They made their way back to the cargo bay hatch. Heathcliff climbed over the luggage, while Benjamin and Marcus waded through the mess again. Once Benjamin had heaved Heathcliff up and climbed the ladder, he secured the hatchway. He needed to get back upstairs and prepare for the first medical drop.

From a safe distance, Herbert Schwartz watched as Marcus and Benjamin exited the cargo bay and closed the door. He then made his way to the panel, opened it, and went below. He traipsed through mounds of luggage until he found what he was looking for. He opened his suitcase and removed his ski suit, then went in search of his skis. Once daylight came, he would ski out of this hellhole. His only dread was finding his skis damaged.

Herbert had always made his own fate. That wasn't going to change now.

★

'Here you are, safe and sound,' Benjamin said, as he arrived back at Joanne's side. Heathcliff barked when he saw Joanne. When he ran up to her, he was rewarded with hugs and kisses. Then he dutifully sat down beside her.

Joanne held back tears as she bent down and rubbed Heathcliff. His tail was wagging profusely.

'Thank you so much, Captain. You don't know what this means to me,' Joanne said, outstretching her hand.

'You're welcome,' he said, taking it in both his hands.

★

Lesley watched the reunion with a sense of relief. It gave her renewed hope. She needed to believe that they would all get out of here alive. Her stomach was hurting, and she was in constant pain. She knew she should say something, but she was afraid. She was hot and uncomfortable. Lesley feared that something was terribly wrong. She tried her best not to cough, as it hurt more when she did. Lesley never liked knowing the painful truth – now was no exception.

She was grateful, particularly, that Rose was safe. Her friend had always been beside her, through thick and thin.

Lesley and Rosemary had flown to Australia for a short trip to see a musical in Sydney and to do a little shopping on the side. As their flight earlier in the week had been cancelled due to the earthquakes back home, they'd decided to spend their free time shopping and sightseeing. Their text earlier that day from ANZAL had confirmed it was time to go home.

Now wrapped up in a blanket, Lesley, in her sixties and Rosemary, who had just turned fifty-nine, had lived privileged lives, but they were not without tragedy. They had been friends since boarding school. Their antics saw them many times sitting outside the principal's office. Their lifelong friendship developed whilst in detention. Together they shared good times and bad. With four husbands between them, seven children and eleven grandchildren, their lives were hectic but blessed. Whenever difficult times returned, they're unwavering friendship had always see them through.

★

Benjamin headed back downstairs to the first-class cabin, to let the doctors know that the medical supplies would be arriving shortly. He then walked into the cockpit to retrieve his coat and gloves. He didn't relish the idea of going outside again. He wished he had some rope. It was something else he needed to ask Linus for. They would have to lower the supplies onto the roof of the plane, and for that, he was going to need help.

As he entered the first-class cabin, the mood was sombre yet busy. They were lucky to have four uninjured doctors on board, as well as a few nurses.

As Benjamin was discussing the medical drop with Dr Carlson, Beth couldn't help but overhear. She walked up to them and told them that her husband, Angus, was an experienced mountain climber. If he needed help retrieving the supplies, Angus would be his man.

Benjamin thanked her and said he would seek him out. As he turned to leave the cabin, he noticed the same woman who he'd helped earlier. She was bandaging a patient's arm. She looked up and smiled at him, and so he returned her smile before walking over to her.

'Are you a nurse?' he asked.

'No, but I had basic medic training in the army,' Annabel replied.

'I'm Benjamin Flynn, the captain,' he said, extending his hand to formally introduce himself.

'Hi, I'm Annabel, and yes, I know. Your epaulets are a giveaway,' she said with a cheeky smile, extending her hand in reply.

Benjamin looked momentarily embarrassed, but recovered quickly enough to say, 'Thanks for helping out in here. I know it can't be easy.'

'My pleasure,' she replied, holding his hand a little longer than strictly necessary. Then she turned back to her patient and continued with her bandaging.

★

'Linus, are you reading me? Over,' yelled the rescue pilot into her microphone.

'Go ahead, Sunny,' Linus replied, equally loud.

'We've located them. They're about twelve kilometres down the Tasman Valley. They're close against the south-eastern side. I'm going to drop the locator beacon as close as possible. Then I'll send you the coordinates.'

Thank God, Linus thought. *And so it begins.*

Chapter Nineteen

Mr Fox's residence, Bellevue Hill, NSW, Australia
5.35 a.m. NZ time

'Do you know what fucking time it is?' yelled Mr Fox into his iPhone, which he'd grabbed from the bedside table.

'Yes. Have you heard the news?' asked the man he knew as Wolf.

'Obviously not.'

'Flight AN224 came down over the Mount Cook National Park.'

Silence followed as Mr Fox took in what he'd just heard.

'Are there any survivors?'

'Yes, and I'm one of them. Worst fucking thing I've ever been through. They're going to start rescue operations at first light. I've seen our target in the cabin – he's unhurt.'

'That prick has nine lives,' Mr Fox said. 'What about Tigress?'

'Alive, but badly hurt.'

'I'll be in touch.' After hanging up, Mr Fox turned over to see his wife still sleeping soundly. Jackson Myer hated his sleep disturbed. He needed to think – this opportunity might not come around again. Henry Adams had to die. There was no question about that. Once he arrived home, Henry would eventually figure out what he had done. Either way, he and Gertrude knew too much.

Chapter Twenty

The moon continued its journey to the northwest. Civil twilight was approaching, and the sun was less than six degrees below the horizon. Their situation hadn't improved, although the thought of approaching daylight gave the passengers the illusion that they would be safer. Although, they still felt that the valley was ready to engulf them. Most of the shutters were closed – people had chosen not to look.

But now, as daylight drew near, the cabin crew walked through the cabins asking people to open their shutters. The APU in the tail had finally died, exhausting the last of the fuel. The soft warm tones that had emanated throughout the cabin earlier had finally faded, and the cabin was dark and cold.

Passengers who had loved ones were still holding onto them. Those travelling alone could only think of their loved ones back home and pray they would see them again.

Chloe Pappas was doing both of these things. She had finally woken from her shock and was recovering well; she was naturally a strong woman. But it was hearing Con's voice that had stirred her awake. The thought of Con's illness and never seeing her family again had sent her into shock. She needed to go home and see her family. Con was now resting his head on her shoulder. He had held her hand tightly for a while, but in the last five minutes, it had gone limp. Chloe couldn't face the idea of calling a doctor. She kept telling herself, *He's just sleeping*.

The dead had been discarded to the back of the plane. Chloe could feel their presence behind her, silent and still. There but not really there. She couldn't bear for anyone to take Con away. So, she decided to let him rest on her shoulder and sleep awhile longer.

★

The flight attendants moved quickly on both decks lifting up the remainder of the shutters. As they did, the eastern side of the plane started to become illuminated. Shards of light started to pierce through the cabin windows, and sparkling rays flickered around the cabins, transforming them from places of bleakness into places of hope. The plane grew warmer with each rising degree of the sun.

Living with the dead had given off an uneasy feeling in the cabins. Occasionally, a couple of male passengers carried someone to the back. The remaining passengers just thanked God that it wasn't them.

Off in the distance, breaking snow and ice still echoed down the valley. A constant reminder of their predicament as yet another tremor gently rocked the plane for twenty-two agonising seconds. Then the plane shifted slightly but didn't move from its comfortable position in the snow. However, it did sink a little deeper into it.

Down in the main deck, the snow was now about two metres from their windows. If they sank any deeper, they would have to be evacuated to the upper deck. Some passengers asked to go upstairs, but the cabin crew regretfully told them that currently there were no available seats.

★

Henry Adams, with the help of an Englishman, Bertie Danbridge, had managed to unscrew the bolts on the seat in front of Victoria Dahl and remove it completely. One of Victoria's legs appeared to be broken, while the other leg was badly bruised. They carried her up to business class, and waited with her, until a doctor examined her legs. Bertie said his goodbyes and left, while Henry chose to stay with her until the doctor arrived. Henry checked his watch. Now that the sun was coming up, so would the rescue helicopters.

He found a blanket and pillow and covered Victoria. He didn't want her going into shock. He was supposed to help relocate the dead, but he had got waylaid, unintentionally. Henry was unsure what to do now. He didn't feel like just sitting around, waiting to be rescued. He needed to keep busy. When the doctor finally arrived, she examined Victoria's left leg, bandaged it, and gave her a painkiller. Doctor Ruby Singh said that there wasn't anything else she could do until she was airlifted out. Victoria and Henry thanked her before she headed off to assist another patient.

Henry was taken in by this woman. She was brave, soft on the eyes, easy to talk to, and full of confidence.

'Were you travelling with anyone?' he asked, trying to be tactful.

'No, it was a last-minute flight,' Victoria said. 'I'm sorry. I never asked you your name.'

'My apologies. I'm Henry, Henry Adams.' He offered her his hand, but all she could do was stare at him.

Victoria had been assigned the case at the last minute. She'd been briefed on the bomb threat and passenger list but hadn't been given any photos of the passengers who'd chartered the Learjet.

'Is something wrong?' he asked.

'No, I'm sorry, forgive me. I'm Victoria, Vicky. Dahl. Is your colleague hurt?'

'Yes. Gertrude was badly hurt, but the doctors are looking after her.' Henry paused for a moment, wondering how she knew he was travelling with a colleague.

'Why were you in Sydney?' Victoria thought that now was as good a time as any to start questioning him. Her motto had always been: a federal agent is never off-duty.

'Why are you asking questions about my trip?' he asked cautiously. Victoria realised she was being too forward. She put it down to the pain. She knew she would have to come clean about who she really was.

'I'm sorry, Henry. I need to be straight with you. I work for the Australian Federal Police.'

'What! Oh. But why would you be sorry about that?'

'I was on my way to Christchurch to question a suspect in the attempted bombing aboard your Learjet yesterday.'

'I see. Look, I haven't told Gertrude yet. I thought I'd wait until we arrived home,' Henry said.

'That's fine, but we will need to question everyone who would have been on board the charter.'

'Of course. But Gertrude Simpson is badly hurt.'

'That's okay. We can speak with her later.'

'I still can't believe it.'

'Did the officers tell you anything about the bomb?'

'Enough to scare the shit out of me.'

'A man named Terry Burrows planted the bomb in the wheel assembly of your Learjet. It would have detonated about ten minutes after the landing gear was retracted, when you were well out over the ocean.' Victoria gave Henry a moment to take in what she had said.

'I'm sorry, Henry. It must have been a shock.'

'Not as much as crash-landing in a mountain range in darkness with avalanches crashing down on us.'

'That's the spirit. The New Zealand Federal Police were going to detain you and your colleague at the airport. I'll also need to question you about your business in Australia, and any potential threats you may have received.'

Henry licked his lips, still stunned at the thought. 'Who'd want to kill me and my colleague?'

'What is your line of business?'

'I've just signed a major deal in Sydney with an Australian software company. We're developing a revolutionary chip.'

'I take it that that's a big thing, then.'

'Absolutely. Cellular phones will never be the same again, and that's only one application. AI technology is worth billions when you have something new that everyone needs. Medical, security, and communications are but some of the areas that will benefit. So timing is everything in this game,' Henry said proudly.

'If your design is as good as you say it is … People have killed for a lot less, you know.'

'But I signed the deal yesterday, in Sydney,' he replied, now a little perplexed.

'Maybe someone wants your technology, but not you. Or maybe a competitor is trying to slow your work down. Has anyone else approached you lately regarding your technology? Has anything happened recently?'

'No. Our offices are in Christchurch, where I live. It's taken me five years to develop the prototype. We've just signed with a company called Cyber Systems, who are funding the manufacturing of the chip.'

'Would they have anything to gain or lose if you weren't around, Henry?'

'No,' Henry said with conviction, but he wasn't wholly convinced.

'Someone wanted you and Gertrude dead. Can you think of anything else that's happened lately that might cause suspicion?' Victoria asked.

Henry told Victoria about the breech in security. He also told her about the private investigator he had hired to look into the hack. Victoria asked for his details so her New Zealand counterparts could follow through and assist at their end.

'I don't know Jackson Myer that well, but Gertrude does, she introduced us. I only know him by reputation.

It was Gertrude who led the negotiations with Cyber Systems. They're an innovative but fairly new company. They had the technology and finance we needed to produce the chip.'

'Well, someone wanted you dead, Henry. We need to find out who before they try again,' Victoria said matter-of-factly. She tried to reach for her bag.

The only person Henry had confided in about the breech in security was Gertrude. He wondered if she had involuntarily confided in the wrong person. It sent a chill down his spine; the thought of someone wanting to kill him and Gertrude.

'Maybe Gertrude confided in someone she thought she could trust?' Henry said, still bewildered.

Victoria put her hand on his arm. 'Could you please pass me my handbag? My satellite phone is in there. I need to call the AFP. They'll look into Cyber Systems and let me know if they find anything.'

Henry passed Victoria her handbag. Even with a broken leg, and the threat of what was happening outside, she was completely focused and resolute. *What a woman*, he thought. Henry sat beside Victoria and recounted everything he could that was relevant. She made hasty notes. He wanted to check on Gertrude and see if she was awake, he thought it was about time he told her the whole truth. He decided, once he'd finished answering

Victoria's questions, he would question Gertrude about Cyber Systems.

As Henry looked around the cabin, he noticed other passengers using their mobiles. Some were making videos for their families. All the same, he found it strange to be trapped high up on a freezing cold mountain, perilously close to death, and to find that people were still using their mobiles. God, Henry loved the twenty-first century. He knew that there was so much more to come, and he was determined to be a major player in it.

★

'Have another swig, Sir Roger,' said Professor Windsor Hounslow. His words were starting to slur as he delicately handed over the bottle. Sir Roger accepted it with gratitude. On this occasion, he didn't mind drinking out of the same bottle, although he did wipe the lid each time before taking his turn.

'Cheers,' Sir Roger replied as he took another swill.

'You do know that we'll be the last off, old chap,' Windsor said, turning to his new friend.

'What are you talking about?'

'Well, the most serious cases will be air-lifted out first. Then the minor injuries. Then it will be the children.

Then the women, then us mere males will be bringing up the rear. Just like on the Titanic.'

'Shit. It doesn't look too good for us, does it?' Sir Roger conceded, realising for the first time in his life that, in at least this situation, being a man wasn't a privilege.

'Let's just hope that we don't sink as quickly,' Windsor said, starting to chuckle.

'It's a pity that we don't have an orchestra to play for us, as we do,' Sir Roger replied, taking another swig after wiping the bottle again.

Just like an aftershock, Windsor Hounslow realised that he hadn't called his lawyer. He couldn't abide everyone squabbling over his meagre possessions. Then again, he thought it might be fun – he decided not to call him after all.

Meanwhile, upstairs in business class, Hugh Mallard raised his hand up and touched the rays of light flooding into the cabin. It felt good – help would be arriving soon. Felix was breathing better, but Jane still hadn't woken up. He was cuddling Ava. He couldn't imagine her growing up without her mum. He couldn't see any of them getting through this without her. She always held everything together. Jane's diagnosis hadn't changed but neither had her prognosis since the crash. Hugh didn't know if that was good or not.

Even though business class was allocated to the injured, one flight attendant allowed Hugh and the girls to remain with Felix and his wife. He had watched passengers carry the dead to the back of the plane. He wouldn't let them do that to Jane. His children understood what was happening. He wouldn't let them go through that. No one was breaking up his family. She'd pull through – he knew it with every bit of strength he possessed. She had to.

The two German models were now resting back in their seats. Their excitement over the *Vogue* shoot had long since evaporated, and now their only thoughts were of going home to Germany. They cuddled up to each other to keep warm, thinking of what could have been.

Rose Banks snuck into the galley and found a handful of little liquor bottles. She dutifully handed some to Lesley, but she only shook her head. Rose could see that Lesley was sweating.

'Hey, Les,' she said, placing her hand on her friend's forehead. It was hot and clammy to the touch. Lesley didn't look good – she seemed to be delirious.

'Lesley. Wake up, please.' Rose shook her friend to rouse her. Lesley responded by coughing violently. Blood spurted from her mouth, all over Rose and the seat in front of her. Rose panicked and screamed for help.

Amy Donnelly raced over to examine Lesley.

'I ... I thought she was okay,' Rose said.

'Did she tell you that she was in pain at all?'

'No, but I've heard her cough a few times.'

Amy called for two of the male flight attendants to help carry Lesley downstairs into first class.

'What's wrong with her?'

'She may have internal injuries,' Amy said with honest uncertainty.

'I'm coming with you,' Rose said, as she grabbed Lesley's blanket.

'No, I'm sorry, but there isn't room for visitors down there.'

'We'll do our very best for her, but you need to stay here,' he said, as she followed the conscripted orderlies to the first-class cabin. Rose sat back down in her seat. She realised that, apart from some bruising, she wasn't hurt and should probably go downstairs to economy. Nobody had told them to move. She indignantly wondered if that was because of their age, but then again, she hadn't looked in a mirror since the crash. If she had, she would have been appalled at all the bruising.

Rose started to cry. She was afraid that she would never see her friend again. All of a sudden, she felt terribly alone.

Further along in the cabin, past the galley and toilets, Chloe Pappas wrapped a blanket more tightly around

Con. She hadn't heard him breathe in a while. *Till death do us part*, she thought, as she continued to stroke his hair and talk about the old days. She'd listened to his breathing for over forty-six years. She knew the sounds of her husband. But now he was silent and still. He was right beside her, as he always had been, but at the same time, he was not. She couldn't comprehend leaving Con behind.

★

Gladys was making a fuss over Dave. The nurse had given him a painkiller, and thankfully his shoulder no longer throbbed. He was glad that he'd only suffered a dislocated shoulder. He wouldn't be able to bare it if he lost Gladys. He wondered if the news of the crash had reached England. What time was it over there? He couldn't remember. He asked Gladys to find her mobile. He hated the idea of his children finding out about the crash on the news. He was going to be evacuated before Gladys because of his shoulder. She'd be frightened up here without him. Dave had resigned himself an hour ago to giving up his seat on the chopper to someone else.

Down on the main deck, Pauline Walsh heard Chyna Day whimpering. She had returned to the lower cabin because it was warmer than business class. She had been feeling better. She found the first available seat and sat down to find she was sitting next to Chyna Day. She tried to re-assure the actress that they would get out of this alive. But she knew that she didn't sound convincing. Pauline reached down under her seat for her bag and pulled out a small plastic bag.

'Have one of these pills. The red ones are the best, but the rest will also settle your nerves.'

Chyna looked down at the pills.

'They're Smarties.'

'Technically … yes … but they always make *me* feel better,' she said with a nudge.

Chyna couldn't help but smile. She took a couple of red ones.

'You haven't got a chocolate bar, have you? I haven't had one in three years.'

'I had a Mars Bar earlier, but I ate it, sorry.'

★

'Her vitals have improved with the transfusion,' Dr Uzer told Millie as he removed the needle from Annie's arm. 'How are you feeling?'

'I'm fine. A little woozy, but fine. Do you think they'll airlift her off first?'

'Yes. She'll be one of the first to go.'

'Thank God,' Millie said, leaning back and closing her heavy eyes.

Dr Munir Uzer looked at Millie. She'd only known privilege. He chastised himself for being so cynical. They were all trapped together.

'You won't be able to go with her. They're only airlifting critical patients first.'

'I know. Just as long as she's safe,' Millie said, stroking her sister's hair.

Munir opened up a sheet of paper containing his notes on Annie Wellington's injuries.

'Thank you,' Millie said, grabbing his arm as he scribbled more notes in doctor hieroglyphics.

'You're welcome. Do you know your blood type?'

'No, sorry, I don't.'

'Don't worry. They'll cross-check her when she arrives at the hospital. You should call your parents – I'm sure they have heard about the crash by now. They'll be worried.'

Millie hadn't thought about that. Her only concern was for her sister. Her phone had been on the table by her chair originally, but she had no idea where it was now.

'Thank you again, and I'm sorry for the way I spoke to you earlier. It was unforgivable.'

Munir accepted her apology and gathered up the rubber tubing and needles. He left Millie to rest while he checked on another passenger.

Millie kept wiping Annie's face with a damp towel. Life had been so carefree only hours before. Now death was staring her in the face.

★

Doctor Philippa Carlson had categorised the injured with a number of one through to five. The ones would be evacuated first, then the twos, and so on. The younger doctors found it difficult putting a number on a human being – it was like playing God with their lives – so it had fallen to her. Once the medical supplies arrived, they'd all be better equipped to stabilise them for departure.

Meanwhile, Lu Ming had remained in his seat in 1K. His leg was bandaged, and he had been given a painkiller, but this didn't stop him from yelling at anyone who walked past. Peng Ming had been happy to move downstairs into economy with Pauline Walsh. She'd relished the idea of getting away from her selfish husband. Lu had been reassured many times that he would be evacuated soon. He was tagged as a number two. He'd offered Charlotte a thousand dollars to make him a number one. Through gritted teeth, she'd declined. It was all she could do not to swear at the contemptable man.

'Hey, you,' Lu said. 'Hey, you.'

Charlotte turned around at his command. 'Yes, can I help you?' She said it with a practiced smile.

'I need my bag from my storage compartment.'

'I'm sorry, sir, but we'll only be evacuating passengers, not belongings.'

'I'm not talking about my bloody suitcase. I want the plastic bag I put in the storage compartment,' he said.

Charlotte stared at him for a moment, but then thought about how it might shut him up. So, she obliged, and handed him the Coles bag. It was heavy. She hoped that whatever was inside it was worth it.

He took it without a thank you and cuddled it to his chest.

Chapter Twenty-One

Mount Cook Rescue, Mt Cook Village
6.07 a.m.

'Hi, Captain Flynn. We're about to take-off. Be with you soon.'

'That's good news, Linus. I have the figures you asked for relating to the injured and dead.'

'Okay. What's the damage?' Immediately regretting his poor choice of words, Linus rephrased the question. 'Sorry, Ben. It's been hectic down here.'

'Don't worry about it. We felt another earthquake up here. Everyone's on edge.'

'We felt it, too. I'll be dropping off some walkie-talkies with the rest of the supplies in case your Sat Phone dies. Mobile coverage can be as unpredictable up there as the weather.'

'Thanks. We'll be ready,' Benjamin said, before disconnecting the line. He was beginning to feel anxious. With rescue operations about to commence, he prayed that nothing would go wrong. Apart from helping Heathcliff, Benjamin felt redundant. The doctors and nurses had worked non-stop. They had everything under control, thanks to June's military guidance. But Benjamin had nothing to fly.

As he walked out of the cockpit, Marcus came running up to him.

'Ben, you better come quick,' he said, before turning around and heading downstairs.

Benjamin followed Marcus all the way to the back of the main cabin. But as he walked down the aisle, a passenger jumped out in front of him and blocked his way.

'Please, Captain, when can we get out of here? I've got twelve children here scared out of their wits. Including myself. What's taking so long?' It was the teacher with the Kiwi school group.

'Please, miss –' Benjamin started.

'Joan. Joan Hollingsworth.'

'Please be patient a little longer, Joan. A rescue chopper is on its way as we speak. Only when it's safe will we start evacuating.' He placed his hand on her shoulder. 'I know you're scared.' He could see that she was under immense pressure – she was responsible for the lives of all the school children. He knew what that pressure felt like all too well, being currently responsible for over 500 lives. 'I need you to trust me.'

Benjamin watched as the tension in Joan's face relaxed a little. 'Okay, yes, sorry,' she said, as she stood aside.

'Get the children ready. After the injured are air-lifted out, the children will be the next to go.'

Benjamin had given her hope, which was what she needed from him. He realised that all the passengers would be needing the same reassurance. He hadn't spoken to them for a while, and knew he'd have to address them shortly. They deserved to be kept informed, whether or not the news was good.

He made his excuses and continued on after Marcus. There was a commotion at the back of the plane, as someone was trying to open the exit door. Two passengers were arguing. Another was blocking the emergency passageway.

'What the hell is going on?' yelled Benjamin as he pulled Herbert Schwartz away from the other passenger.

'I'm leaving, Captain,' Herbert said, who had changed into his ski gear.

'Nobody's leaving. Not yet,' Benjamin instructed.

'Forgive me, Captain, but you can't stop me. This plane is a death trap, and I will not be trapped inside when all of that snow comes down the mountains.'

Passengers nearby were becoming concerned after hearing Herbert's outburst. They looked over at Benjamin for an explanation. Then they all began talking at once. Captain Flynn knew that now was as good a time as any to explain their predicament. He couldn't use the intercom system, so he would have to make the same speech twice, once on each deck.

'May I have your attention, please!' he boomed. When they'd settled, he went on. 'It isn't safe to go outside! We're too high up in the Tasman Valley. The mountains that surround us have heavy winter snow on them, and the earthquakes are breaking that snow up and causing avalanches. That's the sound you've been hearing since we crashed. We're safer inside this aircraft. There could be crevices or sink holes, and God only knows what else out there. Search and rescue will be here in about five minutes. They'll assess our situation and advise us of the safest way out of here.' His last remark was directed at Herbert Schwartz.

Herbert took a step towards Benjamin and spoke quietly to him.

'Captain, I am an experienced skier. I have been skiing for over thirty-five years. I have skied on more dangerous terrains than this. It is my life and my choice. You have no right to decide my fate.'

'While you're in my aircraft, you're my responsibility. I'm the captain and my decision is final.' Turning to the man guarding the door, he said, 'Thank you. See that nobody leaves.'

'Yes, Captain.'

Herbert Schwartz was fuming. He hated being dictated to. He grabbed his skis and walked off down the aisle. Marcus watched him leave with a look of empathy.

The sunlight had now fully illuminated both cabins. Passengers had turned off their flash-light phone apps. Those by the windows were able to see the terrain around them, although what they saw terrified them. Snow upon snow upon snow, as far as the eye could see. The backdrop through their porthole windows showed the colossal mountains, stretching so high up that they couldn't see their tops.

Herbert made his way to the access panel in the floor. He opened it, lowered his skis, and then climbed down into the cargo bay. The plane was on a slight angle. But he still managed to wade through the mangled luggage till he found what he was looking for.

On the portside was a tear in the fuselage. He started to dig his way through the snow that had fallen through it, his strong shoulders ploughing with powerful momentum.

Then he was suddenly interrupted by another passenger.

'Are you leaving?' asked a young Swedish man in English.

Herbert turned around, not wanting to get into another fight, especially with a young, healthy Swede.

'Yes, I'm leaving. Don't try and stop me.'

'I won't. My friends and I would like to come with you. A few passengers have been talking quietly about leaving and taking their chances down the valley. When you ski down the valley, we will follow your ski treads through the snow. Now that it's daylight, I believe we can make it.'

'I will not be responsible for you and your friends.'

'I'm not asking you to. But once you're down, you can let them know that we have followed you, and once we are down, too, they can organise transport to pick us up.'

'It will be dangerous,' Herbert said uncertainly, eyeing the young man.

'Staying inside this tomb will be dangerous. Those mountains are over 12,000 feet high. We will be crushed like a tin-can if heavy volumes of snow come down on us.'

'Your choice. I've leaving as soon as I clear this snow away.'

'I'll organise for some people to come down and help you,' the man said, before he turned and went back upstairs to pass the word around.

Chapter Twenty-Two

After making a replica speech upstairs, Benjamin donned his coat and gloves and headed to the rear of the plane, where it was conspicuously colder. Snow had completely covered the floor directly above the torn fuselage. While Benjamin waited for Angus McWilliams to arrive, he thought about what he'd told the passengers. He believed he'd done the right thing. They deserved the truth, no matter how surreal or frightening it might be. He'd expected pandemonium from the passengers but was instead greeted with quiet resolve.

Before meeting up with Benjamin, Angus had gone in search of Beth. He'd found her assisting a doctor in the first-class cabin. She'd given him a warm kiss and re-wrapped his scarf tighter around his neck and chest.

'Tread carefully, won't you?' she said.

'Always,' Angus replied, before returning her kiss. 'You take care also, Poppy'. He turned and walked out of the cabin.

Angus climbed up and out of the aircraft before heaving Captain Flynn up and outside. They were standing on the ceiling of the plane. The sun peeked through the clouds, illuminating the ash particles still lingering in the air. The sun rose up and over the mountains as both men watched the phenomenon in silence, admiring its beauty. Their predicament aside, they had to admit that the view was amazing.

However, exposed as they were, Benjamin could smell something in the air. It had to have come from deep underground. Angus smelt it too; they knew that it wasn't a good sign.

As they stood atop the giant aircraft, they felt another slight tremor. They both knelt down and waited for it to subside. Behind them, up and off in the distance, they heard what sounded like cracking, as if something was splitting apart. He wondered which mountain was shaking off its winter coat.

It was frightening but thrilling to listen to. Benjamin felt like a goldfish in a bowl – just something tiny amidst a huge, open-glass world.

When the tremor stopped, they heard the sounds of rotor blades off in the distance.

Before Benjamin could rejoice at the impending arrival, the plane shifted, then started to slide down along the snow again. Both men lay flat on the roof of the aircraft. When the plane eventually stopped, it had shifted approximately thirty metres from its original resting place. Above the wind, Benjamin could hear the passengers screaming. Both men stayed low until they were sure the movement had stopped.

'You okay, Angus?' Benjamin yelled, offering him his hand.

'Yeah, I'm all good. That was a thrill ride,' he replied, as he took Benjamin's arm. 'I can hear the chopper coming, but I can't see where it's coming from.'

'The sound is echoing all around the valley. Train your eyes down there.' Benjamin pointed downwind. 'It will be coming up from Mount Cook Village.'

'Will do.'

They waited for what seemed like an eternity. Benjamin realised that the wind was going to play a dangerous role in the evacuation. Even though they were partially sheltered by the valley wall, there was a funnel of air cascading down the valley. He only hoped that it would abate before they started evacuating.

They stomped their feet to keep warm and for something to do while they waited. Finally, they saw a speck approaching off in the distance, barely visible against the snow-white landscape. They watched as it grew in size.

An EC145 rescue helicopter flew up and over their heads. The chopper continued up the valley, so that it could survey the mountains on either side. A film recording would be automatically uploaded to the rescue co-ordination centre back at Mount Cook Village. It soon turned back towards the plane and lowered itself to within fifty feet of Captain Flynn and Angus McWilliams. The rear door opened, and the crew lowered down a crate attached to ropes and a winch. The wind was causing it to swing. It was gusting now at around thirty knots. Benjamin and Angus braced themselves as the crate swung around again. They both ducked instinctively, even though it was still six feet above their heads.

It wasn't going to be as easy as they'd hoped. The chopper lowered the crate even further, to within reaching distance. As it came around again, Angus grabbed it. It pulled him along the aircraft, so he quickly let go. When the crate came around again, the pilot lowered it to within three feet of the aircraft ceiling. Then, on its final turn, it scraped along the roof of the plane. The chopper released the rope cable and both men quickly braced themselves against the crate to stop it from going over the side.

Once the crate stopped moving, Benjamin gave the thumbs up signal to the pilot, who reciprocated the acknowledgement and turned the chopper away before heading back down the valley. The pilot continued filming the terrain as the chopper headed back to its base to pick up Linus and his team.

'We'll drag her back to the opening,' Benjamin yelled.

Angus gave him the thumbs up, and both men grabbed the rope before starting to pull it along the roof of the aircraft.

'I hope he's coming back!' Angus hollered.

'He will, but it's safer for them to keep their distance for now,' Benjamin replied.

As they got to the opening, Benjamin instructed Angus to get back inside. He opened the latch on the crate and started to remove the boxes. He passed them down to Angus, who in turn passed the packages onto fellow passengers below, forming a supply chain back to the critically injured in first class.

Once all of the boxes were inside, Benjamin pushed the crate over the side of the plane. He kept the ropes, as they were over fifty feet in length and might come in handy.

Before climbing back into the cabin, Benjamin looked up at the impressive sight of Aoraki. She was truly remarkable. It towered majestically above all of its neighbours. He felt very small and insignificant as he climbed back inside the Airbus.

The boxes marked with a red cross were taken into the first-class cabin for the doctors to sort through. The remaining boxes – containing two walkie-talkies, a satellite phone, flares, hard hats, gloves, ropes, crampons, harnesses, an ice axe, ice screws, and pitons – remained in Benjamin's care.

Benjamin attached the headphones to his ears and turned on the radio to the frequency hand-written on the box.

'Mount Cook Rescue, this is Captain Flynn. Do you read me? Over.'

After a few seconds of static, the reply came.

'Loud and clear, captain. This is Linus. Over.'

'Good to hear your voice. When can we start the evacuations? We had another aftershock a few minutes ago. Over.'

'I know. Our pilot reported heavy volumes of snow coming down from the Minarets. However, I've got some good news and bad news. The air temperature is rising faster than normal – we think due to hot gas vents that have opened up. Also, Mount Taranaki has awoken from its 168 year slumber. Unfortunately, the higher temperature means more melting snow to deal with. The geologists believe that there's more to come. We'll try to evacuate the injured shortly. The army Chinook has arrived with a team of doctors; they're setting up a MASH unit to help stabilise the injured before they can get medevacked out. Over.'

'That's great. So how do you want to proceed? We have emergency slides on all emergency doors. Passengers can be lowered down on them, then onto the snow. Over.'

'It'll depend on how stable the snow is around you,' Linus warned. 'I'm on my way up to you now. They'll drop me and my team off first so that we can place marker poles around the plane where it's safe to tread. Sunny – the pilot – saw a few large crevices not far from your location, which have opened up. We'll need to tread carefully. That plane of yours weighs over 600 tonnes; I looked it up.'

'Thanks, Linus. Tell me something I don't know. Over.'

'Be with you in ten minutes. Out.'

Benjamin walked into the first-class cabin to update the doctors on their situation. He asked Dr Carlson to prepare the number ones for departure.

'My wife's dead,' a shocked passenger said, grabbing Benjamin's arm before beginning to break down. Benjamin grabbed the man's arm to hold him up.

'I'm so very sorry, sir,' he replied. Benjamin knew that this was of little comfort, but he didn't know what else to say. Nothing would replace his loss.

Suddenly, a gentle voice pulled the man's attention away.

'Come with me, please, sir,' Annabel said, wrapping her arm around the man's shoulder and escorting him from the first-class cabin. 'I'm truly sorry for your loss.' Annabel escorted him into the economy cabin and placed him in a seat. She then walked into the galley and searched for a small bottle of alcohol. Her only thought was to calm his nerves – she didn't care if he drank or not. She felt like a hypocrite, as drinking had never helped her, only turned her into an alcoholic. Seeing the little bottles, she was tempted to take one and put it in her pocket.

Annabel quickly put the thought out of her mind. Now wasn't the time to fall off the wagon. She returned to the grief-stricken man and offered him a bottle of scotch to numb away his despair for a while. Just then, John, who had finished transferring the dead to the back of the aircraft, offered him a blanket and stayed with him for a while. Annabel thanked him before heading back into first class to help the doctors.

As she walked pasted the partition, she noticed the captain still standing there. He appeared to be staring into space; he hadn't moved. She quickly returned to the galley and retrieved a bottle of water.

'It's not your fault. If anything, these people owe you their lives.'

'Thanks for saying that. But I'm responsible for everyone on board. I failed that man and his wife.'

'Most of us are alive because of you. Don't forget that.'

Benjamin looked into her pleasant green eyes. He absorbed their kindness, which he desperately needed. 'When did you leave the army?' he asked.

Taken aback that he remembered, she shifted a fraction and said, 'Over two years ago. Things just got to me a little.'

'It can happen to the best of us. They were lucky to have you,' he replied.

Annabel was about to say something when June Wilson called out to Benjamin. 'Captain, another helicopter is arriving.'

Benjamin turned away from Annabel.

'Thanks, June, I'm coming.' He turned back to Annabel and said, 'Excuse me.'

Benjamin walked back up the staircase. He was finally going to meet Linus O'Rourke.

Chapter Twenty-Three

6.45 a.m. NZ time

Outside the Airbus, Captain Flynn and Angus McWilliams grabbed Linus as he was lowered down. Three more team members followed behind him. Once they were all safely on the roof of the Airbus, Linus gave the thumbs up to Sunny, the pilot. The chopper then lowered down a large bag containing ropes and poles, which Linus needed to mark the terrain around the aircraft. Next, Sunny lowered a number of makeshift stretchers for the first of many injured passengers. Finally, she flew the EC145 up the valley, dropping beacons onto the snow-covered valley floor containing GPS trackers, which Rescue Operations would then be able to use to track the flow of snow down the valley. They would record the snow's speed and movement precisely.

The rescue ops team climbed into the aircraft and made their way down the back staircase, away from the blistering wind.

'It's a pleasure to finally meet you in person, Captain Flynn,' Linus said, shaking Benjamin's hand.

'The pleasure's all mine,' Benjamin said. 'And for God's sake, call me Ben. This is Angus McWilliams, a very resourceful passenger and professional climber.'

'Nice to meet you,' Linus replied, extending his hand again.

'Likewise.'

Linus asked Benjamin to open one of the emergency doors in the main cabin, just aft of the first-class area, so that they could climb down and check the snow around the aircraft. The wind was still gusting, but it was the snow beneath their feet that was of the most concern. Once the chopper returned, they would begin evacuations.

Linus' team headed straight into the first-class cabin to set up the stretchers for the first of many evacuations. Captain Flynn followed, catching Marcus Whitby on his way through and updating him on their current position. He asked Marcus to spread the word that rescue operations would start shortly. He hoped that it would boost morale throughout the cabins, and that evacuations would start soon.

Linus, Angus, and another rescue team member went to one of the emergency doors on the starboard side, opened the hatch, and climbed down onto the precarious snow. They decided to bring some large suitcases up from below to create a series of steps down. Passengers on the starboard side watched from their windows with renewed anticipation.

It was slow going as all three men walked carefully across the unstable snow. Dirty snowflakes were still falling, changing the pristine white into a dirty playground of ash and soot. Linus held out his hand for a few flakes to land gently on his glove. He brought his hand up to his nose and smelt the ash. His expression told Angus that it wasn't good news.

The passengers watched as they placed markers all around the aircraft. They had two distinct colour banners – red for danger and green for safe passage. They appeared to be placing a large number of red banners in the snow in front of the plane and along the starboard side. But a small green corridor of banners led away from the plane towards the opposite side of the valley. This corridor would eventually guide the passengers safely away from the aircraft to the landing site of the choppers.

They slowly headed back into the Airbus as the chopper hovered overhead.

Linus finished his conversation with Sunny. He didn't look happy when he finished.

'What is it?' Benjamin asked.

'Sunny has spotted large volumes of snow and ice on the valley floor behind us. She's top-heavy up there. Any more seismic activity could bring it all crashing down towards us. We're talking about an entire winter's volume up there.'

'We need to start transferring people now,' Benjamin said.

'Flying everyone out will take too long. We have over 500 people on board,' Marcus said.

'I know,' Linus said. 'I would normally suggest guiding people out, down the valley. But with all the seismic activity and ice movement, it's just too risky.'

'The snow is less dense further down, right?' Marcus inquired, pointing south down the valley. 'The further down we get, the better chance we'll have.'

'True,' Linus said. 'But it isn't just soft snow we're talking about. You're dealing with unpredictable ice, large crevices, and ice caves all the way down the valley. Not to mention the cold winds. On top of that, you're risking further aftershocks and avalanches. I can't guarantee that trekking down won't be even more dangerous.'

At that moment, a makeshift stretcher carrying the first of four seriously injured passengers was carried past them to the opened doorway.

'We'll discuss this option later,' Benjamin finished, as he stood aside to let them pass. 'Let's make sure we can airlift these injured people out safely first.'

'Agreed,' Linus replied. He climbed outside the Airbus and helped to lower the stretcher down onto the snow.

The helicopter lowered its safety basket as Linus and his team carried the first of many injured passengers over to it. With experience, they repeated this exercise three more times.

Annie Wellington was the fourth passenger brought to the emergency door.

She held her sister's hand tightly; she was awake for the first time since the crash.

'Are you coming?' she whispered hoarsely.

'No, I can't,' Millie replied. 'But I'll meet you at Dunedin Hospital as soon as I'm airlifted out. The injured have to go first.' Dr Munir Uzer was holding the IV drip bag beside her. Millie leaned down and hugged her sister – a heartfelt embrace that she never wanted to end. Once they parted, Annie was lifted down and across the snow to the waiting basket, from which she was hoisted up and into the EC145 rescue chopper. Millie watched the chopper carry her sister away until they disappeared from view. For the first time in her life, she felt truly frightened. She wrapped her blanket around her shaking body, then started to cry.

Millie didn't know what she would do if Annie died. It would be like losing a piece of herself. She shivered again as the emergency door closed behind her.

Dr Uzer allowed her to cry on his shoulder. Then Naomi appeared beside him and escorted Millie into the economy cabin. Now that four passengers had left, they could transfer four more injured passengers from business class down into the first-class cabin, ready for their turn to be evacuated.

Naomi took Millie over to Leonor and Ava, then asked her to look after the girls until their father returned. Jane and Felix had just been transferred down to first class for the next round of evacuations. Hugh Mallard had accompanied them. Millie realised at that moment that she hadn't yet called her parents. She knew her parents would have heard the news by now and would be panicking, but she'd lost her mobile sometime during the crash.

Millie looked around the cabin – she needed to borrow a phone.

★

Lu Ming was still insisting on getting evacuation priority. Dr Carlson explained to him that there were others with more critical needs, but it made no difference to Lu. He started complaining to another flight attendant, who finally told him to shut up. John had arrived in the first-class cabin assisting an injured passenger. He forcefully told Lu Ming that he would be evacuated once all the grade ones had been airlifted.

Lu was still clinging to his Coles shopping bag as if his life depended on it.

'Where's my wife?' he asked the flight attendant.

'Escaped, I would imagine.'

'What did you say?'

'Oh, shut the fuck up, will you?' John spat out forcefully, extremely out of character. Being fired for vulgarity was the least of his worries. He swore to himself that he would never fly again.

★

Marcus Whitby found the man he was looking for. He grabbed his arm and led him away from his group of friends.

'They don't want to walk people out of here. They say it's too dangerous.'

'Unless you know what you're doing. I've skied all my life, back home in Sweden. So have my friends. We know how to survive on the snow,' Lars Norstrom said.

'Who's going?' Marcus asked.

Lars shrugged. 'Whoever wants to come, but they must be young and fit. And we'll have to leave soon.'

'Passengers don't have the right gear to hike down that valley,' Marcus said.

'They must have covered-in shoes. We're taking the serving trays. We can sit on them and slide down part of the way. We will use our shoes for brakes if it gets too steep. I heard we are about ten to twelve kilometres from Tasman Lake – then there is a road. Rescue can collect us from there.'

Marcus let him go back to his friends. He seemed to know what he was talking about. Marcus was torn between leaving with the Swedes and staying and taking his chances. He needed to see his wife again. He wanted to go with them but knew that Captain Flynn would expect him to be the second-last living person off the aircraft.

It would take most of the day to evacuate everyone. His conscious fought him all the way back to the cockpit. Maybe he should escort the passengers who wanted to leave down the valley? After all, they were his responsibility too …

★

'Are you fucking kidding me?' Linus yelled into his headpiece.

Captain Flynn came over to him with concern on his face.

'What is it?' he asked.

'Sunny just told me she can see someone skiing down the valley. About two kilometres down.'

Benjamin stared at him in astonishment, then realised – 'That would be Herbert Schwartz, a very determined German. I told him he couldn't go. He must have slipped out without anyone seeing him.'

'Sunny can't stick around. She's heading to Dunedin Hospital. The German's on his own,' Linus said matter-of-factly.

'Understood,' Benjamin said. *Herbert would prefer it that way,* Benjamin thought privately.

'Sunny will take the four passengers she has straight to Dunedin Hospital. They are prepped and ready to receive them. Everyone else will be dropped down at Mount Cook Village, then ambulanced to local community hospitals. She won't be back for a while, but the Chinook is on its way. If Herbert makes it to the lake, we can get a driver to pick him up.'

At that moment, June Wilson appeared beside Benjamin and handed him the revised passenger list. Each passenger name had an 'L' or 'D' beside it. 'Living' or 'dead'.

Benjamin briefly scanned the list before handing it to Linus. Thankfully, there were a lot more 'L's than 'D's.

'We have a few missing passengers,' June said. 'I think they might have been sucked out when the fuselage ripped open as we crashed.'

'They'll be further up the valley somewhere. God, we've got to find them, Linus,' Benjamin said.

'We will, Captain.' Linus understood Benjamin's unease. He was also responsible for his own team, so he understood the pressure that Benjamin was under.

'Thank you,' was all that Benjamin could say.

'Now that I have an indication of the dead, it will give us a timeframe for the evacuation,' Linus said. 'We'll mark off passenger names as they're airlifted out. We'll have to leave the dead behind for now. We'll come back for them when it's safe.'

'Understood,' Benjamin said, despondently.

'Once we've found a safe zone, we'll be able to land the choppers. The Chinook will be a godsend,' Linus said, as he walked off towards the first-class cabin.

When he entered the most exclusive part of the aircraft, he wasn't prepared for the extent of the carnage. There were bloodied bandages and medical supplies everywhere. It was like a war zone. He saw blood-stained seats and blood-soaked carpet beneath his feet. The doctors and nurses were diligently moving around the cabin, tending to their patients. They'd gone through the same terrifying ordeal as the rest of the passengers but were still working furiously to treat the injured.

The four empty seats would shortly be filled with more passengers, who were currently lying on the floor upstairs in the lounge. Hopefully, within the next hour, all fourteen seats would be empty. Then they could start air-lifting passengers from the business class section.

The second EC145 could hold nine passengers. It wasn't equipped for medical rescues, but it could still hold four stretchers. Sunny would return in approximately forty minutes – offloading the passengers would take time. The second rescue chopper was refuelling at Mount Cook Village and would arrive in less than ten minutes. The army Chinook would depart shortly thereafter – it had just finished offloading its equipment for the MASH unit.

Upstairs in business class, Joanne was resting calmly, now that she had Heathcliff loyally resting next to her. Amy had felt guilty that she wasn't by her mother's side, but her mother wouldn't have it any other way. She was about to speak with her mother when Heathcliff's ears pricked up. He whimpered, then started to bark.

Linus was in the middle of a conversation with the pilot of the second rescue chopper, when another tremor started. Linus held onto the armrests of his chair and waited, like everyone else on board, for it to stop. It was his first tremor inside the Airbus. It stopped within twenty seconds, but the sound of breaking ice didn't. Jumping up, Linus made his way to the starboard side of the plane.

He opened the door and looked outside. What he saw would remain with him for the rest of his life. The hideous sound drew his attention up towards the majestic sight of Aoraki. He watched as a thunderous avalanche of snow and ice collapsed down the mountain. He was grateful that they were far enough away and across the other side of the valley. Linus watched the avalanche until it slowly came to a stop.

Still, they were running out of time.

Then he heard banging on the roof of the aircraft. Ice had fallen from the mountain directly above them onto the eastern side of the valley. He had believed that they were safe enough, but now immediately realised that the weight of the ice would cause the fuselage to collapse in on itself. He raced back upstairs and headed to the back of the aircraft, then waited until the thumping sounds had stopped. Then he climbed back out onto the roof of the Airbus. Linus called for his team to help remove the chunks of ice sitting on the plane's roof.

A handful of male passengers joined them. They worked frantically to remove them. The rocks of ice left dents in the roof, but the roof hadn't caved in. Linus thanked them as two more choppers came into view. Another EC145 – as well as the army Chinook – were arriving to commence another round of evacuations. Linus inspected the landing zone again, which they had marked out earlier, to make sure that no crevices had appeared during the last earthquake. He was relieved to see that none had.

★

'Do you remember the time when we headed down to Melbourne and were trapped all night in our car?' Chloe asked while she kept stroking Con's hair. 'We pulled out the blankets and cosied up all night as the storm passed by. Remember? This is nothing compared to that hair-raising night. We'll be out of here soon, Con, and back home with our children around us.'

Con's body had shifted during the last tremor. Chloe had quickly put his head back on her shoulder. She needed to keep up the pretence.

Beth McWilliams came up to them and checked Con's pulse. Tears welled up – she couldn't hold them back any longer. She looked pleadingly at Chloe, but she shook her head, as if to say, *not yet*. Beth respected her wishes and left her with her husband.

Beth continued her rounds and checked on her other patients. Victoria Dahl's broken leg was heavily bandaged, and the morphine had eased her pain. Hugh Mallard was with Jane and their son Felix, down in the first-class cabin, while Millie cared for Leonor and Ava. Jane had regained consciousness but was not very responsive. She would be evacuated with Felix shortly. Beth found June Wilson and updated her on Con and Chloe Pappas.

Millie could feel Ava trembling in her arms and decided to tell her a story. Anything to stop herself from trembling, too. A few rows behind them, they heard Chloe humming softly to Con. Beth had returned with June Wilson, to assess Chloe's situation.

'He has cancer,' Chloe said to them, as if needing to explain their presence on the plane. 'He wanted to be buried on Ios, where he was born. I can't leave him here.'

'I'm sure they'll honour his wishes, Mrs Pappas. But you'll be leaving soon,' June said.

'He didn't think I knew about his illness, but I did,' Chloe continued as if not hearing June's last remark 'The doctor's surgery called one day about his specialist appointment. I Googled the doctor. He was an oncologist. You know, we've owned a grocery store all our married lives. All we wanted was one holiday together.'

'I'm so very sorry, Mrs Pappas,' Beth responded quietly.

'Regret is a terrible thing. Don't allow it to happen to you,' Chloe said, looking at Beth intently as she spoke.

Beth had been keeping strict notes on her injured passengers. She had gotten to know each of her patients by name and a little about their lives. She remembered a quote: 'familiarity breeds contempt'. She had never cared for that saying. She knew that she shouldn't get too emotionally attached to patients, but there were times when she couldn't help it. She felt some of Chloe's sadness and despair.

At that moment, Beth needed to hold Angus, just for a moment. She searched the cabins for him. Someone had told her that he was down in economy, preparing for the next evacuation. Beth ran down the staircase and looked frantically for him. Her eyes caught sight of him for just a moment as he climbed down and out of the emergency door with a stretcher.

She knew better than to disturb him. Knowing that he was okay was good enough for her. *Get a grip*, she thought. Beth headed back into the first-class cabin to see what she could do there.

Dr Philippa Carlson asked Beth to ready the next round of injured passengers up in business class for transfer to the first-class cabin. A couple of doctors had gone upstairs to select the new candidates. Most could walk on their own now, but some still needed assistance. Beth said that she would organise it with Sally Keogh. She was grateful that she had purpose.

★

The two German models were escorted downstairs into first class. Jane was to be evacuated next with her son.

Hugh didn't want to be apart from his wife and son, but he also couldn't leave his daughters alone upstairs. He felt like he was being torn apart.

★

07:40 a.m., Mount Cook Village

At that same moment, Major Wilkinson was co-ordinating the setup of his MASH unit in readiness for the evacuees. They already had the medical tent erected, and the triage station was ready to go. The cots were being set up currently. They were also putting together a supply tent, a communications tent, a mess tent, and portable latrines, which were offloaded from the Chinook before it could commence rescue operations.

Major Wilkinson was known by his subordinates as 'the Steamroller'. Nothing got in his way.

The rest of his staff had just arrived via a convoy of army trucks. He wanted the MASH unit ready by zero eight hundred hours. It was ready with four minutes to spare.

In between bellowing orders to his staff, Major Wilkinson periodically turned his attention to the looming figure of Aoraki off in the distance. It peered down on him with contempt.

Major Wilkinson knew who would prevail at the end of the day. He sniffed in the cold air, then turned away in disgust at the strange smell.

Chapter Twenty-Four

7.45 a.m. NZ time

'Help, help me!' Henry yelled.

… *Ten minutes earlier* …

Henry and Victoria had spoken to his private investigator about the bomb threat and his current situation. He was in shock; but confirmed his investigation was escalating fast. He relayed a conversation he'd had with the firm's researcher and press officer who admitted to having suspicions regarding Gertrude and Jackson Myer's association.

'I don't mean recently,' the investigator said. 'She believed that Gertrude has always worked for Cyber Systems. Or Jackson Myer, to be precise.'

'What do you mean?' Henry asked.

'I can't prove anything yet, but I believe that her goal all along was to set you up with Jackson Myer. I think they've played you, Henry. You need to speak with Gertrude.'

'Christ. Keep digging, please,' Henry demanded.

'So far we don't have any direct proof of her collusion. But your researcher said she overheard Gertrude on the phone to Jackson Myer last week, she overheard the name Synergy Holdings. Also known as Samlegðarhlutir. I looked it up, guess who the registered owner is?'

'Jackson Myer,' Henry said despondently.

'Correct. I didn't want to approach you until I had direct proof. I know you think a lot of Gertrude. I know how much this collaboration means to you. Let me dig a little deeper. I'll know more in a day or so. Now that the AFP are involved, we will get to the bottom of it much quicker. I'll speak with you again once you're back in Christchurch. I'm so sorry, Henry.'

'Thank you, but it's not your fault. I was foolish and naïve.' Henry knew his next port of call was to speak with Gertrude. He had finally found his link with Iceland, but to what purpose?

Henry walked into the first-class cabin just as a man brushed passed him. He didn't take much notice, as he was single-mindedly focused on how to confront Gertrude about the latest accusations. The space was solemn, as some of the doctors and nurses were upstairs helping to relocate another round of injured passengers downstairs. The remaining passengers were resting sombrely in their seats.

Henry found Gertrude in her own seat. He didn't care how hurt she was – if she was awake, he needed answers.

'Listen, Gertrude,' he said. 'I want to talk to you about Jackson Myer and Synergy Holdings. And don't lie to me.'

Gertrude's head was facing the window. Her eyes were open, but she appeared to be staring out into nothing. 'Gertrude, look at me,' Henry said, nudging her arm.

Gertrude's head bobbed over to the other side. Her eyes remained open, but they saw nothing. Henry knew instantly that she was dead.

'Help! Help me!' Henry yelled.

Dr Uzer came running over. He felt Gertrude's pulse – he couldn't understand it. She was fine only minutes before. He called Dr Carlson over. They tried resuscitating her, but it was no good. After Dr Carlson examined her, she shook her head. 'Her neck is broken,' Dr Carlson said.

'*What?*' replied Munir and Henry simultaneously.

'See here, Dr Munir. Look at these marks. This was not done in the crash. Someone has broken her neck,' she said.

'I checked her over carefully, Dr Carlson. I assure you that those marks were not there when I examined her less than half an hour ago.'

'Get the captain here now,' Philippa Carlson said. Her tone was not one to be questioned.

Henry raced off to find Captain Flynn. He couldn't believe it – what the hell was happening? He found the captain outside, just as another rescue chopper was headed south down the valley.

He waved to the captain to come inside. 'You need to come with me now, Captain,' Henry anxiously said.

The emergency door closed after Linus climbed back in.

'Please, Captain,' Henry said.

'Okay. I'm coming,' Benjamin replied, hearing the urgency in his voice.

Captain Flynn turned to Linus and nodded his head, indicating that Linus should follow.

As they walked back into the first–class cabin, a new set of injured passengers were being made comfortable and were quietly being attended to.

'What is it, doctor?' Benjamin asked, as they arrived by Dr Carlson's side.

'This woman had a head injury,' she said. 'A concussion and some internal injuries, but nothing life threatening. But now, she's dead – someone has broken her neck.'

'*What!*' Ben said.

'Why? Who would want to kill her?' Benjamin asked, looking over at Henry.

'I'm not sure,' he replied. 'But our original flight from Sydney was cancelled. Initially, we were told that it was due to maintenance problems. But the Australian Federal Police paid me a visit before we departed Sydney and said that someone had planted a bomb on our private jet. They believe we were the party targeted. There is an AFP officer on board – her name is Victoria Dahl. She will corroborate what I've just said.'

'Jesus Christ,' Captain Flynn said. 'There must be someone on board who followed you back to New Zealand. If he's under contract, he won't stop until he's finished the job.'

'Great. That's comforting to know,' Henry said, as he started looking around the room.

'The AFP officer's being brought down into first class now, as she has a broken leg. She was heading to New Zealand to interview a potential suspect,' Henry said.

'With all the dead and injured, what's two more dead bodies? There probably won't be any autopsies,' Benjamin said.

'Did you see anyone in here when you came in, Henry?' Linus asked.

Henry thought for a moment. 'Yes. A man walked pasted me as I walked in. But I didn't get a good look at him. His head was down. Shit, I'm sorry, I wasn't paying attention.'

'Was he tall, short, white, black, young, old? Think, Henry,' Benjamin urged.

'Um, tall, taller than me, about six feet. White. Broad-shouldered. He had a black jacket on and a hat. A beanie, I think. I'm sorry, that's all I can remember,' Henry said, feeling embarrassed. His embarrassment turned to anger when he looked down at Gertrude.

What had she gotten herself into? If she was a part of the conspiracy, why kill her? 'Poor Gertrude. What the hell is happening?'

'I don't know,' Benjamin said, truly bewildered.

'He may come after you next, Henry, before you're airlifted out of here.'

'We may need to get him off, sooner rather than later,' Benjamin said. 'The authorities will need to speak with you. 'I'll radio them and let them know what's happened.'

'I'm not leaving,' Henry interrupted. 'Not until we find the person responsible. Besides, you haven't evacuated all the injured yet.'

'Henry, whoever planted that bomb won't stop until you're dead,' Benjamin said. 'It's my responsibility to keep you safe, and that's exactly what I'm going to do.'

'Every man evacuated from this point on will be treated as a suspect until proven otherwise,' Linus said. 'I'll radio Major Wilkinson down at the MASH unit and let him know what's happened.'

'I'm not leaving until I speak with Victoria Dahl. She'll be able to help,' Henry said with finality as he walked off to search of her. Benjamin and Linus watched Henry as he left the first-class cabin. They didn't believe he truly appreciated the trouble he was in.

'We'll need to keep an eye on him,' Linus said. 'Were there any law enforcement people on board, apart from this Victoria Dahl?'

'The air marshall was injured,' Benjamin said. 'He's being evacuated shortly. He'll have a weapon on him. I'll speak with him and ask him for his side-arm. I'll check with June Wilson and see if there are any other law enforcement officers on board. If so, we'll ask them to watch over Henry.'

'Sounds good. I'll leave that with you,' Linus said. 'I wouldn't advise telling anyone else – your passengers have enough to deal with.'

Benjamin headed off in search of June Wilson. He could rely on her discretion.

★

07.55 a.m. NZ time

'Wolf, I need you off that plane,' Mr Fox said.

'Why? Has our plan changed?' Wolf replied.

'You could say that. The Australian Federal Police are sticking their noses in where they don't belong. They have an agent on the plane. It's too late now. If they have any sense, they'll evacuate him sooner rather than later. You need to take care of him, once he's back in Christchurch.'

'Understood. Tigress is no longer a problem.'

'Shame, I liked her.'

'I might be able to intercept him, before he arrives in Christchurch.'

'If so, get it done.'

Wolf ended his phone call. He had another way off the plane. He needed to find the Swedish backpacker.

★

When Victoria was carried into the first-class cabin, she had already been made aware of Gertrude's death. She called the AFP and asked them to sift through Gertrude's life and find out what they could about Jackson Myer. Victoria asked Henry for Gertrude's laptop and handbag. After her search, she asked Henry to go down into the luggage compartment and look for Gertrude's suitcase. It was likely that she had a second mobile. If it was to be found anywhere, it would be in there. What's more, if there was anything incriminating on it, she'd find it.

Henry was about to leave in search of Captain Flynn when he arrived back in the cabin with June Wilson, followed closely behind by a burly man in his forties.

'This is Constantine Zabinski, your five o'clock shadow,' June said. 'He's an ex-Polish soldier who has military and protection experience. Where you go, Mr Jones, Mr Zabinski follows. I've informed him of your predicament.'

'Thank you, Ms Wilson,' Henry said, who had now decided it was best not to argue. Henry shook hands with the steely-eyed man. He was going to be his constant companion until they were evacuated down to Mount Cook Village.

Constantine had volunteered his help because he couldn't bare just sitting around waiting to be evacuated. He needed to put his own life in his own hands. He was given the air marshal's gun and had put it in his sock and strapped it to his leg. He had initially thought of heading down the valley on foot with the Swedes, however, thought better of it, knowing how unfit he now was.

★

After exchanging formalities with Constantine, they headed to the hatchway, which led down to the luggage compartment.

Once they climbed down, they could see that all the luggage was strewn everywhere. They thought it would take some time to find Gertrude's case, but as the first-class luggage was always kept apart from the other classes of travel, it only took them fifteen minutes. Once they had Gertrude's suitcase, Henry found that they needed the key. He cursed himself for not thinking of it before.

Henry offered to head back to the first-class cabin, but Constantine refused to let him out of his sight. Instead, Constantine went to the hatchway and called out. A female passenger came to the opening and listened while he gave her instructions on what to collect and from whom.

'Okey dokey,' said Pauline Walsh, as she headed off towards the first-class cabin.

Pauline had recovered remarkably well since her fall in the toilet. She was still sitting next to the film star, Chyna Day, who hadn't stopped complaining. Pauline had contemplated moving back to her original seat. But unfortunately, her economy seat was now lost in the 'morgue', along with her coat. She was finally warm and was about to discuss her latest novel with Chyna to help distract her, when she heard someone calling out for help nearby.

As she approached the hatchway, a deep-voiced Polishman had asked her to go into first class and find a woman called 'Victoria' and ask for a key. Pauline had agreed, even though she wasn't quite sure what it was all about.

Pauline entered the luxurious first-class cabin again. There was still a gagging smell of blood in the cabin. The carpet she trod on was squishy with the stuff.

Pauline asked one of the flight attendants if there was a Victoria in the cabin, and the woman pointed her in the right direction. Pauline shared her instructions and Victoria searched Gertrude's bag for the luggage key. Once she'd handed it over, Pauline made a quick exit. She'd written about death many times in her novels, but only as an outsider looking in. She'd never understood what it was like to actually live through the consequences of death. Pauline knew that she would have to re-write a good part of her novel. Her characters had appeared breezily unaffected by their predicaments, and she now understood that they must appear two-dimensional and cold.

Pauline realised, at that very moment, her life wasn't as bad as she thought it was. She had amazing parents, siblings, and friends who were always there for her. The survivors on board were suffering, and not all of them from injuries. Many had lost loved ones. Even now, she could sense them silently resting in the morgue. It made Pauline's blood run cold.

Pauline climbed down the step ladder and handed over the key to Constantine. Not wanting to be rude, she delicately asked what the hell they were doing, opening a woman's suitcase. Henry explained to her what he was looking for and why. It seemed simpler to him to just tell the truth.

Henry was still scrummaging around when Pauline suggested he look in the toiletry bag. He immediately found what he was looking for.

When he turned the mobile on, it asked for a password. He put it in his pocket and hoped that Victoria would know how to unlock it.

Constantine and Henry headed back upstairs, leaving the suitcase on the floor. Pauline could hear a soft howling sound coming from further down in the luggage compartment. She looked up to see a tear in the fuselage – snow had come inside. Oddly, Pauline couldn't leave this woman's luggage strewn all over the floor, so she knelt down and gathered everything up, neatly folding it back into the suitcase.

'Typical men. Can't put anything away,' she said. But as Pauline placed a thick jumper back into the suitcase, she realised that it was her size. She quickly put it on. This was no time for courtesies. She was cold and didn't believe the woman would mind under the circumstances, especially considering her own coat was resting over a dead woman. Her new jumper was cashmere – it felt warm and soft. Pauline thought to herself, *Well, if I'm going to steal something, it might as well be cashmere.*

As she closed the suitcase, she heard some voices off in the distance. She wasn't paying any attention until she heard one say, 'Are you ready to go? It's now or never.'

'How many are going?'

Pauline looked up from her kneeling position and saw the co-pilot talking to two passengers. By their accents, they sounded Nordic.

'About thirty passengers want to leave. The wind is easing, the sun is up, and the temperature is rising. It's now or never,' Theodor Lagerquist said with vehemence.

'I … I don't know,' replied Marcus. 'I can't abandon the rest of the passengers.'

'I understand. But most of us won't be airlifted out until the end,' Lars said.

'You've heard the avalanches. It may be too late by the time it's our turn to be rescued,' Theodor said.

'What about the older passengers?' Marcus asked.

'*Nej*, only the young and strong can go. It will be too difficult for anyone else,' Lars said.

'I'm sorry, but we'll need to move fast out there,' Theodor said. 'Are you coming?' After what seemed like a lifetime, Marcus replied, 'Yes.'

'Okay, we go in five minutes. Be ready,' Lars said.

As they headed towards the hatchway, Pauline ducked behind some luggage. She wasn't sure why she did it. Maybe it was instinct, or maybe she'd read too many suspense novels. She felt foolish afterwards, but she felt even more foolish once they'd climbed up and out and shut the hatchway behind them, leaving her trapped inside.

'Oh shit,' she said, as she ran to the ladder. She climbed up but couldn't get the hatch door open. Banging on the door again felt like déjà vu.

'Help! Help! Somebody let me out!' she yelled repeatedly. No one came. Pauline sat there for a while, contemplating what to do next. Now wasn't the time to become claustrophobic. Pauline finally scampered over to the tear in the fuselage. She had a thick cashmere jumper on, but it wouldn't be warm enough to go outside. She had to warn the captain of what these men were up to. *Idiots*, she thought. But they were desperate. The captain had been right earlier, when he'd warned about the dangerous conditions outside.

Pauline searched through more luggage until she found what she was looking for – a coat, beret, and scarf, which she wrapped around her neck. Before leaving, she noticed a long metal rod, which she picked up and took with her.

The plane was still on a slight five-degree incline toward its starboard side. Someone had dug a trench up and out through the torn fuselage on the port side. It was nearly six feet in length. Pauline crawled up and out, and she found herself outside the massive aircraft. There was already a set of heavy footprints in the snow leading away from the aircraft.

The sun was starting to warm everything around her. The snow wasn't smooth, as you would expect virgin snow to be – it was fractured and broken. Boulders of ice lay everywhere. Pauline was reminded of what the captain had said about ice caves and crevices. She decided to tread carefully. Small ice flurries were falling all around her. It was surreal – they were supposed to be white feathery snow-flaked crystals. Instead, they were the colour of dirty ash.

Pauline made her way carefully across the snow, using the pole to prod the snow in front of her. She kept to the side of the aircraft. Looking up at it, she appreciated the Airbus' mammoth size.

Pauline's thoughts were momentarily distracted as she caught a strong smell in the air. Turning her head towards the stench, she realised that it was fuel. Her hands were freezing – she needed to get inside. She trekked as quickly as she could to the emergency door near the first-class cabin. Using her pole, she started to bang on the door.

Finally, someone opened it.

'What the fuck are you doing out there?' Linus asked.

'Enjoying the view. What the hell do you think I'm doing out here?' she said in response. 'Well, don't just stand there, lift me up. She raised her arms up. Once Linus had hauled Pauline inside, she told him what she'd overheard. He thanked her before racing off to find Captain Flynn.

Chapter Twenty-Five

8.10 a.m. NZ time

'Captain,' Linus said as he waved his arm to signal Benjamin's attention.

Benjamin excused himself before heading towards Linus.

'We've got another problem.'

'What is it now?' Benjamin asked.

'One of the passengers overheard three men talking about leaving. A professional skier, like Herbert Schwartz, might just make it on skis. But a group of people on foot! It's suicide. You have to stop them.'

'Does your informant know who they are?'

'Yes, she said one of them was Marcus, your first officer.'

'*What!*' Benjamin yelled. 'What the fuck does he think he's doing?' Benjamin turned his back on Linus and went in search of Marcus. He finally caught sight of him climbing down through the hatchway, into the cargo bay below.

Once he'd climbed down the ladder after him, Benjamin saw nearly thirty passengers wrapped up and climbing through the hole in the fuselage.

'Stop now!' he yelled.

They stopped and turned to see the captain standing in front of them.

'This is madness. You won't make it. It's too dangerous out there.'

'Sorry, Captain, but this is our choice,' said one man. 'It'll take hours before it's our turn to be evacuated. I'd rather take my chances outside on my own terms.'

'We're dead either way. At least we'll have a chance out there,' Bertie Danbridge said, who had decided to go with them. Benjamin recognised Chyna Day amongst the passengers exiting the bulkhead.

'I understand how you feel,' Benjamin said, raising his arms up to concede the point. 'But you won't make it. It's too dangerous. Even if more snow comes down the valley, we'll still be protected inside the Airbus.'

'What if the plane collapses into a crevice?' Marcus replied, as he came into view for the first time. He moved to the front and came forward. 'Or if we're crushed beneath the weight of all that snow and ice?' The other passengers watched as Marcus challenged Benjamin. 'These people are being penalised simply because they're not injured. They deserve a fighting chance.'

'I'm the captain, and I'm ordering you back upstairs. Please trust me and the rescuers. We'll get you out of here,' Benjamin pleaded.

Some of the passengers looked at each other, now unsure. They didn't know what to do.

Some began to shout defiances at him.

'I need to get out of here,' Chyna said. Captain Flynn knew he couldn't force them to stay. There were too many passengers to restrain. There were risks either way. They were young and believed themselves invincible.

Benjamin pleaded with them to stay. Finally, eleven passengers conceded and walked over to stand beside their captain. The remaining passengers continued outside.

Benjamin looked at Marcus, but Marcus couldn't hold his stare. Benjamin could see that he was conflicted and ashamed about the decision he was about to make.

'Your responsibility is with the aircraft and remaining passengers,' Benjamin said.

'I have to go. I'm sorry, Ben. I have to see my wife again.'

'You're making a big mistake, Marcus.'

'I have to try. Don't you dare judge me. We've flown together, what, three, four times? You don't know me.'

'I'm talking about your conscience. You'll have to live with your decision for the rest of your life.'

Marcus was sweating, even though it was bitterly cold in the compartment. He moved to the opening, then turned and said, 'I've taken the SAT phone.' Then he climbed out of the aircraft without another word spoken.

Captain Flynn escorted the remaining passengers back upstairs. He closed the hatchway, then moved a food cart over the top of the opening. It wasn't much of a deterrent, but it was all he could find. He walked up to two male passengers in nearby seats and introduced himself. 'Would you please let me know if anyone else tries to leave through that hatchway?' Benjamin pointed to the food trolley. 'I've put the trolley on it but it's not much of a blockade.'

They agreed, and Captain Flynn thanked them before heading back to Linus.

★

'I couldn't stop all of them. I think about twenty or so left,' Benjamin said when he found Linus.

Linus immediately contacted Major Wilkinson and Rescue Operations down at Mount Cook Village to update them on the situation. He also notified the chopper pilots to keep an eye out.

'Marcus went with them. He took the plane's SAT phone. If he runs into trouble, he'll call,' Benjamin said. The disappointment was plain on his face.

'Don't take it personally, Ben. Frightened people do stupid things. Come on, the choppers are arriving soon. We need to get the next batch ready.'

'Since when have you been calling my passengers batches?' Benjamin smiled.

As they went to open the door, another aftershock caught them off guard.

The tremor shook the plane, and men and women alike stopped what they were doing. There was no point screaming anymore, it would change nothing. Everyone grabbed whatever they could to balance themselves as they felt the plane shift and begin to move.

Please stop, prayed Benjamin repeatedly. *Please stop*. The plane screeched its way along the snow. Finally, it settled down again. Was leaving such a bad idea? Was he right to convince those passengers to stay? Benjamin didn't know anymore, but he trusted Linus' judgement. He shook all lingering doubts from his mind. His only focus should be getting the rest of the passengers off quickly and safely.

So far, they had offloaded over sixty injured passengers. The plane was slowly emptying. The Army Chinook had arrived, and could take up to fifty people or, alternatively, over twenty-four stretchers. It was larger and much heavier than the EC145, especially when fully loaded, but it was a risk worth taking.

★

Herbert's journey down the valley wasn't turning out as smoothly as he'd thought it would be. He had to dodge boulders and what looked like giant cracks in the snow, which he tried to ski far away from. A few times, he had to stop completely and check the condition of the snow around him before continuing further down the valley. To his right, he saw Aoraki looming. During the last tremor, the ground beneath him had shaken violently. He'd lost control and tumbled down, before he finally managed to slow himself and lie on the snow until it stopped. At least for now, he was still confident in his decision.

Then he picked himself up again and continued on, humming his favourite poem as he did.

'*Aus der nacht, die mich bedeckt,* schwarz wie die grube von pol zu pol …'

Chapter Twenty-Six

Marcus was wrapped up tight against the chill. There was a steady cold wind coming down the valley as the group made their way carefully down the slopes. Lars Norstrom led the way with Theodor Lagerquist and Sebastian Bjork on either side of him. Marcus brought up the rear to make sure that no one fell behind. They trod carefully, watching for any displaced snow. The group had just experienced another tremor. Marcus felt a sense of foreboding as he looked up at the colossal mountain range. In normal circumstances, they would have been impressive and breathtaking, but today they were ominous, leaving Marcus exposed and vulnerable. He only now appreciated the protection that the giant Airbus had unwittingly provided them as he turned and looked back up the valley. He could still see the Airbus off in the distance. Then, thinking only of his wife, he turned back and followed the passengers down the valley.

As they continued their descent, Marcus reassured himself that Lars knew what he was doing. They were using poles to check the softness of the snow. It was still very deep in parts, and no one wanted to fall through the snowy quicksand.

'Stop!' Theodor yelled. He raised his fist in the air.

Lars yelled something back in Swedish that Marcus took to mean, *What is it?*

'Broken snow. Keep to the left.' Theodor motioned with his hand. At times, they'd tobogganed down on their dinner trays. In other times, like now, they had to walk. Marcus realised that this trek was going to take longer than he'd first thought. He pulled up his collar and continued to slog through the snow behind everyone else. The first of many lingering doubts, about his decision, crept into his thoughts.

★

Herbert Schwartz was admiring the scenery as he made his way down the valley. No matter where he skied in the world, he never tired of the picturesque, snow-covered, milky-white tundra. He was nearly home – he had finally caught sight of Tasman Lake. It was massive and covered with new ice floes. Up ahead, on his right, he saw snow falling down the mountainside.

It had been rough going for a while as he'd passed below Aoraki. The Tasman and Ball Glaciers were breaking apart. It wouldn't be long before they completely collapsed and came thundering down into the valley. Herbert knew that there was a road that ran from Mount Cook Village to high above Tasman Lake. The lower end of the Tasman Valley was mostly covered in rock and boulders. But with all the avalanches, the winter snow had lined the valley floor enough for him to ski down. He would call Mount Cook Rescue once he arrived at the lake.

He knew he would get a stripping down for wasting their time, but he was the master of his own fate. As he continued his arduous journey towards the lake, he recited his favourite poem.

'*Aus der nacht, die mich bedeckt, schwarz wie die grube von pol zu pol …*'

Out of the night that covers me,
Black as the pit from pole to pole,
I thank whatever gods may be
For my unconquerable soul.

In the fell clutch of circumstance
I have not winced nor cried aloud.
Under the bludgeoning's of chance
My head is bloody, but unbowed.

Beyond this place of wrath and tears
Looms but the horror of the shade,

And yet the menace of the years
Finds and shall find me unafraid.

It matters not how strait the gate,
How charged with punishments the scroll,
I am the master of my fate,
I am the captain of my soul.

Alas, no one could predict the future. Not even Herbert. When he was no more than three kilometres from the lake, the snow started to turn into slush and break apart around him. He was losing momentum. The snow of the valley floor was slowly melting to reveal rocks and boulders beneath. He hadn't predicted how the temperature would grow the lower he skied. Winter wasn't over, but the seismic activity had super-heated the atmosphere around the ranges, and now the snow was melting at an alarming rate.

Herbert finally had to stop. He cursed the conditions as he unhooked his skis. He would have to trek the rest of the way on foot. He heaved his expensive gear onto his shoulder, above his backpack. This was not what Herbert had had in mind; he would be set back by hours. The ground was getting slippery, and the snow had turned to slush. Up ahead, the valley floor had transformed into a rocky outcrop, with chunks of ice scattered everywhere, which he now had to manoeuvre over. Small streams of water were growing in size as he made his way to the lake. He cursed his luck. It was an inconvenience – nothing more. He would still make it; he was confident.

★

Marcus looked up at the sound of another avalanche. One of the passengers stopped. Marcus walked over to her and asked her what was wrong.

'I want to go back. I'm sorry, but the captain was right. We're trapped, no matter what we do, aren't we?' Chyna Day said, as she looked pleadingly at Marcus, hoping he would reassure her and give her an honest answer. He didn't know what to say to her. He truly thought that this was the safest option. They felt like they'd been walking for miles, but in reality, they had only travelled three kilometres.

Another passenger heard what the young woman had said to the first officer and walked over to them. 'I'll take her back. I can't make it down the valley. I was foolish to try.'

Marcus needed to make a decision.

In that moment, he realised what he had done. He'd abandoned his ship and left his passengers behind. Marcus raised his head towards the sky and cried, 'What the hell was I thinking! Lars! Lars!'

Lars turned around to see a small group of people surrounding Marcus.

'These passengers can't go any further,' Marcus said. 'I'm sorry, but I'm taking them back.'

Lars looked around at the other passengers. Most were shivering with cold. Marcus walked up to Lars and handed him the SAT phone.

'In case you run into trouble, this will get you through to the rescue unit at Mount Cook.'.

'Okay,' Lars said, taking the SAT phone.

'Good luck.' It was all Marcus could say before he turned around.

Ten passengers in total followed Marcus back to the Airbus.

Chapter Twenty-Seven

9.15 a.m. NZ time

Annabel was helping an injured woman to the emergency exit. Her broken arm was resting in a makeshift sling made out of tablecloths from the first-class galley. As they passed the galley, Annabel noticed that some of the drawers were open. The passengers had been helping themselves to the small bottles of spirits.

Licking her lips, Annabel contemplated taking one. Once the woman was lifted down and out of the plane, Annabel walked back into the galley. One cupboard was ajar, and Annabel could see a handful of scattered liquor bottles still inside. She stared down at them. The temptation was too great. Considering what she'd just been through, who would blame her? Just one drink to steady her nerves.

As she started to reach into the draw, she heard Captain Flynn's voice in the aisle. With a singular motion of strength, she withdrew her hand and slammed the door shut. Relief rippled through her when she opened another draw and found some water bottles huddled together. She opened one and drank the entire bottle without taking a pause. Annabel then grabbed a few more bottles and headed back into the first-class cabin.

She found Captain Flynn talking with Dr Ruby Singh about the Mallard family. Jane and Felix had finally been evacuated. However, Hugh was beside himself with worry, and young Ava was still in shock. Annabel offered them each a bottle of water and asked why they couldn't transfer the father and daughters now. What would it matter if three more passengers jumped on the next Chinook ride?

Captain Flynn agreed. The quicker the children were off the plane, the better. Annabel said that she would give them the good news.

Annabel felt proud of herself. A month ago, she would have drunk the bottle of liquor. But today she hadn't. Considering where she was, she was proud of herself for turning away from the little bottles. Life was precious; she'd learnt that in the army. It could be taken away in an instant. Now was not the time for luxuries like self-pity.

Before leaving the cabin, Annabel turned around and watched the captain from the corner of the room. He had a confidence that was reassuring. She wanted to believe that it was rubbing off on her. Her gaze was interrupted by Beth McWilliams, who asked Annabel to help with another patient.

'I think you have an admirer,' Beth said to Annabel, as the passenger was made comfortable in her seat.

'What?' Annabel asked.

Beth nodded her head towards the other side of the cabin. When Annabel turned around, she saw Captain Flynn staring at her. He quickly lowered his gaze and walked out of the cabin. Annabel's heart started to beat faster. She didn't know if it was adrenaline, anxiety, or embarrassment. But this time, the phenomenon made her smile.

Chapter Twenty-Eight

9.25 a.m. NZ time

'Thanks, Harry,' Victoria said, as she disconnected the call. Victoria gave up her seat on the EC145 to another passenger – she still had unfinished business. Someone had murdered Gertrude Simpson and it was highly probable that they'd try to kill Henry. Victoria knew that if not on the plane, then they'd try once he was evacuated. Her last phone call confirmed her suspicions. The AFP had obtained Gertrude's mobile call lists and text messages. They revealed a distinct and ongoing communication between Gertrude and Jackson Myer. They had also obtained her banking records, and one bank account had large, unexplained deposits. They dated back over four years to the present date. Victoria's colleagues were tracing the deposits.

'Jackson Myer obviously didn't want Gertrude talking to anyone. Unfortunately, Gertrude had believed that she was invaluable to Myer, and so untouchable,' Victoria said.

'This is all so unbelievable,' Henry said, still baffled.

'I'm sorry, Henry. The AFP has found an account in Gertrude's name. They're backtracking the large deposits now, but you can guess where they came from.'

'I ... I can't believe she'd betray me like that,' he said, shocked. 'I thought she understood.'

'Understood what?' Victoria asked.

'How important my work was to me. The significance of what I have achieved. This technology can improve billions of people's lives, but in the wrong hands ...' Henry allowed his final words to trail off.

'What do you mean, Henry, "in the wrong hands"?'

'Universally, its applications would benefit all facets of industry, from car manufacturers and aeronautical companies like Boeing and Airbus, to telecommunications, mining, and engineering. Not to mention medical breakthroughs. But in the wrong hands, it could be manipulated and used to interfere with information technology. Sophisticated spyware could be manipulated if not protected. The applications for its use are still in their infancy. Gertrude understood this.'

'I guess she chose to share it with Myer.'

'I've just realised that if I were dead, it would be up to the board to make all the decisions. Cyber Systems now have members on my board as part of the new agreement. They are, after all, funding the testing and production of the chip. They could take control of it.'

'Shit! I need to get you out of here, Henry.'

'How could I have been such an idiot?' Henry asked, feeling naïve.

'My partner at the AFP said that Mr Jackal – a.k.a. Terry Burrows – is talking. He's scared, and rightly so. The New Zealand Federal Police were watching his house when a man broke in a few hours ago. The NZFP are tailing the guy, but they believe he planted evidence inside Terry's home to incriminate him in the bombing. He's guilty, of course, but the evidence is pointing to a rival conglomerate of Jackson Myer. He's obviously tying up loose ends.'

'Has this Terry Burrows confirmed that he works for Jackson Myer?'

'No. He was hired by a Mr Wolf, who we believe is on this flight. Mr Burrows wants immunity – he knows that if he goes to gaol, he'll be killed.'

'If he planted that bomb, then good riddance,' Henry said.

'I don't want to leave you alone here, Henry. Whoever killed Gertrude is still out there. I think you'd better leave with me.'

'There's still more injured to evacuate, plus the women. I'm not leaving before them. I'll wait my turn, thanks,' Henry said.

'That's very chivalrous of you, Henry, but you need protection.'

'I'm not leaving before the women, and that's final. And you're leaving on the next rescue chopper.' Before Victoria could argue the point, Henry got up and walked out of the first-class cabin in search of the captain, followed closely by Constantine. Victoria opened up her mobile and made a call. When Henry found Benjamin with Linus, he insisted that Victoria be flown out on the next chopper.

Constantine knew how precarious Henry's situation was. He had been listening, intently. He knew that the Federal Police would insist he be evacuated as soon as possible. To Constantine's assurance, he knew he would be accompanying him. In relief, he pulled out his mobile and made another phone call while Henry was talking to the pilot and the rescue co-ordinator.

Ten minutes later, Benjamin received a call from Margaret Tennyson at ANZAL flight operations.

'Yes, Margaret?'

'We've received a request from the Federal Police here in Aus. They're insisting we airlift a male passenger, one Henry Adams, out ASAP. He's been flagged as high priority.'

'Yes, I know him. There's also an AFP officer here on the plane. She's injured and will be transferred down to the medivac centre shortly. She has a broken leg and is concerned about Mr Adams. A colleague of his was murdered about two hours ago, right here in her seat.'

'Fucking hell, Ben, when were you going to tell me?'

'Sorry, Margaret. Victoria informed her people, but it's been hectic up here.'

'What happened?'

'Someone broke her neck.'

'Shit. I've just been informed that their Learjet was cancelled yesterday after the pilot found a bomb on board.'

'I know. Henry Adams is at risk. Also, some of my passengers left on foot down the valley. The killer may be among them, or he could still be on board.'

'If you can bag her body and send it down in a chopper, forensics might find evidence of her killer. But that will still take some time.'

'We can send her body down with Henry and the AFP Officer.'

'I can co-ordinate with the New Zealand Police to take a DNA sample from each male passenger as they're brought down, if that will help. We can say it's for identification purposes or something like that,' Margaret said.

'That might help, but we won't get a match until after the passengers have been transferred out of the area. By then, it'll be too late,' Benjamin said.

'Of course, you're right. Right now, our first concern is for the rest of the passengers. Customs will have everyone's passport details, and I'll update the authorities here. I'll speak with the New Zealand authorities to have Mr Adams escorted back to Christchurch.'

'Thanks, Margaret.'

'The authorities want him out of there *now*, Ben. This came from Canberra.'

'Okay, I'll have him transferred with the AFP officer on the next chopper,' Benjamin said.

'Did you say that some passengers left the aircraft?'

'Yes … The chopper pilots are monitoring their progress. I couldn't stop them.'

'Imbeciles.'

Benjamin couldn't tell Margaret that Marcus was one of them. Recriminations would come later. After disconnecting the call, Benjamin went in search of Henry. He was leaving whether he wanted to or not.

★

'We'll be moving you to the exit now, Mr Ming,' Beth said, as she called John over to help Mr Ming exit.

'Be careful, you idiot,' Lu wailed. When John tried to remove his Coles shopping bag, he yanked it back to his chest. 'This stays with me.'

'Fine, whatever,' John said, raising his hands in the air.

They lifted Lu Ming carefully out of the emergency door. He was covered with an extra blanket before getting lowered outside and onto the snow. Victoria Dahl was behind him. Henry helped to carry her, and behind them, Captain Flynn and Linus were carrying a stretcher, which held Gertrude Simpson's dead body.

The EC145 hovered above the ground a metre or so before it slowly lowered itself down. It glided along the snow for a few metres until it finally came to a rest. People outside put scarfs or handkerchiefs over their noses and mouths so they wouldn't breathe in the flurries of churned-up dust and snow.

Linus had re-located his flags to create a new landing zone. His team had to continually re-monitor the snow after each new tremor. There was always the possibility that the snow would become unstable beneath the weight of each new chopper landing.

The helicopter crew opened the side and rear doors and stepped down to help lift the passengers inside. The sounds made by the rotor blades were horrendous.

As Lu Ming was being lifted into the chopper, a sudden gust of wind caused the crew to lose their balance. Lu was only holding onto the stretcher with one hand, as the other was wrapped around his Coles shopping bag. Before he could react, he lost his grip around the bag. Thanks to the continuous swirling wind revolving around him, his bag split open and sent its contents – all 200,000 dollars of it – swirling high into a vortex of gusty wind. Some were torn to shreds by the rotor blades, while the rest chased the wind down into the valley.

Lu's screams could be heard by passengers all throughout the Airbus. Many rushed to the windows to see what had happened.

Peng Ming didn't need to look outside to know what had happened. She sat quietly in her newly allocated seat and continued to drink her gin and tonic. She was now as free as the money.

After Lu Ming was secured in the chopper, Henry wished Victoria good luck. But before he could turn to leave, Benjamin, Linus, and Constantine blocked his route back into the plane.

'Sorry, mate,' Benjamin yelled. 'But I've been ordered by the Australian Government to put you on that chopper.'

'No, absolutely not!'

'I'm sorry, but I have my orders. Please, don't make us put you on by force,' yelled Constantine.

'This is bullshit!'

'Maybe,' Linus said. 'We have too much to deal with up here. We can't guarantee your safety. Now, please get on that chopper. It needs to leave.'

Very indignantly, Henry climbed on board and sat in the jump seat. Once secure, Constantine climbed in after him. He was asked to stay with Henry until the NZ Federal Police arrived at the village to escort him to Christchurch. After another passenger was helped on board, Gertrude's body was placed inside next to Lu Ming. The wind blew the blanket from her face. Realising what had been placed beside him, Lu Ming's screams could be heard echoing down the valley.

The EC145 headed south, overtaking a few hundred-dollar notes that were slowly making their way down the valley. Not long into the flight, the pilot noticed a group of passengers on the snow. They appeared to be sliding along the snow on trays. The pilot noted their location and radioed their coordinates to rescue operations. They continued to the MASH unit on the outskirts of Mount Cook Village.

Lars Norstrom looked up as the chopper flew overhead. His small group continued on their journey, stopping every now and then to check the conditions of the snow. They were making good time, now that some of the slower passengers had turned back.

★

As Benjamin and the others climbed back into the Airbus and closed the door, a number of passengers surrounded them. They had seen through the windows the two uninjured men getting onto the chopper. Word spread throughout the plane like wildfire. They demanded answers.

'What's going on, Captain?'

'Do we now have social standing on board?'

'Are first-class passengers being evacuated before business and poor sodding economy?'

Benjamin couldn't put off telling the passengers about Gertrude. He'd promised them transparency. Earlier, he hadn't wanted to alarm anyone. Benjamin didn't believe that the other passengers were in any danger from Gertrude's killer. He didn't want neighbour accusing neighbour.

Benjamin spoke up. 'Everyone listen to me! An injured woman was murdered two hours ago in the first-class cabin.' Benjamin waited for the shocked expressions and murmurings to settle down. 'This was the second attempt on her life. The man you saw leave just now was also a target. I believed that his life was in imminent danger. I don't have the time to babysit him up here. He was accompanied by an ex-soldier who is guarding him until the Federal Police arrive to escort him to Christchurch. There will also be a man air-lifted down on the next

Chinook run with his two children. His wife and son were both injured. They are the only exception to the evacuation plan.'

A passenger spoke up. 'Did her killer bring our plane down?'

'No, definitely not. We experienced catastrophic engine failure. It's possible that gas vents erupted due to the seismic activity over the mountains recently and, more worryingly, the latest round of earthquakes and volcanic activity.'

The passengers murmured thoughtfully, grateful for the transparency.

'Look,' Benjamin said, raising his hands in front of him. 'Within the hour, we will have finished evacuating the injured. Then the women will be ready to go. The Chinook can carry up to fifty people. Please be patient for just a few hours more.'

As the passengers settled back down, satisfied with his explanation, Benjamin was relieved that one more problem had been solved. And yet, he had no idea whether or not Gertrude's killer was still on board. He hoped not.

Chapter Twenty-Nine

10.00 a.m. NZ time

'I can smell fuel. A man is smoking outside!' yelled a passenger. He was speaking in Mandarin.

'I'm sorry, I don't speak Mandarin. I'll get one of my colleagues for you,' Charlotte said. But before she could walk off, he grabbed her arm, pointing outside.

'*Man, smoke!*' the Chinese passenger said insistently.

The flight attendant still didn't seem to comprehend what he was saying. 'No, sir, you can't go out for a cigarette.' The man tried to explain again as Charlotte still had trouble understanding him.

'Oh, for fuck's sake,' Peng Ming interjected, unable to stand listening any longer. 'He's saying he can smell fuel outside, and that a dumb-fuck Australian guy is smoking a cigarette.'

Charlotte had no problem understanding that. The nearby passengers all looked at Peng as Charlotte swore and bolted out of the galley. She raced to the emergency door at the back of the plane to stop the passenger.

Millie Wellington watched as she ran down the aisle and disappeared around the side of the toilet door. Sir Roger Standish and Windsor Hounslow looked on in amusement, as they were already three sheets to the wind.

Millie had been keeping busy looking after the Mallard girls, Leonor and Ava. She had appreciated the distraction. Ava had fallen asleep in her arms. But now that Hugh Mallard was back with his daughters. She was feeling redundant. Especially now that Hugh told her they were leaving on the next chopper.

Millie had managed to call her father. He had become lost for words, and Millie had ended up talking to her mother. They'd both thought that their daughters had been killed in the crash. When she'd told her parents that Annie was hurt, she'd heard them both crying. Millie knew that they would move heaven and earth to be by their daughter's side.

Now, stroking Ava's hair, Millie knew that her father would have already organised a flight to New Zealand. They were probably on their way to JFK after hiring a private jet. That thought made her smile.

★

… Five minutes earlier …

Benjamin handed Annabel a hot steaming cup of coffee. 'You're allowed a five-minute coffee break, OH&S regs,' he said with an uninhibited smile.

They were standing in the galley behind the first-class cabin. Annabel accepted it with gratitude.

'What do you do now that you've left the army?' Benjamin asked.

'I started an organisation. I wanted to help female military personnel deal with trauma and anxiety. I was on my way to visit a C.E.O who runs a similar organisation here in New Zealand. He was impressed by my work and wanted to invest. I'm going to miss my appointment, unfortunately,' Annabel said, smiling.

'Don't worry. I'm sure he'll understand. If he doesn't, let me know, and I'll have a word with him.'

Annabel laughed despite herself. She was warming to him more with each minute. 'I'll hold you to that.'

'PTSD was the unspoken bane in the military's back. Brave men treated like cowards because the killing got to them. Now it's mandatory in some areas, especially for pilots, to have regular psych evaluations. But you're right, it's mainly for frontline serving men. Those women are lucky to have you watching their backs.'

'Thanks for saying so. I wanted to report the truth about what I saw and experienced in the army. But the truth was hard to take up close.'

'You'll deal with it in time. You need to forgive yourself,' Benjamin kindly said.

'Forgive myself?' Annabel asked.

'Yes. For what you saw and were helpless to stop.'

Benjamin caught sight of Charlotte, running to the back of the plane. Now what?

'Please excuse me, Annabel,' he said, putting his coffee down. He followed Charlotte to the back of the plane.

Annabel watched Captain Flynn move down the aisle. He was right. She needed to forgive herself. She needed to live again.

'Sir, put that cigarette out, now!' yelled Charlotte to the Australian man standing outside in the cold, stamping his feet and smoking a cigarette.

'I'm just finishing up!' he yelled back, tossing down the cigarette.

'Don't toss it, you idiot!' yelled Charlotte, but it was too late. She watched as the cigarette landed twenty feet away from him in the snow. At first, it did nothing, and Charlotte sighed with relief. But a few seconds later, it ignited the fuel, which had soaked into the snow. It took off up the valley, following the same path that the Airbus had travelled down.

The man quickly sprinted back to the plane, slipping and skidding.

Charlotte sighed with relief when she realised that there was no more fuel leaking from what was left of the wing. Without a continuous flow, the flame couldn't reach the tanks. However, as the fuel burned down, it started to melt the snow and ice on the side of the Airbus. The soft snow would turn slushy and unstable.

Captain Flynn leaned over and yanked the man inside.

'What the fuck were you thinking?' Benjamin yelled, shocked at the man's stupidity.

'I just wanted a fag. We've been here for ages,' the passenger responded dumbly.

'Couldn't you smell the fuel?' asked Benjamin in astonishment.

The man looked dumb founded. 'No. My sinuses have been playing up for weeks. Sorry, mate,' he said. He turned to look outside at the flames, finally realising the seriousness of what he had just done.

'I think I just shit my pants, if that's any consolation,' he said, before excusing himself.

Benjamin looked along the length of the plane and noticed some people trudging through the snow. Benjamin was still wearing his coat, but he retrieved his gloves and hat from the depths of his coat pocket before stepping down into the snow to wait for the passengers to approach.

When they drew near, he could see that one of them was Marcus.

They were nearly frozen as Benjamin helped them back into the plane. There was a moment of silence between the two pilots before Marcus finally spoke.

'I'm so sorry, Ben. I don't know what I was thinking.'

'Forget about it. I still have hundreds of passengers to evacuate. What happened to the others?'

'They're continuing down the valley. I gave Lars the SAT phone.'

'All right. Go inside and get warm. I'll let the rescue unit know. How many have continued?'

'About eleven passengers,' Marcus said.

'Do you think they can make it?'

'I don't know,' he said, shaking his head. 'We were making headway using the dining trays. It appears the first-class trays are larger than the economy ones.' Marcus smiled, trying to find some humour in the awkward moment. 'We kept stopping and starting as Lars checked the condition of the snow.'

'It's getting warmer though. They might make it. One of the women wanted to return, so I brought her back with the others. I don't know what to say, Ben. I panicked. I had to do something. I'm so sorry. A captain never leaves his ship.'

'We'll deal with that later.'

Benjamin knew that Marcus would have a lot of questions to answer when he got back home. His career at ANZAL would be over. Benjamin patted him on the back as they walked away from the door.

'You know, the strangest thing happened as we were heading back here. A hundred-dollar bill hit me in the face,' Marcus said, as he removed it from his pocket and showed it to Benjamin.

'It's a long story,' Benjamin said. 'I'll be back in a minute.' He walked off in search of June.

She was busy as usual, co-ordinating the transfer of passengers. He asked her to arrange hot drinks for the returning passengers. The rescue unit dropped off a gas cylinder and cooking pot so that they could heat up water and provide tea and coffee. The cabin wasn't as cold as it had been when they'd first crashed, but with the doors constantly being opened and shut again, a chilly wind was tunnelling through both cabins.

Chapter Thirty

10.20 a.m. NZ time

Lars dug his heels into the snow to slow his speed. He raised his fist to signal the rest of his party to stop. The snow was no longer smooth underneath, but broken and jagged. He could see a giant crevice up ahead.

Bertie Danbridge started to stretch while he waited for Lars to continue. Other passengers stamped their feet to fend off the cold, some of them mumbling that they should have listened to the captain.

Lars walked on ahead, then circled to the right. He'd finally identified a solid section of snow that they could use to continue their descent. He waved the others over.

They started to walk towards Lars but stopped abruptly when they heard the sound of cracking ice beneath them. Paralysed by the sound, they didn't know what to do, or which way to run. Cracks in the snow started to appear all around them. Everyone froze and looked to Lars for reassurance, but none was forthcoming. Before they could take a step forward, an entire slab of snow collapsed from under them and nine of their remaining group fell down into the opened crevice below.

Lars ran towards the sinkhole, then laid on his stomach and crawled the last ten feet before looking down into the massive ice cave below. It was at least thirty feet deep. Two of the passengers were trapped beneath the ice, which had broken away. The remaining passengers were dazed, but conscious.

Lars motioned for the rest of his group to stay away. He pulled out the SAT phone and dialled Mount Cook Rescue.

★

'Benjamin, we have yet another problem,' Linus said, as he approached the captain. He recounted what had happened to Lars and his party. 'They're about thirty feet down.'

'Shit,' Benjamin cursed.

'They're past the Tasman Glacier, but the valley is becoming more unstable the closer to the lake they get. We can't land a helicopter near them, as the ice is obviously unsafe. That cave could go on for miles. We'll drop a team off with a winch, ropes, and stretchers. Any serious cases will need to be air-lifted out.'

'Can you spare anyone, Linus?' Benjamin asked.

'No, but we'll have to. I've asked Angus McWilliams to help, as he has mountaineering experience. You'll need to co-ordinate the rest of the evacuations up here by yourself.'

'All right. Be careful, Linus,' Benjamin said.

'I'll be fine. I've been doing this for a long time.'

Linus patted Benjamin on the shoulder as he walked off to find Angus. Linus hated asking a civilian for help, but they didn't have time to wait for another rescue unit to arrive. Linus' team were needed here on site.

When he found Angus, he was with his wife, Beth, in the first-class cabin.

Angus agreed to help without hesitation. Only Beth looked uncertain. Dr Munir Uzer offered to accompany them, but Linus declined his offer. With no climbing experience, it would be too dangerous. He wasn't prepared to put any more lives at risk. And besides, Major Wilkinson would need all the medical help he could get. Some of the doctors had already been transferred down to the MASH unit. Dr Uzer had agreed to stay behind in case anyone needed him.

When Angus arrived at the emergency door, Beth was already there to meet him. They stared in silence at each other. Angus took Beth in his arms and held her tightly, for what could have been an eternity. She whispered, 'Please come back to me.'

'Always, Poppy,' he said, before giving Beth a tender kiss. They hugged each other again before Angus turned away and headed out the emergency door to find Linus.

The chopper already had three injured passengers on board. Linus and Angus climbed in. Their backpacks were full of equipment that they'd need for the rescue – ropes, winches, and first-aid kits.

The helicopter lifted off and headed down the valley. From up high, Linus could see first-hand the destruction caused by the earthquakes. They saw large boulders and thousands of tonnes of snow and ice resting on the valley floor, broken away from the mountains above. It was all too surreal.

Even though it was daylight, the sky was cloudy and the cumulus cover above them was filled with a gritty, dark substance. Thankfully, the ash-filled wind was heading out to sea and away from the valley.

This country really did beat with every tremor, volcanic eruption, glacial movement, and geyser eruption. Its explosive wrath inspired and invigorated Linus. He knew perfectly well that if it wasn't respected, it could kill him, but he admired its strength and ferocity all the same.

Once the chopper arrived at the coordinates given, they spotted three men waving up at them. Linus hooked Angus up to the winch and then lowered him down to the valley floor. Once unhooked, Linus retracted the winch and was lowered down himself. They made their way carefully towards the opening, and on their stomachs, they crawled to the edge and peered down. They could see nine passengers down in the cave. Two of them were trapped by heavy ice, and two of them were not moving.

The chopper hoisted up the remaining uninjured walkers before heading down the valley to drop off its injured passengers. It would return once they had refuelled.

Linus backtracked to set up the winch and pulley about forty feet away from the opening. They attached the ropes, and once secured, lowered the ropes and harness down to the passengers. Linus instructed them on how to winch themselves up one at a time. They were to use their feet to help crawl themselves up the ice wall.

The operation was taking too long, though, as the passengers were having trouble attaching the harnesses correctly. Then they had difficulty ascending the wall. Linus asked Angus to help lower him down into the cave – it would be quicker if he was down below to help the passengers.

Lars and Theodor helped with the winch and ropes but were told to keep their distance.

Once lowered into the cave, Linus could see tunnels leading off in two separate directions. The ice cave was massive. He was instantly fascinated. It wasn't often that they got to explore ice caves, but there was no time for that. Linus worked quickly to harness the passengers and hoist them up, one by one.

As they arrived at the surface, Angus hauled them out. Parts of the opening were breaking away with each new assent to the opening. Finally, when most of the passengers had been winched to the surface, Angus lowered the harness again so that Linus could attach it around a block of ice that was trapping Bertie Danbridge. He was conscious, but in pain.

Using his walkie-talkie, Linus gave the okay for Angus to start the winch. As it lifted the block of ice, Bertie let out a cry of pain as the pressure lifted from his leg. Linus quickly put his hand over his mouth. He didn't want any more cave-ins. Bertie bit into his hand instead. Linus bandaged his leg as best he could and gave Bertie a sedative to ease the pain before attaching him to the harness.

'Okay, Angus, start the winch,' Linus said.

'Roger,' Angus said, and he started to haul Bertie up. Once Bertie had ascended the wall, Lars and Theo crawled back to the opening and helped carry Bertie to safety. Angus asked Lars to find a stable site for the chopper to land. The Swede used his large pole to poke around in the snow. He was more than fifty feet away from the ice cave. Linus had given him a flare to mark the spot.

In the meantime, the winch was sent back down as Linus worked on freeing the remaining two passengers.

When he checked the pulse of one woman, there was stillness.

He had to save the living. Leaving her where she lay, he turned his attention to the final passenger. He had a serious head wound and was unconscious. Again, Linus used the winch to remove the heavy block of ice trapping the man. Once done, he finally attached the harness to him. Again, he gave the okay for it to be raised. But before they reached the opening of the cave, another piece of ice broke away and collapsed into the cave.

'Stop!' Linus yelled into the walkie-talkie, diving out of the way. He narrowly escaped the falling chunks of ice. He could see the passenger was stuck just below the opening. With the passenger unconscious, Linus would have to bring him back down and go up with him, too, all while using his legs to keep him away from the wall of the cave.

'Bring him back down, Angus.'

'Okay, lowering.'

Once the male passenger was back on the cave floor, Linus attached himself to the harness, then gave the order to be lifted. The going was slow, but as they arrived at the top of the cave, they were unable to be hauled out. There was a protruding piece of ice jutting out of the wall. It prevented Linus from reaching the surface. He tried pushing himself away from the wall, but he couldn't manoeuvre the ropes. Angus appeared at the opening. He had to cut away some of the ice at the opening with a small pickaxe before they could hoist them out.

It worked. The winch continued to lift both men out of the cave.

As Angus and Theo pulled Linus and the final passenger back onto the snow, another tremor started. It rocked the ground beneath them. They all remained flat on their stomachs, not daring to move. Large cracks appeared around Angus and Theo, but before they could lift themselves up and dive out of the way, the ice beneath them ripped open and collapsed into the cave, taking Angus and Theo with it. Linus and the other passenger were dropped a few metres back into the cave, but as they were still attached to the ropes and winch, they dangled in mid-air. More ice and snow tumbled down into the cave, hitting them on the way down.

Lars raced over to the cave opening and worked quickly to bring them back up. Once he was back on his feet, Linus called out to Angus, but there was no answer. Off in the distance, a helicopter could be heard coming up the valley.

Linus was still attached to his rope and winch. As he reached the expanded opening, Linus looked down. His heart sank when he saw nothing. Tonnes of snow and ice now lay on the cave floor on top of Angus and

Theo. He doubted that either man could have survived the cave-in. Linus let out a scream – Angus was a good man, a brave man. They didn't deserve this. Linus' heart sank even further when he realised that he'd have to tell Beth.

When the chopper arrived, the crew transferred six of the injured onto it. It would have to make another trip to collect the remaining passengers.

Sitting on the ice, Linus said nothing. He had seen death many times in the national park – Aoraki had taken numerous lives over the years. But this time it was personal.

Lars Norstrom remained silent until he and Linus arrived at the MASH unit. Those people had relied on him, and those deaths would weigh on him for the rest of his life. Especially Theo's, how could he face Theo's parents?

Linus needed some personal time to compose himself, but he didn't have the luxury of that. The pilot was waiting to take him back to the Airbus, and back to Beth McWilliams. There were hundreds of passengers still needing rescue. He climbed aboard as the graceful EC145 lifted off and headed back up the valley.

As they flew past Tasman Lake, Linus noticed a man carrying his skis on his shoulder. It must be Herbert Schwartz. He was alongside the lake, heading towards the track that led up to the carpark.

Linus could barely make out the track that ran alongside the valley wall. Boulders of all sizes littered the track leading up to the carpark. With the seismic activity, the lake had increased in size significantly that morning. Linus saw how choppy the once tranquil lake was. He hoped Herbert would make it.

Linus rested back in his seat and remained silent for the rest of their journey back to AN224.

★

Herbert Schwartz found the path, he had to climb over a number of rocks. He paused, exhausted. Tasman Lake was before him, but the lake was higher than he'd expected. It was choppy and full of floating icebergs. He felt very small and insignificant all of a sudden, like Gulliver in his travels. Herbert had never liked the sensation of feeling small and unnoticed.

He rested his skis against the side of the mountain and pulled out his mobile. Once his call was concluded, he sat down and took a slow drink. He would have to trek up the path to the carpark and wait for the rescue car from Mount Cook Village to pick him up. He would need to organise another car to drive him to Christchurch. He had no intention of travelling by coach. He needed speed; this whole experience had been a great inconvenience for him. But he wasn't a quitter and would re-organise his meetings and be back on schedule by the afternoon. *Never give up*, Herbert reminded himself.

He sat down on the edge of the path and looked up along the valley. He was very impressed with himself. He decided to have a ten-minute break before trekking along the road. He removed his ski boots and changed into his brogues. Then he took another drink of water. Yet as he did, another tremor started. He stayed motionless and waited for it to stop.

Predictably, the earthquake dislodged more snow directly above him. The avalanche started high up on Mount Kinsey, which peaked at over two thousand metres. The snow started to build up speed and volume as it continued down the mountain.

Herbert's instincts kicked in, and he ran as fast as he could along the path until he found a ridge, which he pressed himself up against. When the snow reached him, he gritted his teeth and clung to the rock ledge. The snow bounced off the ledge and landed below him, in the lake.

The sound was deafening. The force of the barrage of snow caused a massive wind tunnel to build, and Herbert held on for his life. The snow was coming down all around him.

The thunderous noise finally ceased. He turned around and saw that the majority of the snow had ended up in the lake, and in the valley from which he'd just travelled.

Herbert finally climbed over the new piles of snow and rock. He couldn't believe his luck.

'*Danke*,' he said to whatever fates had granted his lucky escape, before he raised his arms up in the air in spite of himself. As he did, a last clump of snow caught up with the rest of the avalanche and landed squarely on top of Herbert, trapping him under its weight.

Chapter Thirty-One

'Captain, where's Beth McWilliams?' Linus asked.

'She's in the first-class cabin. Why?' Benjamin looked behind Linus. 'Where's Angus?'

Linus needed a moment before he could speak. His silence told Benjamin what he needed to know.

'Oh my God …'

'I need to tell her,' Linus said.

'Do you want me to come with you?' Benjamin asked.

'No, I need to do it alone.'

'I'll have Annabel meet you there.'

Linus slowly walked towards the first-class cabin. He could see that Beth was cleaning up in the now empty space. He waited until she stopped what she was doing. He was stonewalling.

Beth looked up and smiled at him, but then her smile slowly drained from her face.

She nodded in slow motion. No words were needed as Beth walked slowly up to him. He took her in his arms, then said, 'I'm so sorry, Beth.'

'*No, no, no,*' she cried as she sank towards the floor. Linus held her tightly. There was nothing he could say or do that he wasn't already doing.

'I'm so sorry, Beth. He saved my life and many others. The ice shelf collapsed, and the tremor knocked him into the cave. He was buried under the snow. I'm sure it would have been quick.'

'Maybe … maybe he survived?' Beth pleaded.

'No, Beth. He couldn't survive that. I'm so sorry.' Linus continued to hold her as she cried into his shoulder.

Annabel arrived to see Beth in Linus' arms. She came up beside him and took Beth away to a quiet corner of the cabin. Captain Flynn sat down beside Linus. He wanted to say something, anything, but he was lost for words.

Before Benjamin could bring himself to speak, they were hit by another vicious earthquake. This one was by far the most violent. They heard a terrifying sound outside, and both men ran unsteadily to the emergency door. They gazed up at Aoraki, off in the distance, then watched in shocked incredulity as the top of the mountain broke apart. The force sent millions of tonnes of rock, ice and snow thundering down its mountain slopes. Boulders of rock exploded high into the air.

The height of Aoraki had been instantly reduced by sixty feet.

Linus turned his attention up the valley. He could see snow being pushed down the valley floor. He ran into the cabin and yelled for the passengers to take their seats and put their seatbelts on. As he did this, Benjamin ran upstairs and repeated the same warnings to the remaining passengers in business class.

The Alpine Fault was destabilising once again, shaking the mammoth peaks all around the park. The force was unbelievable.

Most of the passengers were downstairs in economy, waiting to be evacuated. There was a frantic rush for everyone to get seated.

The plane shook violently as passengers gripped their armrests and were shaken like rag dolls. The plane started to slide along the snow. Its movement was rough and bumpy as it screeched along the valley floor. But as the valley's incline steepened, so did the speed of the Airbus.

Everyone had their eyes closed as they prayed for the plane to stop. But it wasn't stopping – it skidded and slid further down the valley, travelling over 800 metres before the plane's weight finally slowed enough for it to sink into the snow and be brought to a halt. The Airbus had come to rest against the eastern side of the valley, but it was even closer now to the impressive sight of Mount Cook.

But unbeknownst to all on board, the plane had come to rest directly over a massive ice crevice. The Airbus was resting on a plateau, and beneath it was a massive ice shelf.

The heavy volumes of snowfall had covered the ice cave deep below, but the weight of the newly arrived Airbus was causing it to crack and destabilise. It wouldn't be long before the weight of the Airbus destabilised the shelf.

Once the aircraft and the passengers inside it had settled down, Linus and his team left the Airbus to inspect the site. The landing zone poles were now gone, and they didn't fancy trekking back up the valley to retrieve them. They radioed the rescue team to return with more markers and to advise them on their situation from the air.

When Sunny flew over AN224's new resting place, she didn't like what she saw. Time was running out – she informed Linus of a number of sink holes that surrounded the aircraft.

Linus relayed the conversation to Benjamin. 'It's not good but getting the passengers out in the open is still just as dangerous,' Linus said.

'We still have over two hundred people on board,' said Benjamin. 'They've made it this far. I'm not losing them now, Linus. Is that clear?'

'I know, Ben. Let's wait until I hear from Sunny again.'

★

Rose Banks had been semi-conscious during the latest ordeal and had helped herself earlier to a couple of single-serve bottles of wine. Lesley had been evacuated, and she felt afraid and alone.

Rose needed another drink. Her reasoning was simple: if death was coming for her, she didn't want to be sober when it did.

Chloe Pappas was momentarily taken out of her trance by the latest earthquake. She held tightly to Con's hand. But she felt no comfort in it. She knew now he was gone.

Professor Windsor Hounslow, let out a sigh of relief. He thought they were done for. He heard Sir Roger, next to him, praying. He thought it was out of character for the guy. But he listened to him repeat the Lord's Prayer.

Pauline Walsh was buckled in her new seat. Doing anything to be distracted from the terrifying tremors, she had been thinking of a new theme for her latest book.. She would have to write them down. She hated it when she had a good idea, then had trouble remembering it later, simply because she didn't have a pen handy. Pauline made herself a silent promise: never again would she go anywhere without a pen and paper.

★

'You're not going to believe this, Linus,' Sunny said into her microphone, 500 feet above him. 'I can see more rock than snow on the mountain peaks. Most of the snow is on the valley floor. The mountains have taken a battering, but near your current position, I can see that a number of cracks have opened up. Not more than twenty to thirty feet from your plane. I can't land too near – we'll have to land further starboard. You'll need a footbridge to get the people across the crevice opening.'

'Understood. Thanks, Sunny. Out,' Linus said.

He spoke privately with Benjamin, before both agreed to talk to the remaining passengers. They needed to know the seriousness of the current situation, no matter how frightening it was.

While Linus spoke to everyone on the upper deck, Benjamin explained their predicament to the passengers in the main cabin. Everyone listened intently as they were told about their current situation and how long it would take for the remaining passengers to be rescued.

Windsor Hounslow and Sir Roger Standish, who were still a little inebriated from devouring the entire bottle of Glendronach Scotch Whiskey, took the news in their stride. So much so that Sir Roger had forgotten he was still in economy.

'We'll need you to walk across a small make-shift bridge to get to safer ground. Then you can board the choppers,' Benjamin said. 'You'll need to wrap up warm, as you'll be exposed to the elements for some time before the choppers can air-lift you out. Some of you may need masks, as the wind from the chopper blades could sting your face and there is still a strong smell in the air.'

The passengers appeared reasonably calm. They understood what was expected of them. Benjamin asked the flight attendants to explain to the foreign speaking passengers as best they could about their situation.

Even though the sun was now high in the sky, the dust clouds had turned the heavens into a dusty auburn colour. The wind was still blowing down the valley.

Finally, the Chinook returned, carrying the equipment to assemble the footbridge. The chopper couldn't land, so it lowered the supplies by winches. Once down, Linus' team began to erect it.

Along with the equipment, two more team members arrived, as well as three army personnel to help with the building of the bridge.

'The injured are stable down at the village, thanks to Major Wilkinson and his team. A large number of passengers have already been evacuated from the village,' Linus said.

'That's the best news I've heard all day,' Benjamin replied, smiling, as they trudged back inside the Airbus.

'The footbridge is going to take a while to assemble.'

'We could get the passengers to help?'

'No … No passengers are to assist on the bridge,' Linus said forcefully.

'All right. Your call,' Benjamin replied.

'Oh, by the way,' Linus added, 'a driver was called to pick up Herbert Schwartz. He'd phoned us for a lift. Only, when the car arrived at the carpark above Tasman Lake, he wasn't anywhere to be seen. I think he may have died during the last earthquake.'

'There's nothing we can do for him now. He made it that far. If he's alive, he'll find a way to contact us. He's a resourceful man. I'll give him that,' Benjamin replied.

Chapter Thirty-Two

12.18 p.m. NZ time

All the doctors from the Airbus had now been transported down to Major Wilkinson's MASH unit. Except for Amy Donnelly who remained with her mother. The doctors were still kept busy and would be until the last of the injured were evacuated out of the village. The MASH unit was growing in size with every chopper arrival, but they handled the extra arrivals with the help of the newly arrived doctors from the Airbus.

Bertie Danbridge was feeling better. His leg was bandaged. The painkillers had kicked in, and he was on his feet again. His leg wasn't broken, but it had needed stitches.

Now, he headed to the mess tent, where he helped himself to a hot cup of coffee. He wanted to leave with the rest of the passengers. His mobile had finally died, and he needed to make a phone call. If Bertie was anything, he was resourceful.

He saw Constantine talking on his mobile. Henry Adams was beside him, who he recognised from the plane. Bertie overheard Henry telling Constantine that he was going to the hospital tent to check on Victoria. He watched as Henry picked up some bottles of water on his way out.

Bertie walked towards Constantine. Maybe he could borrow Constantine's mobile once he'd finished his call.

'I'll be right behind you, Henry,' Constantine said, as he finally got through to his people.

★

Back on board AN224, Pauline Walsh was living her worst nightmare, only she was wide awake. She was still alive, though, except for the bump on her very hard head. Pauline had moved back up to business class because she liked the leg room better than economy, and the tray table was larger. She had found a pen and began scribbling her new ideas down.

Pauline had come to realise with some humility that she was living the part of a character in her latest novel. She now understood why her previous novels hadn't been published. She hadn't expressed enough deep emotional trauma through her character's state of mind to be regarded as realistically convincing.

Her latest novel was set on a sinking ship. Pauline smirked at the irony.

Pauline was too preoccupied by her novel to appreciate what her current predicament was offering her. Trapped with nowhere to go, with danger at every turn, she was living out the story itself. As a consequence, Pauline's head was pumping with ideas. She wrote diligently in her notebook, telling herself that this was therapy. It was also a distraction, until it was her turn to be evacuated.

Whatever happened to her, her notebook must never leave her side, dead or alive. Pauline quickly wrote her name and address on the inside page should she be the former.

It was quite cold upstairs. All the emergency doors had been left open; in case the plane sank further into the snow. Pauline wrapped a thick scarf around her neck. She exhaled hot air into her hands, then rubbed them together vigorously.

When another gust of wind funnelled through the cabin, something fluttered unexpectedly into her face. She studied it with some surprise – it was a hundred-dollar note. Looking around her, she quickly pocketed it into her jacket. She decided to class it as an out-of-pocket expense. She made a short note and added it to her storyline.

★

June arrived beside Chloe Pappas. She knelt down beside her. She'd been quiet for some time now. She was no longer stroking Con's hair. It had been heart-breaking for the flight attendants to witness. They'd tried the best they could, but they couldn't get her to release him. Beth McWilliams had spent time with her, but after the news of her husband's death, she was herself in need of comfort.

'We'll be leaving the aeroplane soon, Mrs Pappas,' June said. 'You'll have to leave him for now.'

Chloe turned to June with a confused expression. 'I can't leave him here.'

'It'll only be for a short time, Mrs Pappas. We must evacuate the living first.'

'I'm staying with him.'

'What about your family? Your children and grandchildren? They can't lose both of you. How tragic for them. Your husband wouldn't want that, surely?'

'We only just retired. It won't be the same, returning home without him,' she said, turning her attention back to her husband. 'Please help the other passengers. I want to stay with him for a short while longer.'

★

Benjamin and Linus were continuing their discussion regarding the evacuation of the remaining passengers, when a passenger introduced himself. He told Linus he was an engineer.

He offered his assistance with the erection of the footbridge. Linus, at first, said no. He was still feeling raw after Angus' death.

'I know the risks involved, but I'm very experienced. You need all the help you can get.'

Linus looked to Benjamin. It would be his decision, as he was still responsible for the remaining passengers and crew.

Considering that time was of the essence, Benjamin agreed. Linus outlined what they were going to do. Once everyone was up-to-speed, they headed outside to check on the footbridge.

Benjamin had forgotten how cold it was outside. It was a stark reminder of their situation, each time he stepped outside. There was still a strong smell in the air that he couldn't identify.

The plane had settled for now, but that could change at any moment. Benjamin, like everyone else, was praying that the crevice wouldn't open up any more than it already had. Otherwise, the weight of the Airbus would collapse into it.

Linus' team made great work assembling the bridge. It was soon stretched out over the crevice to the far side. It was ninety centimetres wide and sixty feet in length.

The main crevice had opened up even further by the time they were finished, but it was far enough away from the plane to reassure Linus that they could all make it out in time. Cables were attached to each end of the bridge, then plunged deep into the ice on the opposite side of the crevice. Rope handrails ran the length of the bridge. They swayed in the wind.

Once it was tested, they would start transferring the passengers over the bridge, where they could wait until the Chinook arrived. A member of Linus' team marked the landing area with a coloured dye. All they needed was another hour or so, and then they could go home, warm, and dry.

Chapter Thirty-Three

Mount Cook Village
12.30 p.m. NZ time

Henry Adams grabbed a few bottles of water from the mess tent and went in search of Victoria Dahl. He entered a large medical tent, and as he walked through, he recognised a couple of the doctors from his flight. He could see that they were still working tirelessly. He nodded at them, with a silent thank you. Once the doctors gave the passengers the all-clear, they would be transported out of the village to local hospitals.

He heard Victoria's voice before he saw her. She was sitting up and talking rapidly, while making notes on her laptop, which she'd brought down from the plane. Her leg was now heavily bandaged. Henry assumed that the painkillers they'd given her were working. No one who met Victoria Dahl now would suspect that she had just been through a plane crash.

What a woman, Henry thought again. He couldn't remove the smile from his face.

He wanted to say something profound and charming to her when he arrived by her side. He waited for Victoria to finish her call, then he held out his hand and said, 'Water?'

She took it and smiled. Henry started to fidget uncomfortably. He felt like a fifteen year old schoolboy. Of all the things to say, that was all he could come up with? *Water?*

For a very intelligent guy, Henry was feeling inadequate.

'Oh, do sit down, Henry, before you fall down. I have some news you need to hear.'

Henry quickly did as he was ordered.

'I've just heard back from the AFP in Canberra. They're running background checks on some of the passengers. Obviously, they started with men between eighteen and fifty. As Gertrude's neck was broken by a professional, they're checking the male passengers for military backgrounds. But if our killer has a fake passport, well, that's another matter entirely.'

'God, this is so surreal,' Henry said, as images of Gertrude kept creeping into his thoughts.

'You can't blame yourself. Gertrude made her own bed.'

'I know, but I've known her for years. She was my friend. If it wasn't for her, I wouldn't have finished my work.'

'I know, but that was her job, Henry – to get you to finish it for Jackson Myer, who ultimately wanted control over it. Look, my boss said that five men have military backgrounds, not including the captain, of course. Two fit our criteria. A Fred Hammond, forty-seven, from New Zealand, and Lachlan Manus, thirty-three, an Aussie. I have to call Captain Flynn and check whether these men are still on board. I heard that some people came down the valley on foot. The chopper picked them all up. We need to identify them. I need to find out if Hammond or Manus are among them. They must be here, somewhere.'

'So, you're saying … He might try again? Right here, at the MASH unit?' Henry asked, looking concerned.

'It's a possibility. If he was hired to do a job, he won't stop until it's finished. We're also waiting to hear back from someone who works for ASIO. She's looking into the foreign passengers for me.' Victoria would have stood up if she could have. Instead, she shifted herself uncomfortably and waved her hand to catch the attention of one of the orderlies. 'Excuse me! Hey, excuse me!'

Dr Ruby Singh turned around to see who was yelling. 'Yes, is something wrong?' She walked over to Victoria and Henry.

'I need to speak with Constantine Zabinski, who recently arrived with us on the chopper.'

'I left him in the mess tent,' Henry said. He was on the phone to someone. I told him where I was going, and he said he would meet me here.'

'He wasn't supposed to leave your side, Henry.'

'Relax. The mess tent is only 200 feet away,' said Henry, trying to sound casual.

'I'll send one of the orderlies to find him for you,' said Ruby.

'Thank you, Dr Singh,' Victoria said. Dr Singh walked over to an army orderly and asked her to find Constantine Zabinski. 'I need you out of here, Henry.'

'Look … People are hurt,' Henry said, waving his arm in a circle to indicate the tent full of injured people. 'They need to be transported before me. I'll just wait here with you.'

'We can't take that chance. I've got to make a few more phone calls, but I need you out of here. They want to transfer me to Dunedin Hospital soon. I need to know that you're safe.'

'Why don't I come with you?'

'I can't protect you there, Henry. Not like this, with my leg busted.'

Henry was embarrassed. It sounded childish, but he didn't want to leave Victoria. Not when he'd just met her.

'I'll stay here until the police arrive. They're on their way from Christchurch. You'll be questioned by them for some time about the last day's events. But I need someone, preferably with more experience, to watch over you until they get here. Captain Flynn gave Mr Zabinski the air marshal's gun. However, we're dealing with a professional here.'

'I understand. Thanks for everything you've done, Victoria,' Henry said.

'Vicky. Everyone calls me Vicky.'

'Okay, Vicky. I'm … Well, I'm just Henry.' He rolled his eyes again, thinking about what an idiot he was. Just for once, he wanted to say something intelligent to a woman. He decided to just sit quietly on the end of her cot while Vicky phoned Captain Flynn.

Victoria stopped pressing buttons on her phone and looked up at Henry. Vicky could see that Henry's life had been his work, which she knew all too well about. During her career, Victoria had seen the worst of mankind, but at times she had also seen the best and bravest.

★

'What do you want me to do?' Wolf asked.

'The plan hasn't changed. I need his technology, not him,' Jackson Myer, a.k.a. Mr Fox, said. 'Are you in a position to do something about it?'

'Yes, I will be shortly. There's not much security around the village. There's military personnel but they are mostly medical core,' Wolf said. 'I believe Henry trusts me.'

There was a questioning silence.

'I've organised a car. It should be arriving very shortly at Mount Cook Village. See that Henry gets in it. It is a black SUV. I'll have you back on a plane to England within twenty-four hours.

'Understood,' Wolf said. He disconnected the call – he was cold and sore. The wind was picking up, and his shoulder and leg were throbbing. He'd survived worse, he thought, as he headed off in search of Henry Adams. As he zipped up his jacket, a hundred–dollar bill flickered above his head. It floated through the air before landing on the ground by his feet.

Constantine Zabinski never saw what hit him. He had gone to the latrine but woke up with his hands tied behind his back and a gag in his mouth, stuffed inside the tiny cubicle. The only two items missing were his mobile and the air marshal's handgun. He tried his best to undo his restraints, but they wouldn't budge. He cursed himself for being so careless. He thought that protecting Henry Adams was his ticket off the Airbus. As he laid squashed up in the foetal position in the latrine, he thought, *I'm too old for this shit*.

Chapter Thirty-Four

Aboard the Airbus, Flight AN224
12.50 p.m. NZ time

The walk-bridge was finally completed. They were minutes away from transferring the remaining female passengers, although the wind had picked up considerably in the last half hour.

Benjamin was given the thumbs up by Linus to start transferring passengers.

Linus called Sunny on the radio to let her know that the bridge was finished. She said that she would be with them soon, but that she was currently refuelling.

Benjamin walked back inside the plane and asked June to organise the remaining women for the next exodus. He was relieved when he saw the Chinook coming up the valley. It brought back memories of his days in the military. Order, routine, and discipline. That's how you survived.

Once the Chinook settled its mighty body onto the snow, sinking only a few inches, its massive rear door opened up and two aircrew walked out. They indicated for Linus to bring the passengers over.

On cue, June had already organised the women. They were lined up and ready to go. June had agreed to allow them to take a small handbag or carry-on backpack, as long as they could secure them over their heads and shoulders. That had started a mad dash to toss out what wasn't needed.

The women were lined up along the aisle, ready to go. They would need to move quickly on the ice, as Linus didn't want the Chinook's heavy weight idling on the snow for too long. The Chinook took seventy women – they thought the risk acceptable, and besides, their weight was on average less than the men's, so the chopper could carry more.

The female passengers disembarked from the emergency door on the upper deck, as the plane had sunk a little deeper into the soft snow. The main deck windows in economy and first class were now below snow level.

The women stepped out and down into the chilly air, then walked single file towards the walk-bridge. The crevice was deep, and they only had the roped handrails to hold onto. It was like walking a trapeze. They would have to walk single file across it, and the roped handrails were continuously moving, so the women had trouble balancing. Soft prayers were whispered under breaths.

June counted seventy women, then asked the remaining few to return to their seats until the Chinook or EC145 returned. The Chinook would take twenty minutes to offload the passengers and return.

Chloe Pappas was still holding Con's hand.

June Wilson was concerned that Chloe would refuse to leave when the time came. A number of passengers with deceased loved ones didn't want to leave the plane without them. It was heart-wrenching to see. If they couldn't persuade them to leave, they may have to force them.

Thankfully, flight attendant Naomi had managed to coax Chloe Pappas out of her seat. She was now dressed warmly and was standing in the middle of the group of women ready to cross the walk-bridge. June had asked Naomi to personally escort Chloe Pappas down to the MASH unit.

Linus walked in front of the women, demonstrating how to walk safely. It looked simple enough when Linus did it. They just had to keep looking ahead. 'Don't look down,' he said, over and over again. Linus' team were waiting for the women on the opposite side of the bridge. They would escort them in single file to the landing zone.

Peng Ming was in line, stamping her feet to keep out the cold. She had already decided that once she arrived in Christchurch, she was going to head in the opposite direction to which her husband was going. She was pissed off that he had lost all of their hard-earned money, although, being a survivor, she had secretly stashed some aside for a rainy day.

Everyone in line turned around when they heard a dog barking near the door.

June Wilson had forgotten about Joanne Donnelly and her guide dog. She'd been in line with everyone else. June cursed herself for forgetting all about Joanne's blindness and followed Joanne and Amy back to their seats.

'I'm so sorry, you should've been at the front of the queue,' June said, feeling embarrassed.

'It's okay, really. I'll wait my turn. We're all equal here,' Joanne said.

'Maybe, but everyone else has an advantage over you. They can see. Please come with me. I need to get you on that Chinook,' June said firmly.

Joanne started to protest.

'Mum, she's right. You and Heathcliff go. I'll be right behind you,' Amy said.

'No, I won't leave you here alone,' Joanne said.

'It's okay. Both of you are going,' June said. 'I'll explain it to the women at the back of the line. They'll understand. The MASH unit needs all the doctors they can get.'

On June's determined orders, Joanne and Amy went to the exit and were helped down by another cabin crew member. Heathcliff leapt out and landed in the soft snow. He clamoured through it to get to Joanne's side.

June approached the last two women in line and politely asked them to return to the plane. Their horrified expressions conveyed to June that they didn't want to go. Chyna Day had no intention of giving up her spot. She lowered her head and tried to ignore the request. Further up in line, Millie and Pauline overheard June's request. Pauline momentarily hesitated, but then walked back towards June and offered up her place on the Chinook.

Meanwhile, Millie was conflicted. She looked over at the Chinook, which was her ticket home, but chose to follow Pauline back to the plane and forgo her seat for Amy, Joanne, and Heathcliff.

June thanked both selfless women and promised that they would be at the front of the line on the next evacuation. Joanne was embarrassed by the generous bequeaths, although her protest didn't last too long.

Pauline Walsh climbed back on board and searched for another comfortable chair in business class. Once settled, she opened her notebook and continued to write. She hoped that she had the luck of the Irish. Pauline had come this far; she was determined to make it. She had decided to be the heroine of her own story.

But on second thought, Pauline remembered that all good novels usually ended in tragedy.

Millie Wellington sat down next to her. Her hands were shaking.

'That was good of you, to give up your seat. I'm sure we'll be fine,' Pauline said. 'At least we can enjoy business class a little longer, even if there aren't any in-flight services.'

'I was in first class,' Millie said.

'Oh, so you're slumming it, then,' Pauline said.

'And you?' Millie smiled. 'Are you slumming it or tasting the fruits of others?'

'Oh, definitely tasting the fruits of others. I'm an unpublished author. Need I say more?' Pauline raised her eyebrows.

'My sister's badly hurt. They took her down the valley hours ago. I don't know if she's alive or dead. I lost my iPhone.'

Pauline wasn't sure what she'd do if she was in Millie's shoes. She was close to her sister, also.

'She'll be okay. She would have arrived at the hospital by now and has already been operated on. She's probably in recovery by now. You'll see. When we get down to the village, I'll help you locate her.'

Millie looked at Pauline for reassurance. 'Thank you. That would be great.' Millie was on the verge of crying.

'You know, when the plane crashed, I was in the toilet,' Pauline said. 'Funnily, I was only thinking yesterday that my life was a pile of shit.'

'Did you remember to flush?' Millie asked.

'Nope!' They both laughed.

★

Once all the women were on board, the massive Chinook lifted off and climbed high into the sky. It turned south and headed back down the valley.

Time ticked by slowly as the remaining passengers waited for the Chinook to return. When Linus disconnected his call, he was relieved to say that the passengers had arrived safely, and that the Chinook was on its way back. June organised for the next fifty-five people to be evacuated. There were twelve women left, including the female flight crew, and so forty-three men would also be joining them.

Captain Flynn had been preoccupied by Victoria's last phone call. She'd explained who she was looking for and he had agreed to help identify the men in question, discretely.

Benjamin reassured Victoria that Fred Hammond was not the man they were looking for. He couldn't locate Lachlan Manus. When he checked with Marcus, he confirmed that Lachlan was one of the passengers who had travelled with him down the valley. He didn't know if he was one of the passengers injured in the cave-in or not.

Benjamin quickly re-dialled Victoria's number and told her to be vigilant, as Lachlan Manus may already be down at the camp.

★

Further ahead in business class, Dave and Gladys Honeycombe were waiting for their turn to leave. Dave had refused to leave with the remaining injured passengers. There was no way in hell, he thought, that he could leave Gladie here on her own. When the Chinook returned, he and Gladys would be evacuation together.

★

Mount Cook Village
12.55 p.m. NZ time

Wolf found Henry Adams in the medical tent, talking to a woman who he remembered from the plane. He needed to get Henry away from her. The woman was on her phone, barking orders at someone. Wolf picked up some blankets and walked through the medical tent, offering blankets to passengers on his route to Henry. As he approached Henry, he heard the woman speak about a threat on Henry's life.

'Sir, I know, but Gertrude Simpson's killer may already be down here at the village.' After a pause, 'Yes, he's here with me now … No, not yet … If they've sent someone, they haven't made themselves known yet.'

Wolf recognised her accent as Australian. The Australian authorities must surely know that Henry was the target of yesterday's botched attack. Wolf walked up to Henry and offered him a blanket. He kindly refused, but on second thoughts, took one for Victoria. When Henry nodded at him, he seemed to recognise him from the plane.

'Oh, it's you. Thanks for helping Victoria earlier on the plane,' Henry said.

'You're welcome,' Wolf said, shaking Henry's hand.

'Were you travelling to New Zealand on holiday? Your accent tells me that you're from Yorkshire, if I'm not mistaken,' Henry said.

'Yes, that's correct,' Wolf said. 'Very intuitive of you.'

'Sorry. I'm Henry,' he said.

'Bernard. And yes, I'm on holiday. Australia, New Zealand, Hawaii, and then home. What about yourself?'

'I was travelling for business,' Henry said.

'What about your friend?' Bernard asked, nodding over at Victoria.

'Oh no, we just met on the plane,' Henry said. Victoria finished her call and looked up at the passenger. She remembered him from the plane, and he was now wearing army fatigues.

'This is Bernard. Do you remember him? He helped me free you after the crash?'

'Oh, yes! Thank you, Mr …'

'Danbridge. But everyone calls me Bertie, and you're welcome. I was about to go over to the mess tent to get a steaming cup of hot coffee. Do you want to join me, Henry? We can bring one back for you, Victoria?'

'That sounds great,' Henry said.

'I think you should stay with me, Henry. It isn't safe.'

'It'll be fine, Vicky. I'll be with Bertie the whole time.' Henry rose up from the cot.

'What do you mean, not safe?' Bertie asked.

'His life has been threatened. I need to keep an eye on him until the authorities arrive.'

'Oh, my word! Look, the mess tent is just 200 feet away. I'll escort him there and back again if you like. I won't let him out of my sight, if that reassures you,' Bertie said, with his most sincere smile.

'What happened to your clothes?' Victoria asked.

'I came down the valley with a few other passengers. They were soaking wet and torn, so the army gave me these clothes. Luckily for me, they're my size.'

'You were very lucky to have survived,' Victoria said, as she eyed him up and down.

'I'll be fine, Vicky. I'll only be five minutes. Besides, Constantine might still be in there. If not, he'll be in the toilet. I'll keep an eye out for him,' Henry said, wanting to offer Victoria more than a bottle of water.

'Okay. Stay with him, won't you, Bertie?'

'Of course.'

Victoria reluctantly agreed, and Henry and Bertie walked off together. She could see that Bertie was limping, but she was distracted by another phone call. It was Captain Flynn, confirming her suspicions about Lachlan Manus. Victoria sat back as she thought about her options. She would have to ask Major Wilkinson to spare her some of his people to locate Manus. However, something was niggling at the back of her mind. She couldn't put her finger on it.

Victoria wasn't taking any chances. Once she hung up, she re-dialled the number for her contact at ASIO, to get an update on their searches. She confirmed that Lachlan Manus was travelling to New Zealand on business. He worked for British Telecom and was visiting Australia and New Zealand to set up a new deal between BT, Telstra, and NZ Telecom.

Victoria was relieved, but she still had a bad feeling, so she asked Sonya to do a background check on Bernard Danbridge, a British citizen. Sonya told her to hold the line while she checked with her counterpart at MI5. Victoria only had to wait five minutes before her counterpart confirmed that Bertie Danbridge was an ex-SAS soldier, retired, now working for a private contractor in England. Victoria received a picture of Bernard Danbridge via her email on her mobile.

Victoria flew out of her cot, dragging her fractured leg behind her as she limped out of the tent, grabbing a crutch on her way out. Forgetting the pain in her leg, she headed straight for the mess tent. On the way, she saw a soldier helping passengers onto a minibus.

'Hey, you! I need you to come with me,' she yelled at him as she drew closer.

'Is someone hurt?' the soldier asked.

'No, but they will be. There's a man here …' She opened her phone and showed him a picture of Bertie Danbridge in military uniform. 'He's a killer. He's been hired to kill a passenger on board my flight and he's already killed a woman. He was heading towards the mess tent.'

'Okay. I'll notify Major Wilkinson, and he'll send some men to the mess tent,' he said, as he ran towards the communications tent.

Victoria followed behind him, but she was impatient. She could have kicked herself for being so careless. She scanned the campsite for any sightings of Henry and Bertie as she made her way to the mess tent. She doubted that they would have gone anywhere near the mess tent, but she needed to make sure. As she slowly shuffled her way through the camp, something on her left caught her attention. She saw Henry being escorted away from the compound, followed closely behind by Bertie Danbridge.

Henry was walking towards a nearby black SUV. He turned anxiously and saw Victoria in the distance. The wind was picking up, and visibility was deteriorating. Ash particles were still flying around in the air. Victoria could see that Henry had a gun in his back and was being forced into the car. She couldn't believe what was happening. How could Bertie believe he could get away with it?

Victoria wasted no time as she scanned the compound close by for a vehicle. A mountain rescue vehicle pulled up and a ranger climbed out, then walked towards the communications centre. She saw her chance and went for it. Climbing inside, she was relieved to see that the keys were still in the ignition. She put it into drive and sped off, thankful that it was an automatic, as she only had one good foot to drive with.

The ground was wet, and the truck skidded over the icy gravel. She had to cut them off before they headed away from the village. Taking a shortcut, Victoria drove faster. Water, gravel, and stones flew up all around her car. She increased the speed – she needed to catch up to Henry and Bertie. The windscreen wipers were frantically wiping snow and ash from her windscreen. Finally, coming around the last tent at the campsite, Victoria caught sight of the SUV on her right-hand side.

Unfortunately for Bertie, he only caught site of Victoria's jeep at the same time that she ploughed straight into him, causing their car to spin and skid off the road.

The SUV sank into a ditch. Victoria scuffled out of her jeep, grabbing her crutch on the way, and headed round the back to see what she could use as a weapon.

Henry climbed out of the car, dazed but unhurt. Bertie had also exited the car on his side, while the driver of the jeep was slumped unconscious in the driver's seat. Bertie circled around the car to shoot at Henry, but as he did, Henry quickly ran around the other side and squatted down to see in which direction Bertie's feet were heading in. Henry picked up a rock and hurled it at Bertie. It was a lucky shot, hitting Bertie on the side of the head and knocking him down temporarily.

Finding a crowbar in the back, Victoria limped as quickly as she could towards Bertie. She swung for his head, but as he rose up, she only hit his shoulder. Bertie's gun flew out of his hand, but he recovered faster than Victoria. The momentum of the swing knocked Victoria off her feet, and she fell to the ground. Bertie went for Victoria, hitting her across the face and knocking her back down, hard, on the road.

Bertie quickly recovered the crowbar and raised it high above his head. He was about to bring it down on Victoria's skull when a bullet pierced his chest.

Bertie stayed upright for a few more seconds before he fell down onto the slush and gravel.

Henry's adrenaline was pumping as he held the gun tightly. Shaking, he didn't take his eyes off Bertie.

'Well done, Henry,' Victoria said, exhausted.

Henry looked down at Victoria, then dropped the gun and ran to her side. She was dizzy, but coherent.

Once she was in a seated position, she said, 'Please reach into my pocket for my mobile.'

Henry quickly did as she'd asked, and Victoria gave him her pin number and told him what number to dial. Then he found himself speaking to Major Wilkinson.

'Are you okay?' Victoria asked.

'I'm fine.'

'No, you're not. I can hear it in your voice. You've just shot and killed a man, Henry. By the way, thank you for saving my life.'

'Any time,' Henry said, feeling heroic and strangely excited about what had just happened. It was a far cry from offering her a bottle of water.

Major Wilkinson arrived with a handful of his men. They secured the area and stretchered Victoria back to the medical tent, with Henry close by her side. Victoria allowed herself a few moments respite as she laid back and looked up at the cloudy sky. A hundred-dollar bill floated over her head and settled on her chest.

Once they arrived back at the camp, she was informed that Constantine was alive and had been located in one of the latrines. He'd only suffered a bump on the head and a bruised ego. Relief settled in when Victoria was told that the next chopper would take Henry to Christchurch, once it had offloaded the injured – including Victoria – to Dunedin hospital.

Within fifteen minutes, they were strapped in and about to lift off. Victoria looked over at Henry, sizing him up.

'Where's my bloody coffee?'

'Rain check.'

'If you insist.' She smiled.

As the EC145 rose high into the sky, Henry looked out the window. Now that he had calmed down a little, he felt ashamed of himself. He couldn't remember feeling so alive, and yet, people were dead – some still trapped in the plane, up in the valley.

But he couldn't shake the feeling. He knew that his life was never going to be the same again. Watching Victoria, whose eyes were closed, Henry hoped that she would be a part of it. Life was too short for what ifs.

Chapter Thirty-Five

1.10 p.m. NZ time

The remaining female passengers were lined up in front of the makeshift bridge. Rose Banks was second in line, wishing that she hadn't drunk so much. She was swaying more than the bridge, while Millie and Pauline were bringing up the rear.

'Okay, start coming over,' Linus yelled, waving his hand to summon them towards him. The wind was still howling down the valley and was increasing by the hour. The women could feel the wind whipping across their faces. Annabel was concerned about Beth McWilliams – she was in no shape to cross the bridge by herself. She offered to escort Beth across the bridge. They were behind Pauline and Millie.

The women started their walk over the bridge. Annabel was bringing up the rear. She had said goodbye to Captain Flynn and was truly sad to be leaving him. The rope kept swaying in her grip, but she held firmly onto it. The women walked slowly but surely.

Most of the women were across the bridge when another tremor started. Pauline and Millie were two-thirds along the bridge. It shook the bridge violently. Cracks in the snow opened up even wider. It became almost impossible to hold on to the rope as it swayed this way and that. Linus and his team tried to hold the bridge steady from their end, while Captain Flynn and Marcus did the best they could at the other end.

But it was no good. With the bridge slippery and wet under foot, Beth, Millie, and a flight attendant lost their footing and slipped over the side of the bridge. Regrettably, Naomi wasn't able to hang onto the rope and fell down into the cavernous terrain below. Beth and Millie both managed to keep hold of the rope and hung over the side with iron grips.

As the crevice opened up even more, chunks of ice began falling down into the abyss below. They were terrified – all the women on the bridge were screaming as Millie tried to focus by staying as still as possible. She kept her eyes closed and struggled not to look down. Her hands were slipping. The rope was icy and freezing to the touch. Pauline fell to the floor of the bridge and crawled over to the edge, where both women had slipped over. Pauline leaned down to grab onto each woman's wrist, but she wasn't strong enough to pull them both up. All she could do was hold on until help arrived. Annabel joined Pauline and tried to reach Millie's wrist.

Linus tried to make his way onto the bridge, but the women were trying to get off, and there wasn't room for him to manoeuvrer past them. Captain Flynn had no qualms about the danger – no more passengers were going to die. He had started to walk onto the shaky bridge when Marcus pulled him back and said, 'I'll help them. Grab that rope.' He pointed to some climbing rope on the snow near them.

Benjamin didn't have time to argue. He grabbed the rope, then tied one end around Marcus' waist and the other around his own.

Marcus was on the bridge before Benjamin could remind him to be careful. Benjamin understood Marcus' need to make amends for his past mistake.

Finally, the tremor subsided, but their predicament hadn't. Pauline was screaming for help – she didn't know what to do – Millie and Beth were still holding onto the rope with both hands. Then Millie lost her grip. Pauline was holding onto one of Millie's wrists while Annabel held the other. Meanwhile, Beth was grappling with her own grip.

Yet another tremor shook the bridge. Pauline was struggling to hold onto one of Beth's wrists. But she was afraid she wasn't strong enough to hold her with one hand.

Both women held on tight to Millie, who was dangling over the bridge, completely dependent on Annabel and Pauline's strength.

Finally, Marcus appeared beside Pauline and leant over the edge. He grabbed one of Millie's hands. Marcus and Pauline pulled Millie up together, but Pauline lost her grip on Beth's wrist. Once they had Millie back safely on the bridge, they manoeuvred her aside so that they could reach down again for Beth.

'Thank you, thank you, thank you,' Millie wheezed.

But as they leaned over the side to lift Beth up, they saw that she was gone.

'*No!*' Pauline screamed, as she leaned further over the side. A pair of strong arms pulled her back. Linus grabbed her and cupped her head to his chest. They were only allowed a moment to grieve.

Pauline was shaking as Linus escorted her off the bridge. Before she knew where they were, Pauline and Millie were being led to the landing site. Neither of them were able to comprehend what had just happened.

All Benjamin could do was look on in shock. He lowered his head and knelt down in the snow, before letting out a scream of rage. Annabel had returned to the eastern side of the walk-bridge. She came up beside Benjamin and put her arms around him. There wasn't anything she could say. He had to wear the grief for now.

'They were both beautiful human beings. They didn't deserve to die. Not like that,' he said after a while.

'No, they didn't. No one did. Please remember, none of this is your fault, Benjamin.'

Benjamin looked Annabel squarely in the face. She knew pain – she'd seen her fair share of it. He couldn't suppress his emotions any longer, so he didn't try.

'Every single death is on my hands,' Benjamin sobbed. 'I'm the captain. I can't allow anyone else to die.'

'Do you know how many people have died today in New Zealand because of these earthquakes? How many homes and businesses lost? We can't control nature – only human nature. As far as I can see, you haven't made any mistakes. You've been calm throughout this whole bloody mess. You made the right call to stay in the plane. Most of these passengers wouldn't have survived these elements for long.'

'Thank you. But I'm going to be under great scrutiny during the next few months. They'll question every decision I made until I start second-guessing myself.'

'Maybe, maybe not. But I can tell you one thing – every passenger on that plane will testify on your behalf. They're alive because of you, and don't you forget it.'

Marcus had decided to keep his distance from Benjamin and Annabel. He could see that Benjamin needed privacy. He could only imagine the weight of responsibility on his captain's shoulders. He hadn't handled his own responsibilities well – his career was over, that much he knew. No captain at ANSAL would want to fly with him now.

Marcus turned his attention back to the bridge. He made sure that it was safe to cross, then started the transfer of more reluctant passengers. He could hear the Chinook coming up the valley. When the last of the men were across the bridge, they walked as before in single file towards the Chinook. The EC145 rescue chopper was also coming into view. Marcus asked June to organise another six passengers.

June nodded, but before she did, she had a silent moment for Naomi. She would personally call her family and explain what happened. Like she would for the other flight attendants she'd lost today.

All the female passengers had now left, except for Annabel, June Wilson, and two female flight attendants. Annabel chose to stay with Benjamin, and June stated that if the captain and first officer were the last two off the plane, she was going to be the third last.

The EC145 had picked up its handful of passengers and headed down the valley. Apart from the wind, the site had grown eerily quiet.

Pauline was resting on board the Chinook. Someone had retrieved her bag from the bridge and handed it to her.

She hugged it for dear life as she swayed to and fro. Her bag contained what she had once described as her most valued possessions – her wallet, passport, phone, notebook, and laptop – but they now seemed like trivial things. All she kept seeing was the look of fear on Millie and Beth's faces, staring up at her. She couldn't have saved both of them. Why couldn't she have saved both? Why had she let go of Beth's arm? This wasn't how it was supposed to end.

Pauline wanted to tell the world about Beth and Angus. About Linus and his heroic rescue team. About Captain Benjamin Flynn, and everyone else she had met on board. It would be a non-fiction account of their ordeal. She would call it *Cloud Piercer*, the English translation of the Māori word for Aoraki.

Pauline wanted to write a true, heart-felt story of what it felt like to experience and survive such a harrowing event. In time, she would try to contact the other passengers to hear their stories.

Pauline made herself a promise. Once she arrived at her sister's house, she would get in contact with Beth and Angus' family and personally explain what had happened to them. They needed to know how brave they were, and how many people they had saved. As Pauline continued to sway back and forth, Millie put her arm around her. This time it was Pauline who was shaking. They were both thankful to be alive.

★

02.10 p.m. NZ time

Captain Flynn and the remaining passengers waited inside the Airbus for the final pickup. The Chinook had been a godsend. Two more trips had seen a quick turnaround. There were only sixty-one passengers remaining, plus five of the flight crew.

The giant plane was nearly deserted. It felt hollow, full of creaking sounds. All of the remaining male passengers were in business class, waiting for their turn to depart. The plane had sunk even further into the snow since the last tremor, and the snow was nearly up to the emergency exit door of the business-class cabin. At least the evacuation would be easier, as the men only needed to step outside onto the snow.

Time ticked by anxiously, until the call came for the final group of men to line up at the emergency door. Linus had confirmation that the Chinook would arrive in five minutes. The wind was as unrelenting as it had been during the previous evacuations. He could see clouds forming rapidly right across the mountain range. If it started to rain, the snow would turn to slush, making their final evacuation even harder.

The Chinook finally arrived to pick up the remaining passengers. Windsor Hounslow and Sir Roger Standish had moved back upstairs and made their way to the front of the final line of evacuees. They had fallen asleep a couple of hours ago, and no one had bothered to wake them until they were told to relocate upstairs. As they stood up to leave, they wondered where everybody else had gone.

*

Charlotte, one of the last two remaining flight attendants, went to the cabin crew rest area below decks. There were several bunk beds in a semi-circle, which were used by the flight attendants during long-haul flights.

She went below to gather her belongings. It was dark in the rest area. She had to use a torch. Seeing the Chinook lift off last time, without her, had sent a chill down her spine. She was having second thoughts about agreeing to stay to the end. Charlotte had always wanted to be a flight attendant. It was a career for life, and now that she had lived through the worst of it, she knew she could fly through anything.

The rest of the flight and cabin crew would be leaving on the EC145 after the Chinook returned for its final payload, and the rest of Linus' team would travel back on the Chinook with the remaining passengers.

As Charlotte transferred some of her personal possessions into a small bag, she heard a screeching metallic sound, like the crushing or squeezing of metal. She wasn't sure what it was, but it sounded different from what she'd heard throughout the day. Before she could finish packing her bag, the bulkhead beside her caved in. The two top bunks collapsed onto the lower bunks. The crevice that the plane was resting in had begun to shift, which was starting to crush the plane's fuselage.

Charlotte ran from the room, leaving her bag behind. Climbing up the stairs, she ran through the empty, now dark, first-class cabin and up the staircase into business class, yelling all the way. But before she could tell the captain what had happened, the plane dropped further down into the crevice.

It was now or never. The captain ordered everyone off the plane. The remaining passengers filed out of the Airbus quickly. They struggled through the heavy snow and away from the plane. The fastest passengers reached the walk-bridge first, only relaxing once they were securely on the other side.

Standing out in the open, the passengers could appreciate the situation they were in. Some hadn't left the aircraft since the crash, and the temperature was starting to drop again. It was freezing.

Benjamin ordered the flight attendants out. Once they were safely over the bridge, Benjamin told Marcus that he was going to do one final sweep around the Airbus. He wanted to make sure that there were no stragglers. Marcus offered to accompany him, but Benjamin declined the offer – he was done with putting others at risk.

Benjamin quickly made his way through the Airbus and raced down the back staircase. He offered a silent apology to the dead for leaving them behind. They would have to wait until it was safe to retrieve their bodies. When they did this, he promised himself that he would be there.

Benjamin continued along the economy cabin and through into first class. Using a torch and calling out as he walked down the aisles. He checked the toilets along the way. Once re-assured that there was no one left on board, he raced back upstairs and headed for the emergency exit.

Snow had now reached the open hatchway and had come onto the plane. As Benjamin reached the door, the aircraft lurched downwards again. The crevice opened up even more and sucked the aeroplane down into the gorge. Snow and ice came flooding in through the doorway.

Marcus watched in horror as the Airbus slid further down. He raced back towards it, but the entire aircraft was sinking. Linus yelled at Marcus to stop as the first officer ran quickly back over the walk-bridge and grabbed a length of rope. He tied it to the bridge and secured the rope around his waist.

Linus and Annabel ran back across the bridge to join Marcus. Annabel wasn't entirely sure what she could do, but she had to do something.

Linus joined Marcus at the edge of the gorge and looked down. He saw the plane resting thirty feet below the surface. He couldn't see the door, as the plane was wedged against a wall of ice. There wasn't much room to manoeuvre. Snow was still falling down into the crevice.

All three called out to Benjamin, but there was no answer. Marcus wanted to be lowered down, but Linus refused, stating that it was too dangerous. If Benjamin was alive, he would have to escape through the ceiling of the aircraft, not the side.

Meanwhile, inside the Airbus, Benjamin started digging the snow away from the door. He grabbed a dining tray and started shovelling the snow. After five minutes, he heard his name being called. Once the remaining snow was shovelled away, all Benjamin could see was a wall of ice, no more than an arm's reach away from the emergency exit. He looked up and saw Marcus and Annabel leaning over the edge of the cave.

'I'm okay!' he yelled. Benjamin wanted to kick himself for being so foolish, but he had to do one final sweep of the plane.

Linus' team arrived with a winch and more rope. They lowered the rope down, but Benjamin knew that he couldn't make it. It was too tight. If the plane or ice shelf shifted, even by a few centimetres, he would be crushed.

The Airbus was now on an incline of about thirty degrees, with the nose of the aircraft pointing downwards. Linus told Benjamin to go to the back of the plane, and to come up through the opening in the ceiling.

Benjamin headed towards the back of the plane. The angle was steep, so Benjamin needed to use the aisle chairs to help haul himself to the rear section.

Sunny, the EC145 chopper pilot, was on her way back up the valley. Once Linus updated her, she ordered a crew member to ready the winch.

Benjamin heaved himself up through the hole in the fuselage. As he emerged, Linus lowered himself down onto the aircraft. He helped Benjamin up onto the ceiling of the aircraft as the rescue team lowered the ropes and harnesses needed to air-lift them off the plane.

Sunny arrived and hovered overhead. She lowered the winch down, and Linus immediately attached it to his harness and secured himself to Benjamin. He gave a thumbs up signal, and Sunny eased them up off the roof of the Airbus before transferring them over to the other side of the walk-bridge, where Marcus, Annabel and Linus' team jointed them.

Annabel was so relieved that she wrapped her arms around Benjamin tightly, before quickly pulling away and apologising.

'What for?' he asked.

'I don't know, to tell you the truth.' She laughed.

Benjamin gazed at Annabel. Relief was evident in her eyes. He liked that she was concerned about him. He hugged her in return, and it felt good to be needed. The EC145 hovered above as the Chinook arrived to collect its final load.

Once it headed back down the Valley, Sunny landed the EC145 chopper. Benjamin was the last one to climb on board. As they rose into the sky, they all heard a thunderous noise. They turned and looked through the windows to where the Airbus had once rested. She had collapsed deeper into the crevice. The icy walls broke away and fell in on top of the mighty plane, sealing her into its icy grave. It could be months before they would be able to get the dead out of the aircraft, but Benjamin promised himself, he would be there when they did.

Benjamin noticed Annabel was shaking, and so wrapped his blanket around her for warmth. It felt good, holding her in his arms.

★

Down at the MASH unit, Dave Honeycombe was sitting with Gladys on a cot, who was on her mobile, talking to one of their daughters. They were grateful to still be together. Some passengers had to leave their loved ones behind. Amongst the survivors and din of melancholy celebration, Charlotte was reunited with her fellow flight attendants. She told them about Naomi and Beth.

It was finally over. All the uninjured passengers had been chauffeured by coach to Christchurch. Chloe Pappas, Millie, Pauline, Joanne, Amy, and Heathcliff, were among them.

Pauline would eventually escort Millie to Dunedin Hospital, where Pauline's sister had agreed to meet her. Millie's father had organised a private jet, but he only had permission to land in Auckland, due to the earthquakes. When Millie arrived at the hospital, she was relieved to hear that her sister had pulled through. She was lucky to have survived. The doctor told Millie that whoever had treated Annie on board had saved her life. Pauline and her sister Alice, waited with Millie until her father arrived. It was a friendship that would never be broken.

★

The mountain tops, which earlier that day had been covered with heavy snow, were now patched with nakedness. Rocky outcrops were visible on what was left of their peaks, as millions of tonnes of rock and ice lay on the valley floor.

The national park had been permanently scarred. It would never be the same again, as Aoraki and her sister peaks had proven again to be a living, breathing hotbed for nature's temper.

By the time the EC145 landed, representatives from ANZAL Airlines in New Zealand were already at the campsite and ready to meet Captain Flynn and First Office Whitby.

'It's already started,' Benjamin said to Marcus, as they walked over to the mess tent. They knew that they would be under continuous scrutiny over the next few days by every organisation involved.

The black box would take some time to retrieve, but it would verify everything that the pilots had reported in their interviews.

'You've done nothing wrong,' said Marcus, knowing his own actions would be under more interrogation.

'You saved my life back there. Don't forget that.'

'Thanks for saying so, Ben. But I have a lot to answer for. I'll be forever sorry that I left.'

'Come on. I'll buy you all a hot cup of coffee,' Benjamin said to Marcus, Annabel, and Linus.

'Well, they better interview me and the other passengers. If they don't, there'll be hell to pay,' Annabel said, as they all walked off towards the mess tent.

When Annabel entered the tent, she recognised some of the other passengers she had helped earlier that day. She felt only pride for what she had accomplished.

June Wilson was already in the medical tent, discussing the passenger list with Major Wilkinson and making sure that everyone was accounted for. She informed him that one first-class passenger was missing.

Benjamin looked around him. Most of the passengers were in deep thought, but relieved to be down and safe. Some passengers were crying, while others were on their phones speaking to loved ones. The memory of their ordeal would be with them for a long time to come. Benjamin walked up to June Wilson and gave her the longest hug of her life. He whispered a thank you in her ear before releasing her.

June simply straightened herself up and said, 'All part of the service.'

The remaining passengers stopped what they were doing when they saw the captain hug June Wilson. Those that could stand did, as they clapped their appreciation for what Captain Flynn had done. He was momentarily embarrassed. But for the first time since the crash, he felt a moment's relief.

Benjamin poured coffees for Linus, Marcus, Annabel, and himself. He only managed one sip before the ANZAL representatives approached him. Benjamin recognised one of them − he was ANZAL's head pilot. He was relieved that he was with them. He was a good man and wouldn't allow anyone to lay blame where none was warranted.

He asked Benjamin for a quick word before they were scheduled to be choppered back to Christchurch. Benjamin agreed, but he told the head pilot he wouldn't be leaving the campsite until all the passengers were safely away.

Benjamin turned to Annabel. 'Would you allow me to buy you dinner, when you're in Christchurch?'

'Are you sure you'll be available?' Annabel asked. She was looking over at the airline representatives, but she was also smiling.

'I'll make time,' he said.

'I'd love to,' she replied. He grinned and left with the head pilot. Despite the cold, she felt a warm sensation – something she hadn't felt for years. As she drank her coffee, a hundred-dollar bill floated down and rested on her cup.

Epilogue

Herbert Schwartz was getting tired as he climbed over the snow.

'*Fick das fur einen witz*,' he said as he slumped down for a rest. *Fuck that for a joke*. His brogues were ruined, and his feet were cold. It had taken all his strength to haul himself back up and continue on after the avalanche had landed on top of him. He cursed himself for taking off his ski boots. It had taken him hours to climb over the tons of snow that had fallen down the mountain around him.

Finally, he reached the car park. Behind and below him, the lake was rising fast. There were icebergs floating everywhere. He was freezing, and he'd long since lost his skis and backpack, so he couldn't call for help. Four times he'd seen the big Chinook and the EC145 fly overhead. Finally, they had stopped coming. He had planned to be the first passenger down the mountain, and now he was the last.

He looked down at his ruined shoes.

'*Gottverdammt,*' he said, as he started his long walk back to Mount Cook Village. He was pissed off that he wasn't going to make his meeting.

Just then, a hundred-dollar note floated past him. He flicked it away.

THE END

Acknowledgements

This novel was inspired by my imagination and a love of airplanes. However, I can't take credit for all the passengers and their storylines … some of my family and friends created passengers for me to adopt in the novel.

Thank you to Alyson, Sylvain, Emma, Sophie, Alisha, and Angela for your contributions.

To the team at Aurora House, thank you for supporting my characters and ideas, it's been an adventure.

About the Author

Completing a Bachelor of Arts, majoring in Creative Writing and Literature, at Griffith University in Queensland, Australia, brought out Paula Welch's passion for writing, and she hasn't looked back since.

Paula has now written three novels, including *Cloud Piercer*, The *Interlopers* (her first young adult novel), and *A River of Fortune*. Currently, she is working on her next novel, 'another adult fiction, this time a murder mystery'.

As an author, Paula has a passion for research and dedicates herself to finessing the finest details of her characters' worlds. When she isn't researching her next book or writing up a storm, she enjoys spending time with her loved ones and, of course, reading.

As for Paula's future plans and work philosophy? 'What I can say, with 100 per cent certainty, if you want something bad enough, don't tell yourself you can't do it, and more importantly, don't give up. From small things, big things grow.'

For more information visit www.paulawelch.com.au